Advance praise for
The Glint of Light

"The language [in *The Glint of Light*] is music, and the story a song that gets under the skin, lingers long--I'm still singing it. Clarence Major is known as one of our best poets. With *The Glint of Light*, he proves himself one of our most powerful novelists, as well." —Bill Roorbach, author of *Lucky Turtle*

"*The Glint of Light* ...builds to its finale the way a Chekov story unfolds, skillfully told by this master...Major... is uniquely gifted...a national treasure."—Nancy Schoenberger, author of *Long Like a River*

"Told through crisp, sparse, and poetic prose...filled with philosophical insight about life, relationships, and art, this is a beautiful novel." —Jennifer Murphy, Author of *Scarlet in Blue*

"A potent and savvy drama ...Clarence Major delivers a fierce, suspenseful, and unsentimental [novel]... you won't want to put it down!" —Noley Reid, author of *Pretend We Are Lovely*

"...*The Glint of Light* [is] Clarence Major at his best; [it] is a literary event of great importance." —Robert Olen Butler, Pulitzer Prize winner, author of *A Good Cent from a Strange Mountain*

"Clarence Major probes the human condition through the prism of one man's complex interior world where hope and doubt live on every page. Infused with poetic prose and skillful plot twists this page turner brings the reader to an understanding of how it is possible to emerge from loss & hardship. This book is a beauty." —Marcia Butler, author of *Oslo, Maine*

"I couldn't put *The Glint of Light* down. [It's] absorbing and informative... The novel brims with intelligence and insight...The story is uplifting and heartbreaking with some unexpected twists. I highly recommend *The Glint of Light*." —Carol Orange, author of *A Discerning Eye*

"*The Glint of Life* is... gut-wrenching... The result is a hypnotizing tale of the tensions between love, duty and betrayal." —Helen Benedict, author of *Wolf Season*

"Clarence Major's *The Glint of Light* gave me the gift of his intimate story-teller's voice, as if we were sitting across a table from each other, drinking coffee... It moves with poignant detail... There's so much longing in this novel, so much truth-telling. It will wise you up; it may break your heart." —Patricia Henley, author of *Hummingbird House*

"Monumentally moving, *The Glint of Light* offers a spellbinding view into the nuances of the human experience. This novel beautifully captures the length of a life and tackles the lingering effects of loss, the power of desire and the pull to self-discovery with remarkable acuity. This is an arresting read that is not to be missed." —Jennifer Maritza McCauley, author of *When Trying to Return Home*

"This eminently readable novel explores...death [and] love...in a subtly oblique and understated fashion [and] the deeper malaise that afflicts society..."—Charles Lambert, author of *The Children's Home*

"...Clarence Major brings us a quietly stunning new novel as large in its vision as it is subtle in its unfolding. With elegance and grace, Major paints a portrait of America at a particular historical moment (the Obama years), yet the book's concerns are timeless, universal: the loss of a mother, the dance of sibling rivalry, the search for love.... Clarence Major brings the full measure of his powers to this Chekhovian tale of love and loss in an extraordinary narrative revealed through the accumulation of keenly observed ordinary detail. The novel is immersive, the story compelling, the characters memorable. *The Glint of Light* will linger with you long after the book is closed." —Rilla Askew, author of *Fire in Beulah*

"Clarence Major has written a beautiful book about love, identity, passion, family, and forgiveness. *The Glint of Light* is a tour de force." —Connie May Fowler, author of *Before Women had Wings*

"Major illuminates the quotidian, the magnificent, and the ephemeral in sharp and glittering detail. *The Glint of Light* is a beautiful novel of refracted memory, longing, and one man's journey through grief in the wake of his mother's death. This is a powerful divination of a life--its hauntings, astonishments, and mysteries revealed in rich and unexpected ways." —Mary Otis, author of *Burst*

"It's a year of wonder and sorrows for the hero of Clarence Major's wonderful new novel. The mysteries of love and betrayal, unexpected violence, and abrupt encounters with racism give hypnotic immediacy to every moment of this narrative. *The Glint of Light* enchanted me and when I reached the end I was overpowered by its beauty." —Elizabeth McKenzie, author of *Stop That Girl*

"Mark's...journey scatters light on the fractured pieces of life...he seeks renewal..." —Joanne Leedom-Ackerman, author of *The Dark Path to the River*

"With a cast of memorable characters and skillfully drawn background... [this] novel's authenticity is hard earned. This powerful story of coming to terms with grief will resonate with you long after reading." —Elena Gorokhova, the author of *A Train to Moscow*

"Clarence Major's novel is a tale of the search for love in the midst of grief... with accumulating power and urgency. It's like having a close friend talking to you at a kitchen table – at once intimate and universal – and with a note of grace." —Susan Jane Gilman, author of *Donna Has Left the Building*

"Clarence Major's... coming-of-age novel captures *The Glint of Light* reflected in... remembrance, grief, and revelation." —Jayne Anne Phillips, author of *Machine Dreams*

the glint of light

the glint of light

CLARENCE MAJOR

WINNIPEG

The Glint of Light

Copyright © 2023 Clarence Major

Design and Layout by Matthew Stevens and M. C. Joudrey.

Published by At Bay Press May 2023.

Library and Archives Canada cataloguing in publication is available upon request.

ISBN 978-1-988168-99-9

Printed and bound in Canada.

This book is printed on acid free paper that is 100% recycled ancient forest friendly (100% post-consumer recycled).

First Edition

10 9 8 7 6 5 4 3 2 1

atbaypress.com

"Don't tell me the moon is shining;
show me the glint of light on broken glass."
—*Anton Chekhov*

Part One

"We learn the rope of life by untying its knots."

—*Jean Toomer*

1

Mother died today three years ago. It happened on the second Monday in April, the month she was born, sixty-eight years earlier.

Mother was born Adella Bischoff in Waverly, Nebraska, two years after the end of World War Two. Nobody in Waverly knew her father and mother each had "one drop."[1] Who knows to how many it would have mattered? Townsfolk couldn't tell they were people of so-called "hypodescent."

Nothing about the Bischoffs seemed to set them apart. They were largely of Russian, German, and French ancestry. They enjoyed all the same small comforts of their conservative milieu. They belonged.

---

[1] *The "one drop rule" was an early twentieth-century legal rule of human classification designed to identify Americans with sub-Saharan African ancestry. Since for this purpose appearance was unreliable, the law relied on "knowledge" of the fact. The thrust of the law resulted from the eighteenth and nineteenth centuries' custom of keeping as many people in bondage as possible for the purpose of perpetuating free labor. The effects of the legal principle lasted well into the twenty-first century.*

(In South Carolina once the issue was: should a white-looking person [known to have African ancestry] be allowed to marry a person assumed to be white—that is one with apparent total European ancestry? Senator George D. Tillman of the South Carolina State Senate, speaking to the lawmakers gathered before him, in part, said, "It is a scientific fact that there is not one full-blooded Caucasian on the floor of this convention. Every member has in him...colored blood... It would be a cruel injustice and the source of endless litigation, of scandal, horror, feud, and bloodshed to undertake to annul or forbid marriage for a remote...obsolete trace of Negro blood." [South Carolina News and Courier, October 17, 1895.])

They carefully kept secret what they thought was their parallel world. Nothing was going to render it asunder. They were relatively comfortable with their lives, with what *they* saw as their private stigma.

Dad's parents came only once to Chicago to visit us. Marie, my twin, and I weren't yet one year old. When Marie and I were very small, maybe six or seven, Dad drove us to Cedar Falls to visit his parents, Effie-Marie and Spencer. Their folks came from Virginia. I don't remember much about the visit.

Marie was named after Dad's mother. I don't remember much about Dad's parents except that Grandmother Effie-Marie's mother Clementine was living with them. She was a very old woman in a wheelchair. After Dad died, we never saw them again.

I was named after Dad's grandfather, Clementine's husband, Marc; he spelled his name the French way; he was named by his New Orleans father, whose name I never learned. Dad's folks were descended from New Orleans slaveholders and slaves. When Marie and I were born, Mother insisted on spelling my name with a "k" instead of a "c."

My grandparents, Muriel and Jake, owned and ran Bischoff Hardware in Lincoln, Nebraska, a short distance from Waverly. While Adella was a teenager, after school, she helped out at the store; the store carried just about everything. People came from all around, Raymond, Greenwood, and Murdock, to buy things from Bischoff Hardware.

The Bischoff family house was near the border between Waverly and Lincoln. This made it easier for them to get to and from their store in Lincoln.

The store sold rakes, shovels, spades, picks, screws, tape, ladders, step-stools, drills, drill bits, saws, saw blades, seed, sanders, grinders, wire, cords, nails, lumber, nail guns, impact drivers, drill presses, routers, wrenches, fence posts, barbed-wire, chicken fence wire, poles, poster boards, poster board paint, sprays, rope, tar paper, sandpaper, putty knives, clamps, tape measures, bolt cutters, staple guns, work gloves, circular saws, hammers, cordless drills, screwdrivers, filters, screens, fans, bathroom fixtures, signs, mailboxes, propane, locks, light bulbs, wallpaper, bolts, florescent tubes, paints, linseed oils, motor oil, handmade wooden stools, saw-horses, and shoe-taps.

The Bischoff family was highly respected and well-established in Waverly. Like most people in Nebraska, Muriel and Jake were Republicans.

Most of the 310 people living in Waverly were of European descent; there were a few Native Americas from the Omaha, the Winnebago and the Great Sioux tribes, and a Chinese family that ran a laundry on Dovers Street.

Waverly was a very small, rural, conservative town. Highway 6 ran through it. Most people went to Lincoln to buy things. There was a tractor supply distribution center, and there was also a large poultry processing company. Watts Electric was probably the biggest company.

One street sign was in both English and Chinese. A plaque said: "Waverly: The forested land was patented in 1726..." At first, the town was called "The Mistake" then was renamed "Waverly" in 1811.

It was in the early 1960s that Mother started openly rebelling. Adella believed she saw deficiencies all around her. She was determined nothing misfit in her upbringing would stymie her. She loved the Beatles.

She was a great believer in Martin Luther King Jr. and his message. She admired Rosa Parks for not sitting at the back of the bus. Thurgood Marshall was one of her heroes. She was also against the Vietnam War.

In college at the University of Nebraska in Lincoln she marched against racism and racial segregation. Mother became the recipient of a new cultural revolution, even before she fully broke from the authority of her parents' influence. Her mother called her "headstrong and uncontrollable", even "hedonistic."

A large part of Mother's battle was against the mores of Waverly. Mother said the town was first a "mistake" then a *fictional* place. What she meant was it was named after Sir Walter Scott's first novel, *Waverly*, published in 1814, and set in Perthshire, Scotland, between 1745 and 1746. People in Chicago, who had never been to Nebraska, had a hard time trying to image what she was describing.

When Mother told this story, most people had never heard of the novel *Waverly*, but they were likely to known about Scott's *Ivanhoe*, even if they had never read it. Many had seen the movie *Ivanhoe*, at least on reruns, or *heard* about the movie.

The irony was: the novel's story was one of high adventure while the town was quiet and reserved. Some people said it was a "dead" town. Mother called it "snail-town."

Another irony was Mother left Waverly carrying its regionalisms and its crotchetiness with her for the rest of her life. She also had in her accent the Nebraska nasal whine and the tendency to jabber on beyond reason.

It was around this same time that her parents told her she had African American ancestors. They showed her two photographs: one of Muriel's grandmother, Helen Webster, from Louisiana, a strikingly lovely woman of olive-tan complexion, with a strong intelligent face; the other, of Jake's grandmother, Patsy Bischoff, a beautiful, brown-skinned woman of "obvious high moral birth," from Kansas.

"This is something we don't talk about," Mother's father said to her, "so don't go talking about it with *any*body."

She mulled over the dilemma; and in a short amount of time, she decided to embrace her African American ancestry.

Mother proclaiming African American ancestors seemed to her fellow college students odd. The "one drop" law became her stumbling block. I doubt that Mother ever consciously realized the paradox she placed herself in. Given the world we lived in, and her white appearance, passing for black would be far more difficult for her, than passing for white.

At the same time, Adella also rebelled against the Lutheran religion her parents raised her in. I always suspected her rebellion against her parents' religion had more to do with her *parents* than it did with Lutheranism. Martin Luther, like Mother, was a rebel. In some other context, she might have found compatibility with the thirteenth-century ecclesiastical German friar.

Mother thought it was a good idea for Marie and me to attend church; but she left it up to us to decide where. So, we chose the United Church of Hyde Park, a beautiful white stone church on the corner of East 53rd Street. Many different kinds of people made up the congregation. Marie and I felt comfortable there.

I grew up believing Mother was a beautiful woman and she was. She loved compliments. As an only child, her parents doted on her and spoiled her. They gave her everything they could afford. And she grew up feeling she deserved special treatment. As an adult she still had this attitude. It caused others to see her as a person of excessive pride.

No matter how hard she tried not to, Mother had to fill any room she happened to be in; she filled it with her happiness or with her grief or her boredom; or just with the sound of her own voice; and she was so self-centered she rarely heard or saw anybody around her. Most of the time I felt like Marie and I were supporting actors in her stage play.

Dating? Adella claimed she went out to dinner or to the movies with a boy or two while in college. Then she met Alfred Smith, Dad, in her second year. They quickly became exclusive and soon fell madly in love. Dad was handsome and tall and strong and very athletic. He'd played football since elementary school. He loved sports and had a head for business and math.

Mother and Dad graduated together with MBAs. They wore their caps and gowns and stood in line together to receive their degrees. Mother got lucky; during their last year in graduate school, she was recruited for a staff position at the prestigious Gerdts University in Chicago.

With MBAs in hand, Mother and Dad moved to Hyde Park, to be near Gerdts. Plus, she was already pregnant with us, and Gerdts was located across the park from the University of Chicago.

When Marie and I were old enough, Mother was able to drop us off at the Gerdts's highly-rated nursery school, Osborne Child Care Center. She picked us up on her way home.

The years went by quickly. Dad was managing a second-rate restaurant, The Tasty Palace, on 50th Street, but was on the lookout for something better. In the intervening time, he ran ads in the classified section of the *Hyde Park Herald*, to no avail.

Then, suddenly, when Marie and I were ten years old, Dad was killed in a horrible car accident. After much grief and the funeral, life had to go on.

About a year after Dad's death Mother bought a used Buick Roadmaster, a car big enough to haul us around in.

After we'd finished the sixth grade at Montessori Lowell Private Academy in Hyde Park, Mother wanted to enroll us in a private high school or college prep school.

She spent hours screening the various preparatory schools, University of Chicago Laboratory Schools, Jones College Prep High School, Morgan Park Academy, Chicago Waldorf and the like, before deciding on Luke Marco Academy, which was one of the highest-rated private prep schools in Chicago.

Marie and I resisted. We knew preppy kids, and we didn't like most of them. They tended to be snooty. We preferred the neighborhood kids we knew from Hyde Park High. It was an integrated public school with very high ratings.

After much wrangling and arm-twisting, we convinced Mother to let us attend Hyde Park High.

Soon after we started there, Marie and I took private driving lessons after school; and we earned our driving licenses at the same time. I felt this to be a milestone. It was like an earned status: like getting our social security numbers, getting legal permission to drive was part of becoming validated as an *adult*; and it was a secure step into the world of grownups.

One Sunday afternoon, Mother, Marie and I watched the old movie

Imitation of Life on TV's Turner Classic Movies. It was about a white-looking "colored" girl, Sara Jane, who wanted to escape her "colored" past and fade into the white world. Instantly, Mother became angry with Sara Jane and said, "What a misguided fool!"

Mother often said, "People are just people." Sure, people were just people, but I was skeptical. Even as a teenager, I concluded it would take self-discipline to survive in this world. No matter who you were, you had to find your own way; and you had to create your own lexicon of survival as a guide through the labyrinth.

The high school Marie and I attended was at first populated by students of many ethnicities; then by the time we graduated, reflecting the shift in Hyde Park demographics, it was mostly African American. Yet, at school the consensus remained: cultural and ethnic variety was always better because it prepared one to live in the modern world as it is.

Our little high school universe was only a tiny, tiny part of that ambiguous world that was fast becoming postmodern, a world more and more complex.

In high school, I decided I wanted to be a scientist. As a scientist, I believed I could help make the world a better place; but for a long time, the question was: What kind of scientist?

All around me at school there was a profusion of cultural signals saying I was aiming too high. They were echoing the mantra of an earlier generation of advice to "the Negro": "go slow."

They said: Why not aim to *be* something "your people" are more accepted in? Because I was tall, strong, athletic-looking, and olive-skinned, they said: Why not play basketball or football or baseball, or become a preacher?

These well-meaning people were quick to assure me that these were "high" positions worthy of attaining. I had no doubt they were, but the adults weren't seeing *me*. They were seeing their vision of me.

Naïve or not, I believed Mother's words back when I was six or seven when she told us we could be *anything* we wanted to be. I wanted to be a scientist.

Would it be more difficult for me *because* I was African American? Sure, it was a given, I would have to work harder *because* of who I was.

2

In those high school years, I collected theories! Hegelian idealism appealed to me. Humes's *A Treatise on Human Nature* obsessed me. Newton's theory of gravity kept me up at night. Einstein was my main hero. I didn't fully understand them, but I loved the theory of general relativity and the theory of special relativity. I pondered the laws of physics. What was the structure of space-time?

I also went through a period when the whole universe fascinated me. Were there universes within universes? Was there a beginning? How did it all start and where was it all going? I wanted to spend my life studying stars and planets, the cosmos and galaxies and black holes.

Mars and Mercury and Neptune! The horrible fate of Mars fascinated and terrified me. Why had its water and atmosphere disappeared? Hot Mercury and hotter Venus amazed me, and why were there planets without stars?

I was also interested in music, especially rock'n'roll, then blues and jazz. I learned to read music while taking private piano lessons. Marie took ballet lessons. I was taking piano lessons, but I was more interested in playing the guitar.

I saved up enough money to buy my first guitar. It was an acoustic Yamaha I got on sale at Chicago Music Exchange. Later, I bought a better one, a Fender. I wanted to make music, and the Fender served me well. I felt there was a crazy wonderful relationship between music and science.

With three other guys, Thomas Fernandez, James Atkinson, and Timothy Brownell, from high school, I helped form a rock'n'roll band. The guys and I called our band Hypoallergenic. I was on guitar; Thomas was on tenor sax; James was on clarinet; and Timothy was on drums. James was also our singer. His range went all the way from soprano to baritone. He was a vocal wizard.

Tim's first-year high school sweetheart, Ann Murdoch, dubbed Tim "Sweetman." Not just pretty, she was a great cheerleader and an all-around popular girl. Once we heard her call Tim "Sweetman," we all started calling him by that name.

Whenever we had free time, we practiced in Mother's parking space in the garage of the apartment building my family lived in. Mother's parking space was directly under our apartment.

The Roadmaster was big and very long, almost too big for Mother's allotted space. She was always afraid she might hit the wall or another car while trying to park in that narrow space. After parking in there she had to be very careful opening the car door.

Lucky for us, Mother usually parked the Roadmaster on the street out front. Besides, she believed that dangerous fumes from her car, when she started it, were seeping up into our apartment.

Sweetman and I were tall and athletic; Thomas and James were short and skinny; and we four were the best of friends. Sweetman and I were African American. James's mother was Korean, and his father was of Anglo-Saxon descent. Thomas's mother was from Ireland and his father was from Mexico.

Mother tolerated the "noise" most of the time; then there were times when she couldn't stand it any longer, especially the drums. When we could, we would get our practice done between three and five, before she got home.

When she was there, we'd pile the instruments in Sweetman's old VW van and head for Washington Park.

People from the area, from Cottage Grove to Martin Luther King Drive, would come and gather round to listen to us practice. We never passed the hat. Money wasn't why we were there. "Music gets us in the zone," Sweetman used to say.

The neighborhood around the park, north of my own Hyde Park one, was a working-class neighborhood. We rocked the park. People clapped their hands and some even danced to the music. James sang, rapped, and recited poetry.

I was closest to Sweetman. We hung out together more often, killing time, usually around Old Lake Park Avenue and 53rd Street; we visited music and video shops; at the lakeside we daydreamed about the future, but it bothered me he was a smoker, a chain-smoker. He got adults to buy cigarettes for him; and I doubted that his parents knew he smoked.

Sweetman was also interested in science. He was interested in what made things tick. He too wanted to understand the riddle of the universe and to unravel the mystery of life.

Since both Sweetman and I were big for our ages; bullies never picked on us, but there were times when we had to protect James and Thomas from them. Once I made a boy named Drago apologize to James for calling him by an ethnic slur. After that, whenever Drago saw me, he went the other way.

Music was great, but my dream was never to be a professional musician. I knew I would be some kind of scientist. There were days when I wanted to be an astronaut; I dreamed of flying off beyond gravity and becoming weightless in space. I would look back at the earth in all of its smallness. I would probe time and space as one, to see what Shakespeare called "forever and a day." For me the ultimate question was: What is beyond *forever*?

A week later I wanted to discover a cure for cancer. I read all I could find on cancer research. Soon it became clear it would be a daunting task. Many brilliant people were already working on the cure. I needed my own frontier.

At another time I wanted to be a geologist and spend my life studying the history of the earth as recorded in rocks: limestone, obsidian, marble, quartzite, conglomerate, shale, scoria, gneiss, and siltstone. At the Field Museum of Natural History, I marveled at the textures of rocks, the mystery of their hardness, their age and relationship to time and the earth.

As a geologist I would also be able to make important discoveries on the surface of Mars and on the surfaces of other planets; never mind how I might get to those planets.

I kept shifting. For a while astronomy interested me; then physics and then chemistry took hold. By the time I was ready to graduate from high school, I was sure I would go into molecular biology.

3

While we were still in high school, one summer Mother took Marie and me on a tour of France, Italy, and Spain. Mother said, "This will be your birthday present." It made no sense to us since Marie and I were born in the winter, March eighteenth.

Of course, I wanted to visit the science museums, but Mother kept taking us to the art museums and to fancy restaurants we didn't want to go to. Our flailing did no good. Acting infantile did no good either. Marie and I opted for trying to make the best of the experience.

Mother said to us, "Where are the manners I taught you?" She wanted us to be two examples of bourgeois refinement and we were acting like ordinary American brats.

That reminded me of what one of my teachers said: "Bad things about any minority individuals are generalized and made to apply to the whole group."

I needed to be on my best behavior. I didn't want my bad behavior to reflect on every other African American who ever lived or who would ever live. Marie followed my lead.

Once in the Paris American Express Office, an American tourist woman accosted Mother and said, "What beautiful twins! Did you adopt them?"

Mother's smile was cynical. She had heard similar questions regarding us all our lives. Mother said, "No, I hatched them."

The woman's eyes stretched in alarm; she was not sure if she had been insulted. With a grunt she turned and walked away.

The tour for me remained a nightmare. I had little interest in the things we did or saw. I missed making music with my friends; but I missed, most of all, my new high school girlfriend, Christine Debra Werner. We were in our senior year.

In the last year of elementary school my first puppy love was with a lovely bronze-skinned girl named Tnika Joletta Jackson. Tnika had dimples and she wore her hair in corn-rolls. She grew up to become a wealthy supermodel with her picture on the cover of *Vogue*! But Christy and I had gone "all the way." It was my first time. And I was dying for more.

Early in our relationship, Christy told me all about how she grew up Catholic. She and her family attended St. Thomas the Apostle Church in Hyde Park on South Kimbark Avenue.

"We were casual Catholics," she said.

Her years before public high school in Hyde Park, where I met her, consisted of all things Roman Catholic: rosaries, scapulars, Saint Teresa gifts, daily prayers, mass, nuns, priests, confessions, crucifixes, saints, angels, miracles, martyrs, table tennis, and those starchy school uniforms she hated.

As a little girl she was deeply steeped in drawing and painting and reading stories; she loved the Nancy Drew mysteries; and she especially loved *A Little Princess* and *The Cat in the Hat*. She also went through a Barbie Doll phase, collecting several fashions or phases of them.

In many ways Christy seemed to be a typical American girl: she loved love stories, both consummated and broken-hearted. She spent a lot of time doing her fingernails and toenails, putting up posters of rock stars in her bedroom, daydreaming about her dream love, and a comfortable future in which she would never be tripped up by life.

In Europe we walked a lot. Enraged, Mother would walk on ahead of us. It was a hot summer. Diesel fumes were everywhere. Marie and I also disagreed a lot. We didn't enjoy the same food Mother enjoyed. Mother had hoped for a lighthearted vacation and we caused her to burst into tears.

Mother apparently sensed what was bugging me. I think it was at this point Mother developed a flagrant disdain for Christy, a girl she'd never met. Later, I cringed when Mother asked me about her.

In our senior year, Christy's family moved from Hyde Park to nearby Evanston. They bought a redbrick house, but Christy wasn't happy with the move. She and I believed her family moved in order to try to break up our relationship. They didn't succeed but they made it harder for us to see each other after school.

4

Mother went back to work and we went back to school.

For her last twelve years in Gerdts's History Department, Mother was chief executive officer in charge of all twenty-two personnel in the department. She saw chairs come and go; but Mother talked most glowingly about Professor Laura Steinberg, the incumbent, saying she was the best. Laura had earned her B.A. from Harvard and her Ph.D. from Yale. She specialized in early modern history of Spain and Italy.

Mother was also in charge of managing the department's budget, purchasing, and scheduling. She made arrangements for visitors, booked their hotel rooms. She handled confidential documents, and she selected faculty for subcommittees; and she generally assisted the chair in representing the department.

Sometimes it felt odd being Mother's olive-skinned twins; but the three of us had shared so much. Marie's face was the first face I ever saw; and mine was the first she saw. Then we saw Mother's face, then Dad's face. The three of us were each other's confidante. Despite conflict, we were close. We often laughed at the same time.

Marie and I were extremely close. It was also odd to share something so deep in nature as *duality*. Some tribal peoples worshipped twins. Odd because there was a logical scientific explanation for twins: the mother's body produced too many eggs.

I learned of the infamous Janus head looking in two directions at the same time. One Janus face was Marie's and the other was mine.

Nothing remained the same. Marie and I were headed in different directions.

Growing up she flirted with the idea of becoming a fashion model. She had the required height, the poise, the slenderness, and pretty face. Never mind that her thighs touched when she walked. Because of that flaw, the fashion world told her, she was not acceptable.

Growing up I watched her change. I watched her discover her period; I was witness to her first lipstick and her first bra; I noticed when she started wearing eye shadow and mascara; I saw her apply eye pencil and blush; I saw her buy her first stockings and high heels. I watched her go through uncertain periods about her own attractiveness. I watched her also recover from such doubt.

When Marie started shaving her legs and under her arms, I saw those acts, and similar acts of hers, as evidence our *alikeness* was diminishing. I watched the stirrings of femininity in a girl becoming a woman; I saw a young woman discovering jewelry, pretty clothes, and cute shoes.

I watched her go through a period of anorexia, which she successfully overcame. In high school she flirted with older guys. They knew she was jailbait and they kept their distance. I watched her attempts to gain attention with her body, to be validated, to find reassurance that, because of her attractiveness, she was of value in the world.

By the time we were ready to graduate from high school, Marie and I felt sure education was the key to a better future. That notion propelled us to college. We were also absolutely sure that we would never again be as close as we were when we were younger.

She was absolutely female; I was absolutely male. The terms of our relationship changed; yet we would always confide in each other, and we would always stay in touch.

5

After growing up, I wanted distance––distance from everything that Chicago and family represented.

I moved to California to attend the University of California at Berkeley. I went every summer, for a week or so, to visit Mother and my twin sister. Going back was my way of reassuring myself I was still who I started out being. At the same time, I could keep my distance.

Now Mother had died. I thought about her voice. I talked by phone with her every day up till two or three days before she passed. Those last conversations were calm and consolatory. They hinted at forgivingness.

At one point she was growing thinner and losing her appetite. "My hair is falling out by the handfuls," she said. She sounded tired, tired of living.

Her breathing became sketchy. She was plagued with self-doubt, something she had rarely shown before. Now her defensiveness was gone. She seemed mortally disarmed.

The last time I talked with her on the phone she said, "I had a dream last night. I dreamt I neglected you. I don't think that that is true, but if it *seems* I gave Marie more attention, I'm sorry."

She had clearly favored Marie; but it didn't matter now. I reassured her she had always been a good parent to both of us. She said nothing in response. Her silence was pregnant with defenselessness.

After going away to college, talking with Mother by phone kept me informed on what was going on in the family; she told me who did what, where and when; she also kept me abreast of what was going on at Gerdts and in her neighborhood. This went on for the seven years I was a student at UC Berkeley.

It helped me to live with my guilt for living so far away, for enjoying the distance I had placed between them and me.

When the call came, at the end of two or three days of being unable to reach Mother, it came from Marie who lived on the North Side near the lake.

She said, "Hello, Mark. Elsie called me Saturday night and said Mother was having trouble breathing. I told Elsie to call 911 right away and let them take Mother to the hospital. I'm with her here at Mercy now. She's sleeping but the doctor says it won't be long before she's gone. The cancer has spread far beyond her stomach. I knew a week ago when she stopped smoking the time was near."

Knowing Mother's death was imminent didn't prevent shock. Something in me tried to deny that it was happening. Marie was in the room with her, and she called minutes after Mother passed.

I knew Marie's and my immediate plight was unexceptional: people died all the time, and relatives and friends dealt with it without falling apart. Yet the news overwhelmed me.

When Marie hung up, I went to my window facing 19th Street and watched the traffic pulling up to the stoplight by the hardware store across the street. I was in shock. I watched three teenage boys together strutting along the sidewalk passing the hardware.

All three had disdainful eyes, yet there was a kind of comic gallantry and bravado in them. They were very much alive: to them death was unthinkable. I'd been like them once. To me now, it was suddenly *real* for the first time.

I had to make reservations and contact a lawyer. I would also ask my next-door neighbors, Ralph and Sid, a couple I trusted and depended on, to keep an eye on my apartment while I was away. I did as much for them whenever they were away.

The next day, Tuesday, I got online and made reservations to fly to Chicago on Wednesday. Marie told me Mother's body was moved from the hospital to the morgue, then to O'Connor & Sons Funeral Home, on East 78th Street. I looked them up. They had a respectable online presence. Probably they were going to be just fine for us.

If they weren't already embalming Mother's body, they would do so soon. I tried not to imagine her a corpse, cut open, cleaned out, and stuffed with preservatives. I couldn't help shuddering at my mental image of her laid out on a table, dead.

Despite my rational mind, and despite being a scientist, the image shook me rigorously.

I knew Marie and I would have to start thinking about an array of other issues: Mother's house, her furniture, her valuables, such as jewelry, her clothes, her bank accounts, her investments, stocks and bonds, her insurance policies, her other belongings. And what about Mother's caregiver, Elsie Jones? She would still be living in the house.

Though my sister was a lawyer, she wasn't open to the idea of handling Mother's estate. "We need an estate lawyer," she said. Nor did she want her law firm to do it. I didn't ask why. I told Marie I would locate a lawyer. Following through, online, I searched for Chicago lawyers with offices in the Loop.

I would leave Sacramento on Wednesday; and though I had a return ticket for the following Wednesday, I wasn't sure when I would return. But practicality had to rule. I couldn't take off from work for an indefinite amount of time.

I knew I would be at a hotel in the Loop, probably the Hilton Chicago, and Marie lived just north of the Loop, so a lawyer there would make more sense. I wrote down the telephone numbers of several estate lawyers.

I called two or three, getting secretary after secretary or answering machine after answering machine before I got one whose secretary sounded sufficiently friendly: her name was Samantha. The lawyer was attorney Steven Daniel Berg.

His company was Berg, Armstrong, Gray & Foy. They were on West Harrison Street.

I told Samantha about Mother's death and that I would be arriving in Chicago Wednesday and that once I was settled, I would like to call and make an appointment to see Attorney Berg. I said I would be at a hotel in the Loop, probably the Hilton Chicago.

She offered her sympathy for my loss and took my name and number. "Attorney Berg will be expecting your call," she said. "We look forward to working with you."

During this time, without giving it a name, I was in the first stage of grief——denial——and I knew I would soon begin going through the remaining four classic stages: anger, bargaining, depression and, hopefully, acceptance.

Shock was apparently part of denial. Yet shock seemed odd since Mother's death wasn't a surprise. Marie and I had been anticipating and fearing it. Now we had to deal with the aftermath without things going haywire.

We had to try to keep rational and ignore the inner shrieks threatening to throw us off, to tumble us to the net, or worse.

The sense of freedom I was feeling was troubling; a sense of freedom accompanied by guilt. I hadn't wanted Mother to die. So why did I now feel free of her restraints and ties, free of her voice, free of her very presence, a presence that filled any room she was in?

All my life I had felt indebted to Mother; she had instilled in Marie and me the feeling that we owed her something for giving us life. I resented feeling that way. The anxiety I felt around the debt was gone now. Was a malediction suddenly lifted?

Slowly over time, I realized Mother's life had profoundly underscored my beginnings; and now I was quickly realizing her death signaled an urgent new beginning with endless possibilities for me; but one not without an emotional and psychological price.

I was sequestered in my own loss, with few moorings; I was floating without anchor. The original meaning of freedom was to be without safeguards, without the protection of kin. My connection to Mother had defined me more profoundly than I ever imagined.

At times I felt inadequate, not sure that I could go forward without my shackles: dying, she'd taken with her my leg irons, my fetters, and my iron collar, but was I truly now free?

Mother's death was also having an effect on my relationship with Marie. The death of the one person who linked us might now become a catalyst for widening the distance that had grown between us. I mean, I worried that Marie and I might disagree over Mother's estate; and that might be only the beginning of a deeper gulf.

Marie told me she suspected Mother's death might be a metaphor or catalyst of some kind. Soon after Mother died, she said, "There has to be some comic relief in all of this sadness somewhere."

If so, I wasn't sure what kind of metaphor or catalyst it might be. Sure, Marie recognized the possibility for humor: Mother kicked the bucket; she bought the farm; she will soon be pushing up daisies. But to me none of it was metaphoric, catalytic, or funny.

6

In my senior year at UC Berkeley, the Sacramento division of the Department of Water, Air, and Soil Resources (DWASR) recruited me. When Mother died, I'd been at DWASR for three years. Now, as an alumnus of UC Berkeley, I was constantly getting requests from the school for money.

DWASR was in East Sacramento. It was a good place to work. After living in Berkeley with its mild weather, it took a while to adjust to the hottest summers I had ever known; I had to adjust to northern California's cycle of long periods of drought followed by short periods of excessive rain and snow in the mountains.

I also had to adjust to the politics surrounding the cycle. If we weren't dealing with water control or a water shortage, we were dealing with air pollution or soil erosion or lake pollution or broken spillways or runoff problems.

I knew there were no easy solutions. Air pollution and unclean water had long adversely affected human populations. Greenhouse gases and global warming were problems.

I believed the area's water was part of the environment, and I resented the way it was being politically manipulated. I kept a close watch on the symbiotic relationship between rain or the lack of rain and northern California's bodies of water. The limited supply of clean water was a big issue.

In seven years, I earned three degrees at UC Berkeley: a bachelor of science degree, a master's degree in Environmental Studies, and a graduate degree in Environmental Science, the latter from the College of Natural Resources.

I truly loved the UC Berkeley campus and my classes, not just science and math; I loved my literature classes too. As an undergraduate I took enough lit courses to come away with a good sense of early and modern literature in English.

Berkeley for me wasn't all work and no play. I enjoyed walking across campus on a rainy day or, on a warm sunny day, walking through Memorial Glade and Faculty Glade, walking Campanile Way, Glade Street, Sather Road; and I rode my bike on the bike paths, getting to and from classes.

I felt comfortable on the Berkeley campus. The campus science museums were a favorite. Those were intense but lovely days, the days of my coming of age. I was always serious about my studies; and I wasn't going to whittle away my precious time. I tried to keep diligent and focused.

I also believed in *balance*. During graduate school days, my friends, Clifford, Ashley, and Garth, and I were together a lot. We went to football and basketball games; we played tennis, chess and just hung out drinking beer in bars near campus.

We were keen followers of the San Francisco 49ers football matches and the San Francisco Giants' baseball games. We went out big-time rooting for our teams.

Clifford, Ashley, and Garth were later among my Facebook friends. After college, that was mainly how we kept in touch. Other Facebook friends were scientists I'd met at conferences. I also had a few Facebook friends I didn't know personally, environmental scientists I knew only by reputation.

Clifford, a laid-back redhead, wore raggedy jeans in college all the time; and he usually had a friendly twinkle in his eyes. Cliff was now living in Davis, a few miles from Sacramento, and working at Winik Technologies LLC. He was developing software.

Ashley was blond, sharp-witted, ambitious, and cynical. After college he moved to New York to work in the promotion department at Wells & Chase Publishers, one of the biggest publishers in America.

Garth was prematurely bald and was now in Paris. He'd married a Frenchwoman. I had no idea how he was making a living, and I didn't ask.

The last time the four of us got together was in March of the year I graduated. All of us piled into Cliff's van and drove to Arizona to see the baseball teams in spring training. We had a great time together.

Right after college, I had moved to Sacramento. At first, I was renting an apartment on G Street at McKinley Park. After saving for a few months, I had enough to move to a larger, more comfortable apartment on the top floor of a two-story house at 19th and J Street. Getting to work from there was easy.

The DWASR facility was in a long dark gray barracks-like structure with a light gray metal roof. Inside, there were twenty small offices strung along a long hallway. Herb was in charge of our division. His office was number one. I was in number three.

I was on a team of people focused on water. Others handled air and soil. Thirty of us in the facility were assigned to various aspects of the agenda. There were six other facilities statewide with as many or more engineers.

The facility was set on a gigantic lot containing our vehicles and machinery. At the far end were two warehouses full of supplies and tools we needed to do our work.

We often worked in correlation with the United States Army Corps of Engineers, a federal agency, under the Department of Defense, in the protection of dams, lakes, rivers, and in flood protection.

The Corps had many other concerns around the world, but in

northern California they sometimes assisted us at DWASR. Some of our main sites were Lake Tahoe, Tahoe Dam, Truckee River, Donner Lake, the Klinkhoff Dam, the Jensen Power Plant, and the results of snowmelt in the Sierra mountains.

My duties occasionally took me to Mount Whitney, Donner Pass, Sonora Pass and Mount Langley, to measure snow depth and to advise local officials on problems I saw. In this way most of the resource services tended to assist each other.

In the various towns and cities, local TV news people sometimes interviewed me; they wanted to know what was going on with water, especially during drought periods or after floods and other water-related problems.

I had to be available to explain what was happening with water control, water pollution, lake debris, and the like; to tell them the results of snowpack measurements in the Santa Cruz de la Sierra, and the results of my electronic sensor readings.

We also instituted cleanup programs. As a state agency we were in touch with the Environmental Protection Agency in Washington, D.C. Because it was so big and bureaucratic, our parent agency wasn't always easy to contact and work with.

At the time of Mother's death, I was making a little over eighty thousand a year. Not much, I know, but I felt I was doing work that mattered.

Herb was part of an organization of scientists from all over the country and many from foreign countries, working on a plan to march on Washington to try to get our government to take firmer steps to protect the environment. I was planning to join the march. The date was yet to be set.

7

When I made my booking at the Chicago Hilton, I asked for a room overlooking Grant Park. Marie would pick me up at the airport.

I took a taxi to Sacramento airport, and after passing successfully through the now commonplace indignities of airport security, boarded the plane. Luckily, my seat was on the aisle. I sat and watched the other passengers coming on. Most of them were big like me. I thought this will be a very heavy ship moving across the sky.

I buckled my seatbelt; and I noticed that the cabin had the usual metallic smell, and the air was listless. A young woman in denim jacket and pants was already by the window. She was buckled in and seemed to be already asleep. College student, I thought.

Between her and me, in the middle, was a man with a sheepish but friendly smile. He was dressed in a homemade-looking green jacket and red cotton pants. He seemed almost apologetic for smiling or for his very existence.

Once we were airborne, he said, "Hello, I'm Viktor Weinberg..." He spoke in a near-whisper, like somebody atoning or feeling remorseful.

"Mark Smith," I said, extending my hand, but he didn't take mine. Instead, he looked at it intensely and with an apologetic smile.

He said, "Sorry, I don't think you want to touch me. Germs, you know. I would be happy to shake your hand if I could, but I can't. It's that's... well, you see, I don't want to give you anything. I'm pleased to meet you. You live in Chicago?"

"No, Sacramento. How about you?"

"Chicago. I'm returning home. I visit Sacramento twice a year to spend time with my old math professor, Pierre Rothschild. He's well known in the math world. It's a pity, he's now in an asylum. He's perfectly normal but they keep him there against his will. What's the occasion for your visiting Chicago, if I may ask?"

I noticed he was holding his hand over his mouth as he talked. It wasn't that he had bad breath. He had a rather soapy clean smell.

I said, "My mother died. I'm going to her funeral."

"Oh," said Viktor. "People do die, don't they?" He chuckled sardonically. "Is your father living?"

"No," I said, thinking I was revealing too much to a stranger, a *strange* stranger.

"When your father was living, did he ever take you to see baseball games at Wrigley Field?"

"Yes. I was ten years old; it was the year he died. It was a great experience seeing the Cubs play. I'm a big Cubs fan."

He said, "My father didn't like me." He chuckled sadly. "My mother died too, maybe *because* I was born."

And, again, he laughed, this time with a twinkle in his gray eyes that looked like two rhinestones. "My father died last year. I'm a Jew and I grew up in the Deep South, in Mississippi, and it wasn't easy."

"Oh?"

"Oh, I got by a lot of the time because, although I'm a Jew, I'm also white. The average person in the street couldn't tell if I was a Jew. I only had trouble when people heard my name."

I nodded.

"But I kept to myself as much as possible. I read books, books on mathematics. I hid out in the local public library to keep from being harassed."

I nodded again.

"I love mathematics; constructivism and such. I am also interested in match theory. Do you know match theory?"

"No."

"It's rather interesting. It's about mutually beneficial relationships."

I said, "That doesn't happen very often does it?"

He chuckled. "Not as often as it should."

I said nothing. No response was sometimes the best response; it could be a declaration, a proclamation, louder than a murmur or a shout.

Viktor was still covering his mouth as he talked, and I wondered why: a pathological fear of germs? Which germs? I suspected he was more afraid of *catching* germs than spreading them.

Viktor said, "I'm not well, but I'm not *meshuga*. Anyhow, thank you for listening to me."

I nodded and said, "You're welcome."

He laughed, all the while watching me closely. "I'm really harmless. I don't bother anybody. If you would rather not be bothered, Mr. Smith, I will shut up. It's all right."

"You aren't bothering me, Mr. Weinberg."

"Call me Viktor, it's okay. Mr. Weinberg sounds *so* formal. I don't deserve that much respect." This time he chuckled as his face turned red. "I am seeing some doctors and I think they've secretly implanted devices in my brain. They keep changing my medicine. I don't trust them. I'm sure they're trying to control my thoughts."

"How do you mean?"

"I don't know how they do it but they have a lot of control. They're very smart and they hate me. They dismiss me as a mathematical neophyte. They think I don't know. Nothing matters anyway. I won't be around long."

At this point I knew he was schizophrenic, and I began feeling sympathy for him. He seemed harmless enough and my interest in him actually increased. I said, "Do you work?"

"Oh, I can't work. I'm on disability. No, no, I can't work. Look at me. I'm a mess. How could I work? Who would hire me to do anything? Years ago, I taught in a high school on the South Side. All my students were colored. They were good kids. I do have a master's degree in mathematics, and I am intelligent, but what good does it do me? What use is there in anything? What do you do?"

I told Viktor about the work I did. With his hand still covering his mouth, he was nodding as I talked about my work. When I finished, Viktor said, "Water is the light of life. Nothing lives without it." He paused. "What caused your mother's death?"

The girl by the window suddenly opened her eyes and gave both of us an annoyed look.

I said, "She had cancer of the stomach."

"I'm sorry. What was her name?"

"Adella Bischoff Smith."

He kept nodding and with a secret smile he said, "Death is really what life is all about, isn't it? We are all aiming for it. Don't you think?" He didn't wait for me to respond. Instead, he said, "I've thought about killing myself, but I always stop since, in a way, I am already dead—I mean with death living inside me. It's been with me from birth."

I said, "Oh, I don't know."

He suddenly nodded then said, "I'm going to stop talking now and do a bit of reading. Thank you for listening to my rambling. People don't usually respect me enough to listen to what I say. Thank you, Mr. Smith."

I nodded.

He laughed again. "I'm reading a really interesting book on the relationship between math and nature. It's quite good." Then he reached down and pulled the book out of his bag on the floor and held it up in the beam of light from the ceiling. The dust jacket was red.

I nodded approval, and Viktor opened his book and started reading. Then I closed my eyes and rested my head against the headrest.

Part Two

"So the darkness shall be the light, and the stillness the dancing."
—*T.S. Eliot*

8

Right away, I saw Marie standing at one of the O'Hare luggage carousels. Behind her the carousel was moving with its perpetual efficiency, around and around, as ex-passengers snatched their luggage from it in mid-motion. Marie was holding her smartphone.

Seeing her on occasions like this, I always saw her with fresh eyes. She was wearing a blue jumpsuit and a white scarf around her neck and blue heels. She was tall and slender, tall like our father, and tall like me. Always thin, she looked like she had lost weight. I hoped she wasn't becoming anorexic, something she had flirted with during her teen years.

I remembered that for a couple of years she had daydreamed about becoming a fashion model. At the time beautiful women of color, like herself, were being featured on the cover of popular fashion magazines like *Vogue* and *Glamour*.

Now, Marie was running to meet me. Tears were in her eyes. We embraced and I kissed her on her cheek.

"I feel so miserable over Mother's death," she said.

"I know, I know. I do too."

She said, "Wait! I want to take a picture of us together." She was holding her phone out in front of us and she clicked the picture. I had my arm around her shoulder.

We laughed together as she showed me the picture while we heard beyond the glass doors a few yards away the banging and clatter and chatter and the honking and roaring and groaning of vehicle traffic and people outside on the street. Luckily, the shot wasn't bad. I looked tired and Marie looked a bit wild with too much mascara.

While we waited, Marie said, "We're using, for the funeral services, both at the funeral home and the burial, a friend of Mary's, Dr. Julia Pallas. She's a non-denominational minister, a bit of a freethinker. She compliments Mother's thinking perfectly. I think you will like her."

"That's fine," I said, but I was wondering how could one be both religious and freethinking? I said nothing. As a secularist, one thing I never discussed was religion or the lack of it with anybody, not even my twin sister. Such a discussion could only lead to an impasse or worse.

The luggage conveyor was still turning. While we waited, I looked at Marie. I was surprised at how much older she looked; and I thought I must look older too to her. Hell, we were older.

She and I were now thirty-four, yet she looked older than I thought she should. Thirty-five was the big number coming up soon. It signaled time passing and aging.

"How are you?" she said.

"I'm doing okay," I said. "How is Mary?"

Mary was my sister's wife. Mary Novakovich was of Serbian-Croatian descent. She was a forty-three-year-old professor at Northwestern University in Evanston, a short distance from where she and Marie lived.

Mary taught in the history department, and her discipline was the cultures of Russia and Poland and to a lesser extent Croatia, Hungary, and Romania.

The idea of same-sex marriage at the time, which some people were calling The Obama Era, was still relatively new. Not surprisingly it had taken Mother a while to accept the marriage, but even she came around.

"Mary is fine," Marie said. "No, I shouldn't say that. You know she had breast cancer? I told you that. Right?"

"Yes, you did." I saw my luggage coming toward me.

"She's in remission now. Thank God! We're taking it one day at a time. It's all we can do." She took a deep breath and let it out. "We're grateful for the remission."

I reached down and grabbed my luggage, pulled it up and off the conveyor and sat it on the floor. "That's good she's in remission."

"Mary's son, Roswell, and his girlfriend, Celosa, are at the house. I think you met them the last time you were here."

"Yes. Twice. Are they both still in college?"

"Yes, they drove here from New York. She has two more years of graduate work at NYU and he has one more year at City. Roswell is now twenty-two. Celosa is twenty-one. Time flies."

"I know Mary's proud of him!"

"Why haven't *you* found a girl to marry? You're gainfully employed. Don't forget, 'It is a truth universally acknowledged, that a single man in possession of a good fortune, must be in want of a wife.'"

I laughed, remembering that Jane Austin sentence. "But I don't have a fortune."

"It's all relative, Mark. You have fortune enough. Plus, you're a handsome young man; and you're strong, tall, and athletic; you're long-legged, copper-complexioned; you're clean-shaven, and already facing the world with confidence."

"That doesn't sound like me."

"That's the way I see you, brother. Countless women find those qualities attractive."

I shook my head in disbelief.

My sister was giving me a coy look. She was also clearly being ironic. In other words, "messing with me."

I blushed and said, "It's the roll of the dice."

We were now walking out onto the sidewalk where taxis were lined up, and buses and hotel limos were double-parked. People were standing or lining up waiting for taxis or particular buses or specific hotel limos.

The roar of traffic was intense and engulfing. Vehicle fumes were thick. Attendants blew their whistles, calling for taxis. Annoyed people, with their luggage, stood eagerly waiting.

Marie said, "I saw your old high school girlfriend Christy Werner yesterday at the supermarket in Evanston. Mary and I shop up there because we like the choices better, and it's only a ten- or fifteen-minute drive from our home. She asked about you. She asked about Mother too. I told her——"

"Christy Werner. I've often thought about her. Is she married now? Does she have kids?"

"Don't know..."

The last time I saw Christy, with her long, fluffy, auburn hair, was the day before I left for Berkeley. We were deeply in love. That night we made love in the back of Sweetman's old VW van, which was parked under a tree in his family's backyard; by then the VW was permanently out of commission.

Christy and I wept together; I was leaving the next day. She had already been accepted at the School of the Art Institute of Chicago and, while attending classes, she would be staying in Evanston with her parents.

I had only our idyllic romance to take with me to California. During the first year we kept in touch.

Then, during my second year, I stopped hearing from her. I was puzzled. I felt something had gone wrong. In time, I assumed she had gotten interested in somebody else, and I stopped trying to get her to respond.

"I'm parked way out. It's a bit of walk," Marie said. "You want me to pull your carry-on?"

"No. I can handle both." We crossed the street at the crosswalk. "I've learned to travel light."

While riding toward the city in Marie's red Porsche——which still had its new smell of new leather and new cloth and plastic——I was preoccupied with questions about Mother's death. "Tell me about Mother," I said.

"I told you everything. She stopped smoking, after a lifetime of smoking, and I knew something was up. Elsie had become very protective. In recent years she became more and more secretive about Mother. I couldn't find out much about what was going on. To see what was going on, I decided to spend a few days living in the house. So, I slept in the guestroom."

"Wasn't that Elsie's room?"

"No, she sleeps in the other bedroom. She liked it there. That narrow stairway always gave me the creeps. I stayed in the house just to see what was going on. I could see Mother really wasn't being cared for the way she needed to be. For example, she wasn't getting bathed every day."

I said, "Mother told me bathing every day, at her age, wasn't good for her skin. Her doctor told her that. She had very sensitive skin, you know."

"I know that," Marie snapped, "but not getting bathed for a whole week is downright neglect; and she wasn't eating properly either."

"Mother was always a picky eater; and you know she was stubborn. No one could make her do anything she didn't want to do."

"Elsie wouldn't tell me things I needed to know. I'd ask if Mother was sleeping okay. Elsie would just say, sure, she's fine. Every answer was, sure, she's fine; but Elsie did cook every day, and she did the shopping; even after Mother's car wasn't running, Elsie would take a taxi to the supermarket to do the shopping. And she kept the house clean."

"Well, I'm glad she was there for Mother. We could have done a lot worse than Elsie."

9

Marie said, "How about you? How are things going with you? Still seeing...what was her name, Nina?"

"No, we broke up." I knew how that sounded to my sister. I knew my sister suspected I was just out there hooking up, in other words having casual affairs, but "hook up" and "casual" were never in my romantic vocabulary, and never in my romantic aspirations or actual life.

After I stopped hearing from Christy, I hoped to meet a young woman I could have a relationship with and trust completely and marry at some point in the future, but my luck so far had been bad. I was hoping to drop anchor in new waters and find consolation in love and marriage. I wanted to have a family and children. I was earnestly still trying to get there.

In my first year of graduate school, I was trying to move on when I met Nina-Momo Ishikawa at an annual February conference. It was the Conference on Climate Change in a Changing World; that year it was held at the University of Colorado in Boulder.

Nina was about my complexion, and she had thick black hair. She was thin and small and full of energy and intellectual vitality. She wore very simple clothes: cotton skirts and blouses, nothing fancy. She was strong and energetic and given to sudden outbursts of nervous laughter.

Nina and I happened to be sitting side by side listening to Dr. Payton Rexford speaking on the increasing phenomenon of earthquakes around the world. After the lecture, Nina and I introduced ourselves. I could see her nametag and she could see mine. We decided to go to one of the kiosks for coffee in the lobby.

With our coffee in hand, we found seats in the open area of the lobby, and we told each other about ourselves amidst the medley of many voices and the clicking and clanging sounds of the open area where attendees by the hundreds were moving back and forth, going to and coming from sessions.

I learned Nina was born and raised in Minneapolis, and she got her M.S., in Environmental Studies, or, as some said, Environmental *Science*, at the University of Minnesota. She was now teaching at Baxter State College in Tulsa, Oklahoma.

Nina was very open about her life. She was a couple of years older than I. She was divorced and had a six-year-old daughter, Ryo. Nina's parents were divorced. Her mother lived with her and helped her with Ryo, and her father was remarried and still lived in Minnesota.

That first night Nina and I had dinner together at a Japanese restaurant on the mall in Boulder. We had a wonderful meal that started with miso soup and then we shared small portions of sukiyaki, ramen, onigiri, soba, yakiniku, tempura, yakitori, udo, natto, edamame and a dish of tofu skin. The aroma was delightful. Most of these things I was eating for the first time.

Then after dinner we went to my hotel room. She had a room in the same hotel, but she ended up spending the night with me. The bed sheets were brand new and crisp and so were the pillowcases. I hadn't been in bed with a woman in a long while and it took a little while to adjust to it, but by morning it felt fine.

The next morning was a Saturday, and rather than getting up and rushing off to the conference, Nina and I stayed in bed and again made love.

"Mark," she said, "I like you. I hope we can do this every year." She smiled, waiting for me to respond. Her smile was sad, but her face was hopeful. I felt like I was on a ship looking through a porthole at a loved one on shore as the ship was slowly pulling out to sea.

Unsure if I really meant it, I said, "No reason why we can't." Clearly, with nothing better in sight, I was trying to hold onto a possible relationship far inferior to the one I dreamed of having. Was that a bird in the bush?

That next February the conference was held in Taos, New Mexico, a place of big endless skies and sudden storms followed often by flourishing sunlight and fast-moving clouds. As a person who worked with the natural world, New Mexico interested me. They had good reason for calling it the "land of enchantment."

I admired New Mexico's ancestral pueblos, its Anasazi ruins, its Mogollon ancient cliff dwellings, and its Aztec ruins. I marveled at the rugged landscape with its scrub brush and cacti. Nina and I toured the national parks and we shopped in the cultural centers and went to trading posts on reservations. We bought souvenirs.

Nina and I hung out together throughout the whole Taos conference and we slept together all four nights. This time we shared the same room. I was getting used to being with her. Despite knowing there was no closer relationship possible, I was comfortable with her.

On our last night in Taos we went to Bib Bob's Restaurant for dinner. Our waitress was an elderly woman who, somehow, looked familiar. She was clearly Native American, and logic told me I had never seen her before. When she brought our steak and fries dinners to the table, I said, "I'm Mark. What's your name?"

"Mary."

"Just Mary?"

"Mary Etawa," she said hesitantly.

Funny how people you've never seen before can look familiar.

Nina and I kept in touch by email, but she loved to write letters with her fancy ink pen. I received from her dozens of long chatty letters during the months we were apart. I hardly ever answered by so-called snail mail.

I answered mainly by email. My penmanship was awful. I myself could barely read it. Most of my generation grew up without penmanship skills. We were born to the technology that begot computers, mobile phones, and other electronic instruments.

The last time Nina and I met, the conference was held in San Francisco, a city of hills and trolley cars, a city teaming with good people on the move. Again, she and I got together for four days.

At the beginning of our relationship, she had told me she wasn't interested in marriage. On our last night together I said, "Nina, have you by any chance changed your mind about marriage?" I was hoping she had.

She gave me a puzzled look. "No." Her "no" was emphatic.

Our correspondence dropped off, and Nina and I stopped seeing each other. She didn't come to the conference the next year, in New York City. I was there, but I wasn't at the one following the New York City conference. I think she went to the next one in Los Angeles. I knew something in me sabotaged the relationship because from my point of view it was going nowhere.

Then I got a long letter from her saying in effect she wasn't looking for a serious relationship. She wanted to raise her daughter. Later she might consider something more serious. It was the end of my relationship with Nina-Momo Ishikawa.

Months passed. While I was still a graduate student at Berkeley, I met Ida Eldred, a nineteen-year-old undergraduate from Seattle.

Ida and I met in the campus coffee shop, a place smelling of strong, often burnt, coffee and sweet rolls––a place with the clamor and busyness of students coming and going. Ida happened to walk over to my table and ask if she could sit there. To be sure there *were* other seats available. "Yes, of course," I said.

Right away, I liked her peachy complexion. In terms of her dressing, she didn't stand out from the usual appearance of students there: cotton tops and jeans. She had a square jaw and a Dutch boy haircut. Her eyes sparkled when she talked to me.

She also had a way of turning her head slightly to the side, so she was looking at me from the corners of her eyes while maintaining the twinkling, even teasing, look. Her Valentine-shaped lips were a pleasure to behold.

I later found out her family had money and she was in line to inherit some of it but for now her older brother, Kevin, was in charge of her portion of the family money till she reached the age of twenty-one.

I invited her to dinner at Eureka, a bistro not far from campus. We ate gourmet burgers, and I talked a lot, and she laughed a lot. That was our first date.

She lived off-campus in an apartment that smelled of cat-pee, and she had a roommate, Jill. The cat was Jill's. I also had an off-campus apartment and I also at the time had a roommate, Clifford—Cliff with the bright red hair and dirty jeans. We were roommates for about a year.

Since Ida and I both had roommates, whenever I could afford it, we opted for a hotel or motel room usually near campus.

When her roommate was in class or at work, we made love at her place, and we made love at my place when Cliff was in class or at work.

Ida was at the beginning of her senior year when I graduated. Now I had my graduate degree and a job offer in Sacramento, and I was ready to leave Berkeley.

"Can I come with you?" said Ida.

"What about your classes? You're close to graduating."

"I know and that's a problem, but I want to be with *you*."

"I want to be with you too, but I wouldn't advise you to drop out of school at this point."

"Maybe I could commute?"

"I wouldn't be able to drive you and you don't know how to drive nor do you have a license."

"I could take the train."

"If you want, we could try it," I said, thinking for the first time it might be possible for us to continue to be together and for her to stay in school till she graduated.

When I moved to Sacramento, a few days later, Ida followed. She had some trouble getting out of the lease she had with Jill, a nice tall girl from Ann Arbor, Michigan; but Ida found another girl, Arleta, an economics major, to take her place.

I knew it would happen. Ida dropped out of college. "I want to spend more time with you," she said.

Ida and I lived together in my G Street apartment. She scoured the Sacramento SPCA and the county animal shelter looking for a cute puppy. She picked up a one-year-old brown and black mixed-breed puppy from the Front Street Animal Shelter, and she named her Lottie. Despite my initial hesitation, I enjoyed the puppy, but our apartment began to smell of dog.

I felt guilty about Ida because I knew she loved me, and I wasn't in love with her. I feared her love for me was ravenous. I adored her and I needed her at a bad time in my life after the loss of Christy and Nina. I was kind to her, and I felt compassion for her. In her presence I felt a blurry serenity and a serene comfort. At the time I thought love had to be fireworks, the kind I felt with Christy. In retrospect, I was wrong.

The guilt weighed on me. After Ida and I were together almost a year her family convinced her she was ruining her life and she needed to go back to college. So, when she left for New York to attend New York University, I was relieved. She took Lottie with her, but Lottie's odor remained for a long time.

After Ida was in New York several months, she sent me a letter: "Mark, I forgive you. No hard feelings. I will always cherish our time together. Love, Ida." That "forgive you" was a bit ambiguous: forgive me for what for letting her go, for not convincing her to stay? I would never know what she meant, but I suspected she meant, *I forgive you for not loving me.*

Françoise Germaine and I met in a movie theater in Sacramento. We happened to be sitting side by side. The feature was a classic Francois Truffaut film, *The 400 Blows.*

When the lights came on, a pretty blonde turned to me and said, "An amazing film!"

"Yes," I said.

"*Bonjour! Parlez-vous français?*"

"Just a little," I said.

"I'm Françoise. Your name?"

"Mark."

"Mark, this is the *tenth* time I've seen this film and every time it astonishes me."

"I've seen it three times," I said. I had seen it once in Chicago in an art cinema theater on the Near North Side and twice in Berkeley.

That's how Françoise and I met. I liked her instantly, liked her face, her voice, her French accent, her poise.

All of this I learned later: Françoise was originally from a small village in western France about three hours by car from Paris on the Loire River in Upper Brittany.

She'd come to America as an exchange student to study creative writing, which she said wasn't available at any French university, and she decided to stay. She fell in love with California, and she decided to live there.

Her father, Maurice-Henri Germaine, was a famous filmmaker with a long list of well-known French films to his credit. His films were both artistic and highly commercial. They were seen all over the world.

Many of his films had won French film awards such as the French Syndicate of Cinema Critics, the Grand Prix at Annecy, and other awards. One of his films won an Academy Award in the foreign film category.

Her mother, Damela Beauchêne-Germaine, was now retired from a clerical job she had held during the early years of her marriage to her struggling filmmaker husband. In those years she'd supported the family.

Françoise's family was now wealthy. Her family owned a villa in

Cetona, southwestern Tuscany; an apartment in Paris on Rue Saint-Honoré, Louvre-Palais Royal; a farmhouse in Bordeaux, in central France; and a cottage in Newquay, Cornwall, England.

Françoise was two years older than I was. She was a sophisticated young woman. She walked gracefully like a ballet dancer. As a child she had had ballet lessons: shoulders back, stomach in, chin up, back arched; and while walking her feet, with each step, pointed to the side rather than forward.

We started out dating— going to movies, eating dinner in fancy restaurants up and down J Street between 20th and 25th; and we frequented cafes and bistros; we saw plays at Sacramento's Community Center Theater and elsewhere. We drove to San Francisco to see opera. She *loved* opera.

One sunny day in April we went to the Asparagus Festival in Stockton, San Joaquin County. We walked around in the crowds eating the crispy deep-fried vegetables and enjoying the festivities. Doing such things, we spent a lot of time together.

We dated for six or seven months. She and I never argued; so, what happened? Simply, she left for France to visit her parents and stayed a long time. While she was away, we drifted apart. I wasn't aware when she returned. That's what happened.

10

Marie was in a good permanent relationship. It seemed to her that I was living a frivolous love life. She was worried about me. Mother, too, had wanted me to get married; but I said, why marry just to marry? I needed first to find the *right* woman.

Foolishly, I daydreamed about my high school sweetheart, Christine Debra Werner; a girl I still thought about. I couldn't help hoping for what seemed impossible.

"So, what are you doing *now*?" Marie said.

"I'm being celibate," I said. "Working hard. Playing video games on my computer and watching TV; catching a football game now and then; basketball too; going to the gym and staying in shape; and getting my proper sleep. I don't have a girlfriend. I'm not dating. It's okay. I'm not unhappy."

Marie drove to the Hilton and turned off the motor. I told her to wait for me in front. One of the bellhops came over and placed my luggage on a four-wheeler while I entered the lobby. He waited at the front desk as I checked in.

Then we rode up together in the elevator. He placed the large luggage on the luggage stand, opened the heavy blinds; I tipped him, and he thanked me and left. I used the bathroom, then went down and got back into the car with Marie.

We drove for a while in silence and before long we were on Marie's street in Old Town on the edge of the Historic District.

She and Mary owned a grand old hundred-year-old renovated north side mansion within walking distance of the beach.

Marie pulled into the driveway and parked behind what I assumed was Celosa's black Honda Civic and turned off the motor. Marie turned to me and said, "Here we are!"

I looked at the house and its surroundings. The front garden was decorated with well-cared-for shrubbery and hedges, and the flowers were beautiful. The aroma of sparkling dahlias, creeping thyme, gloriosa daisies, marigolds, pineapple lilies, and yarrows was pleasant. Mary was the family gardener.

I was as impressed this time as I had been the first time a few years earlier. The house was a two-story, Tudor-style, red brick structure, built in the 1920s. The façade was of white stucco square and triangular panels with oak wooden claddings on the upper floor gables.

The front door was equally impressive: it looked like a door from a medieval castle with a tiny round painted-glass window top-and-center and a large black metal doorhandle.

By now Mary had come out onto the walkway and was smiling and waving to us. She was thinner than she was a year earlier. Had the cancer taken its toll? Smiling was unusual for her, but I was happy to see it. Even before cancer she had been a rather somber if not grim person.

Marie and I got out of the car.

It was hot and getting hotter, unusual weather for April in Chicago. I met Mary in the walkway and we embraced. I said, "How are you, Mary?"

She knew what I meant. She nodded, giving me a faint smile. "I'm almost finished with the chemotherapy."

"Glad to hear it, Mary," I said.

"Some of the cells had spread beyond the breast, that's why they had to use chemo. The radiation treatments worked only so far, in just a targeted area; but, to answer your question in an answer longer than you need I'm doing okay."

Mary and I stood together looking at Marie. She was taking our picture with her phone. A bee was swarming around her head.

Mary smiled and with fervor said, "Mark, you don't look a day older. You look splendid!"

I wanted to say, Mary you looked great, but I couldn't because she didn't. The cancer had taken a toll. With barely disguised angst, I said, "Thanks, Mary!"

She said, "Welcome home, Mark! Sweet home, Chicago! Wish the occasion was happier."

"Me too," I said and didn't know what else to say.

Roswell and Celosa met us at the front door. The house smelled of freshly baked oatmeal cookies. I first met Roswell at Marie's and Mary's wedding five years earlier. I met Celosa last year when visiting Mother during the time she was very ill and had lost a lot of weight.

Roswell and I bumped fists and Celosa hugged me.

Roswell was as good-looking as ever, with red hair like his mother's. He was a carefree, easy-going fellow with a quick smile. He smiled or grinned almost all the time. A smile was his default; but at times he could be sarcastic with the stab of a quick joke. Most of the time his eyes showed him to be a kind person who was shy and pleasant.

Mary had spoiled him. Before she and Marie married, Mary raised him as a single parent and doted on him. She also played the martyr. "You have no idea what I went through to bring you into this world," was one of her favorite accusations.

The day of his birth was essentially her day of sacrifice and victory. In other words: more *her day* than his. Mother held the same philosophy of childbirth. No wonder she and Mary got along so well.

When he was about fifteen, Mary and her son went through a

garrulously angry period. They quarreled bitterly. She was often sancti-
monious when she wasn't playing the martyr. He often flung recrimina-
tions at her.

Shortly after Roswell turned eighteen, mother and son declared a
truce. After Mary and Marie married, Roswell's snarky volubility was
somehow kept in check. This was the way Mary and Roswell were on my
arrival: in a state of peaceful détente.

There was no father in the picture. Mary went to a clinic to be
artificially impregnated. While Roswell was growing up, they lived in
Evanston, near the university where she taught. When she and Marie
married, they bought this house and moved in together.

Marie moved from her apartment in the Loop, where she was living,
because it was close to her workplace, Calloway, Tate and Associates.
Earlier, while she was a student at the University of Chicago's Law School,
she'd lived on the South Side in Hyde Park with a roommate, near our old
neighborhood.

Celosa Johnson was an alluring, slender, brown-skinned young
woman with lots of beautiful black hair framing her apple-shaped face.
She was charming and engaging and graceful. She also had pretty dimples
and held a secret smile as though she knew something nobody else knew.
She was cute-small, even petite, and fond of wearing sarongs, giving her a
glamorous and winsome appearance.

She also changed her hairstyle a lot. One day it was a big, glorious
Afro, the next it was in African braids. She went from mambo twist to
box and from braided-up-do to corn-rolls, from synthetic to braided
Mohawk and from tapered to simple twists. Her hair was a live changing
art show.

Celosa was from a well-to-do family on Long Island. Her father was
a medical doctor and her mother an elementary school teacher. She grew
up attending private schools and was an A-student. She carried herself
with a great deal of self-assurance.

She and Roswell had been together now for several years and everybody expected them to marry when they finished college.

11

The next morning Marie and Mary picked me up at the hotel and we headed for Mother's house at 83rd and Lockwood Avenue.

When Mother bought the house, the neighborhood was classified as "safe." Because of recent gang activity, police and real estate people now classified it as "unsafe."

Marie was driving. The three of us fitted comfortably in her Porsche. I was in the back and the two of them were in the front.

Roswell and Celosa were in her car behind us. I could see them in the rearview mirror. I remembered that he was a very careful driver, but my sister's distracted driving was making me nervous. I was cringing.

Marie was talking about Mary's doctor. Then Marie's phone rang a couple times, and she answered it. She was still talking when she nearly ran into the rear of the car in front of her because she hadn't noticed the rhythm of the traffic had slowed.

As we approached the South Side, Marie said, "When Mother first moved into this neighborhood it was one of the best on the South Side. Now, I hate taking my car out here. The neighborhood has become so dangerous. Gangs, you know; but I risk it in the daytime. I *definitely* wouldn't park out here on any of these streets after dark."

It was a sunny, warm morning, not yet hot. It felt good to be on Lake Shore Drive again. People were out running, and I could see blue and red and orange sailboats with white sails far out on Lake Michigan. The expressway wasn't yet congested, as it would be later in the day

Roswell and Celosa were now farther behind us and they soon disappeared from the rearview mirror. By the time we were out as far as Oakwood Boulevard they reappeared.

When we came off the expressway and entered the neighborhood streets, people along the sidewalks looked at us. Marie's fancy Porsche stood out from all the other cars. No wonder she worried about driving it out here.

We parked in front of Mother's house. It was a white stucco with black shutters and Dutch windows. The house was situated back from the sidewalk with a walkway running from the sidewalk up to the stone steps. The front lawn was small and well-kept with a plot of green grass on either side of the walkway and steps. It was one of the best-looking houses on the block.

Marie and I never lived here. After Mother retired, she gave up our Hyde Park apartment. She chose this Greenwood Avenue house because she fell in love with it and she said she was "tired of living in an apartment." This was the ideal, comfortable home she had always wanted.

Elsie Jones came out onto the front porch to greet us, but she looked as grim as a homeless dog. Elsie was a heavyset dark-brown-skinned woman with shoulder-length black hair just beginning to turn gray. If she ever had any vanity it was now gone. Elsie was wearing what used to be called a housedress. It had sunflowers printed all over it.

She must have been in her mid-to-late fifties. She had relatives down south, an aunt on her mother's side, an uncle on her father's side, and a large group of cousins, most of whom she hadn't seen in many years.

Elsie was hired by Mother the year she retired. Over time the two women became best of friends.

Marie called out to her, "We're here!" She chuckled.

Up on the porch, I shook Elsie's hand. She gave me a tight timid smile. I said, "Thank you, Elsie, for taking care of Mother all these years. I can't say thank you enough."

Marie smirked and snapped, "Elsie already knows we are grateful."

"Excuse me?"

"She doesn't *need* you to tell her what she *knows*," said Marie angrily.

Elsie said, "It's all right, Marie. Mark didn't mean no harm. This is a very dark time, but remember what Dr. Martin Luther King, Jr. said, 'Only in the darkness can you see the stars.'"

Elsie smiled at me. "Your mother was happy she lived long enough to see President Obama take office. She lived long enough to see him *re*-elected too."

"I know," I said.

"Adella was something else."

"I know."

"Your mother even visited the president in the White House. Did you know that?"

"Yes, I know. Thank you, Elsie. Yeah, she talked with me about it a lot."

I remembered Mother saying, "I used to see Mr. Obama walking in the neighborhood when we lived in Hyde Park. I saw him several times." We were having one of our hour-long telephone conversations shortly after the-president-to-be won the first time. Mother was very excited. I was more amazed than excited.

Now we all went inside, and Elsie locked the door. There were two doors to lock: the inside door and the outside iron-grated door Mother had had installed after the neighborhood's streets were taken over by gangs and drug trafficking.

The house was full of the hot and pungent cooking smells of sweet cornbread and collard greens with fatback. Behind those odors were the remains of Mother's cigarette smoke. Whenever I thought of collard greens, I translated it to "colored" greens. It was my own little private joke.

We were in the dining room when the doorbell rang. Marie went to see who was there. It was three of Mother's neighbors: Anna Belle Johnson, Ruby Mae Williams, and Carla Ann Carter.

Marie opened the door. The ladies came in greeting us warmly. Mrs. Johnson said, "Marie and Mark, we just wanted to let you guys know we in the neighborhood *loved* your mother. She was dear to our hearts; and we are going to miss her so much. We just stopped by to offer you our condolences. We're not going to stay."

Miss Carter added: "She was the first person in this neighborhood to accept me without question. I'll always be grateful to her for that." Tears ran down her cheeks.

Mrs. Ruby Mae Williams said, "We all someday have to pass on and because Adella was such a good person, I'm sure she is already in a *better* place."

"Amen," said Anna Belle.

Elsie offered them lunch, but they said no thanks.

Miss Carter said, "We know you folks have a lot to take care of and we don't want to take up any more of your time. We'll see you at the funeral. God bless you all."

With that said, they left.

"That was nice," said Mary.

Marie sneered and said, "Things weren't always so sweet as they make it out to be now that she is gone."

Mary said, "What'd you mean?"

"Oh, they were friends all right, but not without the usual squabbles and altercations," said Marie.

Elsie said, "They loved Adella, Marie. I don't know what you're referring to. I don't know anything about no fallings-out between your mama and those women. Adella was the first person in this neighborhood to accept Miss Carter. You know she was born male."

"I know," said Marie. "I shouldn't have said anything."

Mary went to the kitchen with Elsie to make coffee; Marie, Celosa, Roswell and I went to the living room.

Mother's living room was bright and cheerful. Like so many living rooms, it seemed unlived-in. The red, yellow, and blue carpet in the center of the floor was antique Persian. A large painting of an Impressionist landscape by local artist Joe Walker, who had taught briefly at Gerdts, hung over the couch.

Mother had expensive taste. A chair was teal midcentury modern. The sofa was Visconti gold. An armchair of the same color was made of tufted linen. The fireplace hadn't been used in many years. The curtains were bright golden yellow. It was a room to look at, not one to use.

I walked over to the mantel and looked at the framed photographs. Among them was one of Marie and me as infants posed together resting against a stack of pillows. The others were of her mother and father, our grandparents, and several of Mother and Dad together at various times during their brief marriage.

"Marie, you should send all the photographs to me and I will have them duplicated and return the originals to you. In that way we can both have all of them."

"Now is *not* the time to talk about something like that! *How could you?*" And she burst into tears.

"I'm sorry," I said.

"Don't be so insensitive!" she snapped. "Mother just died!" She sobbed, covering her face with both hands.

I walked over and put my arms around her, and she rested her head on my shoulder, still sobbing. Her hair smelled of shampoo. Although I was hugging my twin sister, I wasn't feeling any of the closeness we shared as children; but I knew she was suffering with grief.

I knew also Marie had always been subject to spells of quick anger and crying.

Celosa got up and went to the kitchen.

Roswell had a silly grin on his face. Was he embarrassed by Marie's crying? Was he laughing at my annoyance? What was going on with him? Why was he grinning? Perhaps he grinned when he felt discomfort. Some people were like that.

I sat down on the couch and folded my arms.

Restless, in minutes I was back on my feet. While the others in the living room drank coffee and talked, I went to Mother's deserted bedroom to look around. The room smelled clean as if scrubbed with Lysol.

12

Mother's abandoned bed had been stripped and the bare mattress looked new, but the emptiness and starkness spoke sharply of Mother's passing. Over the head of the bed on the wall hung a small silver crucifix. Mother left the church but apparently not her faith.

I opened the walk-in closet and stepped inside. It was full of Mother's robes, pajamas, nightgowns, shoes, belts, hats, scarfs, dresses, skirts, pants, and an assortment of other things, and in a corner, in its case, my Fender guitar. I picked it up and examined it, remembering the pleasure it gave me; but I had no desire to reclaim it. I put it back in its place, leaving it to its new fate.

I came out and looked around. The unoccupied room was spare and desolate and glaring. The spirit of the room gave me a chill. Only the wall photographs were left with a kind of *still* life.

On the wall adjacent Mother's bed was the familiar framed photograph of her posing with handsome President Obama. The summer two years after he became president, she had gone with a group of tourist ladies from Chicago to Washington D.C. The White House visit was part of a tour of historic locations.

It was just pure luck that President Obama had walked into the room where the group stood listening to the tour guide in the Blue Room.

Mother told me she was admiring things in the Blue Room when the president stepped into the room. He said, "Hello, ladies." They returned his greeting and then Mother was quick to ask the president if he would take a picture with her. He said, "Of course."

I walked around Mother's bed and stood close to the picture. The expression on Mother's face was one of happiness and satisfaction. For her that was a rare expression. It brought a smile to my lips. Seeing that picture, I felt a wave of kindness toward her. Whatever her faults, she usually had good intentions.

On the dresser I noticed her photo album. I opened it. On the first page was a black and white photo of Mother as an infant, a beautiful baby in a crib in Waverly. On the same page were large color photographs of her parents: Jake, her father, a craggy handsome man with brown hair, and Muriel, her mother, a good-looking modest woman with large pretty eyes; but she looked permanently alarmed. Her graying hair was pulled back in a bun.

Mother and her parents looked like they contained all the ethnic groups of the world. I knew, from having had my own DNA ethnic makeup mapped a couple years before Mother was diagnosed, that both sides of my family were made up pretty much with contributions from a multitude of ethnic groups.

I was *fifty-two percent* European and *thirty percent* African; and the remaining percentages were Middle Eastern and East Asian. The breakdown of the African ancestries was of the Niger-Congo area and East Africa. The Middle Eastern ethnicity was of the Anatolia and the Caucasus. In Europe my ancestors were of France, Germany, Spain, Sweden, Denmark, Norway, and Russia. Like Mother and Dad, I proudly called myself simply African American. It was also the way the world saw me.

I turned the page and there were pictures of Mother from her high school days and later pictures of her at the University of Nebraska as a young business major. In one of the college pictures, Mother was posing with a group of other girls, all waving and smiling. In another she was riding a bicycle along a tree-lined lane in Lincoln.

Then I came to the page with pictures of Dad, Alfred Smith. While growing up, Marie and I were told Dad's family had been the only African American family in Cedar Falls, Iowa. They were Presbyterian. Later, at the University of Nebraska, Dad became what he called, "a liberal thinker."

I loved Dad. Marie and I were very little when he died, but I still had vivid memories of him. He loved to make Marie and me laugh. He took us with him on walks around Hyde Park and across the Gerdts campus and over to the lake. I remembered him pushing us in the swings in the park.

Mother had pasted several photos of Dad in her album: their marriage photos, one of Dad standing by his new white Ford Escort with its front-wheel drive, and several pictures taken before Marie and I were born, of them on vacation in the Caribbean.

He looked cocky and handsome. Several pictures were of them while students in college. He sat behind her, talking in her ear, and playing with her long hair. They loved each other dearly.

The accident happened in 1992 when Marie and I were ten years old. Dad was returning on Highway 137 from Wilmette, Illinois where he had been for an interview for an assistant manager job at Midwestern Industries, a company that made a variety of car parts, such as hubcaps, steering wheels, and door handles. It was winter, nighttime, with a hard rain from a powerful storm on Lake Michigan. Visibility was poor.

Dad likely never saw the semitrailer coming. It was later determined, the driver, Eugene Dekker, forty-two, of Kokomo, Indiana, probably fell asleep. He had been on the road with only a couple of hours sleep. He survived the accident, suffering only minor injuries. Dad lost his life.

We were devastated. We never fully recovered from the loss. For years I felt like I was marinating in my own sorrow. I grew up and went away to college still suffering the loss. For years I had nightmares about the accident. I could see the truck coming toward me and I would wake just before it hit.

My memory of his funeral was cloudy. I remembered standing with Mother and Marie and other people at Manifest Memorial Gardens Cemetery in Thornton, Illinois. Dad's Star Legacy copper non-rusting casket was suspended over the open grave, ready to be lowered into it. I remembered Mother crying.

I often thought of returning to the grave to honor him. At the same time, I felt it might be too painful to bear. In my heart every day I honored him. Now we would soon take Mother's body there to be placed in the ground alongside his.

I turned the page, still feeling pain. At this point Marie came into the room and said, "*What* are you doing?"

"Looking at Mother's photos."

"Why are you *so* obsessed with photographs?" She was angry. Then she whispered, "I *don't* want Elsie to hear us talking about removing *anything* from the house. It might upset her. This is *her* home too. You have to remember she lives here. We have to be very careful with her feelings. She's suffering the loss just like we are."

I thought about it. Marie was right. I said, "Yeah, you're right. I'll be careful," I whispered, "But we have to sell the house. You know that, right?"

"I know, but let's not talk about it right now."

I whispered, "Elsie will eventually have to move."

Marie hissed, "*I said let's not talk about it right now.*"

"Sure."

"How long will you be here?" Marie said.

"I'm scheduled to leave Wednesday." I paused. "And now you tell me we aren't going to settle anything anytime soon."

"That's *not* what I said. I said not right now."

"Well, I am going to hire a lawyer," I said. "Elsie doesn't have to know about *that*. We need legal advice."

Marie nodded her approval and turned. I watched her walk away back to join the others. On Mother's dresser was a framed photo of Marie and me at age eleven. I gazed at the photo and wondered how those two kids became us.

For some reason I remembered Marie had reached puberty before I did. We were eleven. She became curious about sex. Girls at school slightly older than her were telling her things about women's and men's parts and babies and things adults do in private. I wasn't yet curious about those things.

My sister had seen that my parts down there were different from hers. One day when she was well into puberty, she asked to see me pee. She was curious about how I did it. Since she and I were so close, I thought there wasn't anything unusual about her request.

I said okay. We were at home alone. This was after Dad's death. Mother was at Gerdts. Marie and I went into the bathroom and I took it out and started peeing into the toilet bowl. Marie watched with fascination. When I finished, she said, "May I touch it?"

"*No!*" I shouted.

Ignoring me and before I could respond further, she reached for it, but I quickly withdrew sensing that something wasn't quite right about what we were doing. This was something you didn't do with your sister. I knew that much.

About a year later one day Marie came home from school and whispered to me: "A boy touched me down there." She giggled. "Wow," I said. "You let a boy touch you down there?" I was shocked. She looked embarrassed, but her embarrassment seemed only in response to my astonishment.

I began to worry for my sister's safety. From an early age we both had heard on TV so much about children being molested. When we were very young, Mother always told us to be careful because there were monstrously wicked people who kidnapped children to do awful and sometimes deadly things to them.

There were dangers lurking everywhere. When Marie told me that a boy touched her down there, I puzzled for days whether or not to tell Mother. I was hoping Mother would find a way to stem Marie's curiosity.

Marie was at her ballet lesson when I told Mother about the boy touching Marie. Rather than going directly to Marie to question her, Mother suspected *me* of mischievous behavior; she put me through the third degree. She asked me if *I* had touched my sister "down there." I said, "No!" I was shocked and hurt.

Here I was trying to save Marie from her own carnal curiosity and Mother was accusing me of molesting *my own* twin sister.

Mother took me with her to see a family therapist, Dr. Consuela Lopez, on Hyde Park Boulevard at Woodlawn Avenue. The doctor was young and attractive, and her office was smart and modern.

Mother told the doctor what I had said. Mother still hadn't questioned Marie.

Dr. Lopez gave Mother an astonished look and said, "Mrs. Smith, why would your son tell you a boy at school had sexually molested his sister if he himself had actually done it? It's not *logical*. He would not have said anything at all. He came to you for help."

Mother apparently saw the mistake. She looked embarrassed and apparently felt ashamed of having accused me of misconduct, but she never said she was sorry.

And she never questioned Marie. Deep inside I was hurt and I never fully forgave Mother. Now she was dead, and I thought it might be time to forgive her for her poor judgment.

The gulf between Mother and me deepened even more. As my hurt feelings simmered and my resentment grew, Mother's anger toward me grew. I felt her disdain and at times her scorn. I felt her derision. Sometimes I thought she couldn't stand my presence.

When she was feeling particularly hateful, she deliberately pitted Marie and me against each other. In retrospect, I suspected it was her way of trying to overcome her own private anger or self-pity. When she wasn't feeling well, she scrawled the graffiti of her disposition large across everything and everybody in sight.

At a certain point during my teen years if I started to speak to Mother, she would start coughing *hak, hak, hak*, as if to cut herself off from hearing what I was about to say. I waited till the coughing stopped and tried again.

At the sound of my voice the coughing started again. She never at the end of the coughing said she was sorry. She never asked me what I was about to say before I was interrupted by her coughing. No matter what it was she didn't want to hear what I had to say. Later, Marie picked up this habit from Mother. She too would start coughing to forestall hearing what I was about to say to her.

13

I entered puberty at the age of fifteen. I'd just turned sixteen when Mother opened the bathroom door and caught me masturbating. I was sitting on the edge of the toilet and holding a picture torn from a girlie magazine I'd bought at the drugstore in one hand and myself in the other. I was shocked to see Mother and I felt humiliated and embarrassed. After that my anger toward her grew.

I was in the bathroom because this was the only place in the house where I had any privacy or so I thought. Now it was clear even the bathroom was no longer a place of refuge. As a sixteen-year-old I had *no* privacy. I was embarrassed and humiliated and angry. I was learning I didn't have the last word on what happened to my life and my body.

Mother, too, was angry. She shouted at me: "Don't you know playing with yourself will *ruin* your health?" She went on about it: "Don't you know you can *damage* yourself down there?" And: "It can cause you *mental* problems too." And: "I've heard it can even cause blindness."

Later I thought: how could an educated woman have such a backwards view of something that was so natural? Even monkeys and dogs and many other animals masturbated. Wasn't a human being also an animal?

As an educated woman Mother might have acknowledged that much. On second thought: Mother probably thought of human beings as higher beings, not animals. But at sixteen I didn't believe human beings were "higher" at anything. We were animals, smart animals.

After this incident, I began to notice Mother was micromanaging my activities and my body and trying even to micromanage my thoughts. If I went to the kitchen to make a piece of toast for myself, she would be right there with a question: "What are you doing now?" "I'm making myself a piece of toast." She would say, "Oh." She continued in this way with each and everything I did.

I believed that Mother in her passive-aggressive way was bullying me. I told myself she was doing this to disguise her resentment and insecurity and need to control me. I later realized she saw Marie and me as her life. She felt we owed her everything for giving us life. At the same time without us she had no personal life.

The Christy worry, she said, was making her ill. She continued to try to convince me to stop seeing Christy. Not doing so she said would only lead to cruel consequences. She said she was being completely impartial. She also said she was thinking only of my wellbeing and my future.

Things got worse. While Mother was at work at the university, one day I took Christy home with me.

While we were making love on my bed, Mother walked into my bedroom. She had left work early on the suspicion something like this might be happening. No doubt she had come home at lunchtime many times before, expecting to catch me misbehaving.

This time she actually caught me. Christy and I were fluttering sparrows in the storm of her rage. She was furious. "*Get out! Get out!*" she shouted to Christy. She drove Christy half-dressed and distressed out of the house.

Poor Christy! She was as humiliated and angry and anguished and embarrassed; as was I.

That night Mother gave me a talking-to. I shrank before her verbal assault. I was anxious and sad, and angry, too. Mostly I was sorry I'd been caught.

"*That girl* is no good for you. Why are you wasting your time with her? Any time a girl will lie down with you like that she isn't worth much. She has no class. You're ruining your life! If you keep this up, you will never amount to anything!"

Hearing Mother say I would not amount to anything because of Christy was gut-wrenching and deeply disquieting.

"Where is your *self-respect*?" she said.

"So, you think I'll never amount to anything and I've no class and no self-respect. Right?"

"I didn't say *that*. I said *if* you keep doing things like this you will amount to nothing in life. Mark, you're too young to be doing that kind of thing with a girl. How old is she?"

"My age. She's seventeen, almost eighteen."

"Well, she's being very reckless and so are you. What if you get her pregnant?"

I started to lie and say we used protection but said nothing.

"I'm disappointed in you, Mark. Promise me you will stop seeing that girl?"

"I have to see her at school. We have some of the same classes."

"You *know* what I mean," she hissed.

Lying, I said, "Okay, I'll stop seeing her."

There was no way I was going to give up Christy. The promise simply deepened the mistrust and lies between Mother and me. I became more secretive. I feigned truthfulness to Mother just to appease her, but she remained suspicious and I continued to see Christy.

Once, early in our relationship, when Christy thought she was pregnant, I had Sweetman drive me to a drugstore on the West Side, where nobody knew me, and I bought a pregnancy kit for Christy.

The next day at school she told me the result was negative. Being reckless juveniles, we celebrated with a cheer, as if we'd achieved some sort of victory.

The war between Mother and me continued. She was never fully convinced she had succeeded in making me into what she wanted me to be. The way I behaved suggested I was never going to be the prodigal son, coming back, begging for forgiveness, read to obey.

Many things I did continued to annoy her. If I stood with the refrigerator door opened, looking in for a time longer than she thought normal, she complained. If I left the TV on in a room I'd just left, she complained. If I forgot to turn off a light, she complained. She watched my every move. Time after time she walked behind me to see what I might do next.

Mother also tried to micromanage Marie. She was self-righteous about it, too. As soon as Marie started having her period Mother monitored Marie's every move. Marie resisted as strongly as I did. Mother was terrified some boy would get Marie pregnant. Like many girls her age, Marie was sure she knew everything and believed she was safe from harm.

At the same time, Mother was against giving Marie or me prophylactics. She constantly warned Marie against having sex and even against kissing boys. "And be careful of men in cars offering you a ride to or from school," she said. This was good advice.

It was true. There had been many reports of men in cars stopping and grabbing girls off the streets. Many of those girls never returned alive. Bodies were sometimes found in remote places. Some of Mother's worries were well founded.

As Marie matured it became clear she was more attracted to her girlfriends, at first in a platonic way, than she was to boys. I think I became aware of this before Mother. As twins, Marie and I could read each other's thoughts and finish each other's sentences. By the time we were sixteen I knew she preferred girls.

Despite the bad blood between Mother and me, we loved each other in our painful way. Ironically, and in her odd way, Mother also valued my opinions. Two years after Dad's death she started dating. She would try on dress after dress and parade herself before me asking for my opinion. She often selected the one to wear that I liked best. When she was doubtful of a man she'd dated, she came to me for advice. I was her confidant.

When I was older, say seventeen, there were late night sessions when she and I would sit at the kitchen table talking quietly. Getting ready for a date she would tell me about her worries and fears. I would try as best I could to console her with words of reassurance.

"Sometimes I feel very lonely," she said once. Another time she said, "Sometimes I feel like life has been very unfair to me."

I wasn't pretending or trying to manipulate her, and for a moment she wasn't trying to control me. In turn Mother would listen to my worries and fears and offer her words of comfort.

She started dating two years after Dad's death and she was careful to keep a distance between her dates and us. Only once did Marie and I come home and find her in bed with a man. We were about twelve then.

We had gone to a neighborhood movie matinee. We didn't stay for the second film. Instead, enlivened, we rushed home to tell Mother about the comedy with its goofy tricksters and risk takers.

Her bedroom door was open. It was hot. I ran in and saw her leaping up naked, trying to cover her white body, while her brown boyfriend was sinking lower into the covers. The brown hairy triangle between her legs shocked me.

I had never seen a grown woman's body; and I had never imagined *that much* hair grew between a woman's legs. I relegated the incident so far back in my mind as to be essentially forgotten.

14

I returned to the living room where the others were gathered. Marie was weeping again and Celosa was trying to comfort her by hugging her and patting her on the back. Except for Marie's sobs and the ticking of Mother's grandfather clock in the corner by the armchair, the room was silent.

Mary was sitting on the couch with her hands folded on her lap, watching with an expression of resigned pity.

Roswell was standing at the window looking out at the street.

Curious to talk with Elsie, I wanted to get her version of Mother's final days and hours; I wondered about the horrible pain Mother must have been suffering.

Elsie was alone in the kitchen at the sink. She turned around when I entered. I stopped and stood by the table.

I said, "Elsie, Mother never talked with me much about pain. Was she in a lot of pain?"

"Oh, yes, Mark, she was in great pain. Of course, she had the pain pills, but they didn't kill the pain completely. I'd go to the drugstore to pick up her prescriptions and I would rub her shoulders and her back for her, but I couldn't make all the pain go away. She suffered a lot, especially during the last days."

"I thought so." Tears came to my eyes, tears for Mother, tears for our relationship, tears for myself.

Elsie and I were silent for a moment. She turned and looked out the window. I stared at the floor.

Elsie said, "Mark, I was thinking about what I'm going to cook for after the funeral. You know how people like to eat after a funeral." She chuckled. I nodded in agreement.

"I'm sure you will think of food everybody will enjoy." I paused then said, "Elsie, I know Mother gave you a salary. I don't know if she left any kind of arrangements for you to continue to be paid, but…"

"Not that I know of Mark; but Marie told me you guys are going to try to give me a little something each week to get by on at least for a while. She said you won't be able to do it forever and I wouldn't expect you to, either."

I happened to have my checkbook with me, so I took it out of my jacket pocket and wrote Elsie a check for five hundred dollars. "Here, I hope this holds you for a while."

Elsie looked at the check. "My goodness, Mark, this is so kind of you. How generous! God bless you, son! I appreciate it *so* much!"

"It's the least I can do."

I had known Elsie for years without knowing her. I knew the basic things about her. She was from Atlanta or rather a small town called Calhoun near Atlanta.

If you asked her where she was from, she always said "Atlanta" because she rightly assumed few people outside the state of Georgia had ever heard of Calhoun. Elsie once said, "My town was named after a defender of slavery. I was taught to pray for people like that." If she had nightmares, I suspected they were sober and without malice.

"Elsie," I said, "I was just wondering if you could tell me about Mother during her last days here in the house. I mean, before they took her to the hospital."

"Not much to tell, Mark. She was sleeping a lot. Had been sleeping pretty much all day for the last two or three weeks. She would get up to go the bathroom; but she never once wet the bed. She was determined she wasn't going to be an old woman wetting the bed."

"Was she eating well?"

"Pretty well. She was never a big eater."

"What was she eating?"

"She liked fruit and stuff. Her teeth had gotten so they hurt her mouth, so she wouldn't wear them except when somebody other than me was here. She couldn't eat things like apples, but she liked bananas and peaches, and she liked to eat them little tiny sardines out of the can. She ate them on saltine crackers."

"I sent her a walker. Did she ever use it?"

"No, sir." Elsie laughed. "It's in there in her bedroom closet where she put it when it arrived. Never took it out of the box. Same with the walking cane you sent. It too is still in the box."

"That was my mother, stubborn to the end."

As Elsie talked, she continued cooking, moving about the kitchen in a meticulous way while at the same time keeping a carefree focus on me.

"Adella was determined she was going to walk on her own till the very end." Elsie laughed again. "Oh, she fell down several times trying to get to the bathroom, but it wasn't nothing serious. She got so she learned how to hold onto the wall to get to the bathroom and back to the bed. Good thing the bathroom was just outside her bedroom."

"Was she sleeping well?"

"We stayed up pretty much all night most nights. I stood guard at the windows. You know the neighborhood has turned so bad with the gangs at war with each other. They kill people, anybody, on sight. Human life means nothing to them. We could hear them out there on the street. She and I were worried half out of our minds most of the time at night, worried bullets might come flying through the window."

"When did *you* sleep?"

"Adella and I both slept in the daytime. I told you already she slept a lot. She never missed out on any sleep. She just stopped doing it at night. You know she was in a lot of pain, especially after the cancer became more advanced. I got used to sleeping in the daytime too."

Many times, Mother told me about the gangs. I knew she was worried about Elsie's and her own safety. That was why she had had another front door, made of steel, installed over the existing wooden door.

"Was she still smoking?" Mother was a smoker since age sixteen and only in her sixties did it seem to affect her health. Dad, too, was a smoker. Marie and I grew up in a house inhaling their smoke.

I was sure their exhaled smoke compromised our health. It made me feel sad. My own childhood asthma probably stemmed from their smoke. Luckily, as an adult, I no longer had asthma; instead, I had its repressed form: eczema, but only a mild form of it.

"Adella stopped smoking about a week before she passed on into the next world," Elsie said.

"Into the next world." What a curious expression. I'd heard it all my life, but now in Elsie's mouth it sounded strange and new. I'd also heard people say their loved ones had moved on "to the next realm."

I myself had long said, "passed away." Which meant finished, completely finished. After courses in philosophy and biological evolution at Berkeley, "finished," sounded right to me. "Next realm" or "next world" sounded like cliché storybook stuff or simply melodramatic.

15

In my hotel room I watched a wrenching football game, waiting for Celosa and Roswell, trying to keep my mind off Mother.

Since we needed an obituary, I'd suggested Roswell and Celosa come to my hotel room so the three of us could work on it together. As they were college students and wrote papers all the time, I thought they would be more practiced at constructing good sentences.

Death was very much on my mind. My own mortality suddenly seemed so fragile. Death came at you like a bull with deeply shaded eyes and with a downturned nose and flaring nostrils; it came bringing searing pain and permanent nothingness; it short-circuited everything you might have planned. Class didn't matter, age didn't matter; it came at you with an absolute and indifferent force.

It was generally assumed people as young as I, thirty-four, didn't think about death but that was a false assumption. Ever since Dad's death, I occasionally thought about it. Now Mother was gone. Life now seemed so elusive, so ephemeral.

My own life now felt dangerously breakable. I didn't want the kind of spectacle Mother's death was going to be--her corpse an imperfect object in an open casket.

Cremate me, I thought. In death I didn't need the triumphal exaltation and plodding ceremony. My body and my death would not be for public display. I remembered the opening lines of Shakespeare's "Sonnet 71": "No longer mourn for me when I am dead/Then you shall hear the surly sullen bell/Give warning to the world I am fled/From this vile world, with vilest worms to dwell".

Roswell and Celosa arrived around eleven. I had already showered, dressed in a light blue cotton shirt and brown seersucker trousers, and gone downstairs for the buffet breakfast of whole wheat toast, jam, two sunny-side-up eggs, three strips of bacon and a glass of orange juice. I was ready, with paper and pen, reading *News & World Report* when they knocked at the door.

Roswell came in with a big smile. They were both wearing pullover shirts and jeans. Roswell's smile seemed more nervous than friendly. His shirt said: *Think!* We shook hands. Celosa kissed me on the cheek. I said, "Come on in and have a seat. Make yourself at home. My home is your home." My attempt at humor fell flat. They didn't laugh.

We gathered around the desk. Celosa took the pen and turned to me. "We should probably keep her age and place of birth and parents' names out of it," she said.

"Why?"

"Because there are bad people who search obituary columns looking for the recently deceased in the hope of stealing their identities. The more information you give the more ammunition you give them to steal her identity. It happens all the time in New York where we live. A neighbor of ours on Long Island died last year and the family put a lot of information about her in the obituary. Thieves opened a credit card with that information and charged thousands of dollars to the dead woman's name."

"Really?" I said, feeling naïve but I recognized the truth of what she was saying.

After three or four drafts, this was what we called finished:

Adella Smith, of Chicago, passed away in hospital a few days ago. She was born in Nebraska. At her bedside was her daughter, Marie. Adella was the daughter of Jake and Muriel of Nebraska—both deceased. Adella earned a degree in Business Administration. She worked as a secretary for forty years at a liberal arts university. Her daughter, Marie, of Chicago, and her son, Mark, of California, survive her. The funeral service will be held at O'Connor & Sons Funeral Home on East 78th Street, Chicago. Check with the funeral home for viewing schedule or check their website. She will be laid to rest in Manifest Memorial Gardens Cemetery, in Thornton, Illinois, alongside her husband, Alfred.

I read it several times. It wasn't great, but it served its civic purpose without revealing personal information such as date of birth, date of death, address, Mother's maiden name or her mother's maiden name.

We finished at little after noon. Downstairs, in the hotel restaurant, I treated Roswell and Celosa to lunch. The restaurant soundtrack was spouting "Sketches of Spain," by Miles Davis, followed by Billie Holiday singing, "I Cover the Waterfront." They were musicians of my parents' generations, but I loved listening to their music.

Roswell and Celosa each ordered burgers and fries and Diet Coke. I ordered salmon and wild rice and a beer. I asked them how things were going in their lives. With riveting candor, they said tuition and other school-related bills at the moment were the most pressing issues on their minds. They also were worried about the state of the world.

Roswell said, "Why can't college be free?"

They shared a cozy apartment in historic Brooklyn. It was cheaper than living in expensive Manhattan. Celosa took the rumbling BMT subway every day to the 8th Street Broadway stop in Lower Manhattan and walked from there to New York University. Roswell did the same thing, taking the MTA, getting off at the 135ᵗʰ Street stop and walking to City College.

Roswell said, "Last week we took part in a big protest march in New York City against violence. We felt we couldn't just sit back and not speak out."

I told them about the forthcoming march on Washington to raise consciousness about our troubled environment.

Celosa said, "That's wonderful."

Roswell said, "Terrific!"

I remembered the protest marches I took part in at Berkeley, the place of the historic "Free Speech Movement" in the mid-1960s. Eating lunch with them also took my mind off the ordeal of Mother's death and the angst and stress I was feeling.

Although I wasn't much older than they, their relative youth and commitment and hope and optimism and idealism impressed me. Despite their lack of money and the hassles they felt and faced, listening to them made me feel a bit nostalgic for my own college days.

16

Roswell and Celosa left; and I walked out into the lobby; I bought a box of powdered doughnuts in the Double Tree shop, just to have in the room for snacking; then I took the elevator back upstairs to my room to relax for a bit, waiting for the next step in this process.

An hour later, I called Marie and told her I was going to try to make an appointment for us to see Attorney Berg Saturday afternoon. She said, "Okay. That works for me."

The TV was at the foot of the bed. I turned it on, undressed and stretched out on the bed in my T-shirt and boxer shorts. Before long I dozed off. Often when I dreamed, I was lost and wandering around in an unknown area, a desolate place looking for a way to get back to the place where I made the mistake of choosing the wrong path. My dreams played variations on this theme. This time my dream was different.

In the dream a giant motorhome pulled up in front of a house that looked like Mother's but was also my apartment building in Sacramento. I was a little boy and at the same time myself as I was now. It suddenly occurred to me Dad might be coming back, but back from where? In my consternation, I was speechless.

The sliding door opened and Dad and Mother and Marie and Mary and Roswell and one or two teachers from high school and an assortment of people I didn't know, started stepping down from the vehicle, waving to me and smiling. I didn't know how to respond. I felt nervous.

I couldn't believe my eyes. All these people coming out of that one vehicle! With fervor and on my best behavior I invited them all inside a house I wasn't sure was mine.

The anxiety of the dream woke me, and I lay there trying with no success to make sense of it except I knew it was an anxiety-ridden *fear* dream and at the same time a *desire* dream, a desire to have known Dad better and a desire to have had a better relationship with Mother.

What was the meaning of Marie's presence? What was the meaning of this amalgamation of people and of so many strangers too coming out of the motorhome? I had no idea.

I called Attorney Berg's office and Samantha answered in her usual friendly voice. "My sister and I would like to come by Saturday afternoon just to make in-person contact. Is Saturday afternoon good for Attorney Berg?"

"Let me see," she said, "Yes, three o'clock would work."

"Great! See you then!"

Just then the hotel phone rang. I assumed it was Marie and picked up. "Hello?"

"Mark, hi, this is Christy!"

I was shocked. "Christy! Long time! How are you?"

"I'm doing well. I ran into your sister at the supermarket out here, and she told me you were staying at the Hilton downtown Chicago. I thought I'd call and say hello."

"Nice to hear your voice, Christy; it's been a long time."

"Am I calling at a bad time? Should I call back later?"

"Oh, no, no. It's fine." I felt nervous and excited and astonished to hear from her after so many years of no communication.

"I'm not sure I'll be able to come to your mother's funeral, but I am going to try. It's pretty complicated. I was wondering...I mean, uh, I was wondering if I could see you, you know...it's been a long time."

"Yes, it has been a long time." I paused and looked at the clock. "You're still out in Evanston?"

"Yes, I still live in Evanston." She paused. "I could stop by and we could have coffee or something, I mean there at the hotel, in the café. They do have a café, right? I'd love to see you, Mark."

"I'm sure there's a coffee shop. Sure, come on over. It'll be great to see you too."

"Okay. What's your room number? I'll come up without stopping at the desk."

I gave her the room number.

"I'll be there in less than an hour."

Waiting for Christy, I continued to feel nervous and excited but also elated. I paced around the room, around and around the room. Several times I checked my appearance in the mirror.

I turned back to the TV and watched a flickering crayon rainbow in a commercial; then I turned off the TV and sat down in the armchair by the bed and closed my eyes and tried to relax.

Then I got up and paced the floor from window to door and back. All the while my pulse seemed to be beating throughout my whole body.

A short time later, I heard a gentle knock at the door. I looked through the peephole. There was Christy's distorted face, a face in the shape of a valentine, a face surrounded by a reef of long and radiant auburn hair, but an older Christy yet unmistakably Christine Debra Warner.

Still feeling a bit nervous but also very excited, I opened the door. I could see my high school sweetheart in the face of this woman, essentially a stranger, standing before me. She was wearing a white cotton shirt and a long blue cotton skirt and white sandals. She was smiling and I, nervous, smiled in return, happy to see her.

It had been more than seven years since we had seen each other. So,

I wasn't sure a conventional gesture of affection applied at this moment. I wondered what to do or say. Maybe Christy was now a married woman with children. *Who* was she now; *what* was she?

One wrong move on my part and the whole meeting might go south. This was all so unexpected! I had to be careful. I had to control my impulses and go slowly even with curiosity.

"Come on in!"

Ladylike and gorgeous as all-get-out she walked inside still smiling and not taking her eyes off me. Her perfume was interesting and pleasant. White Orchid? Gardenia? Juniper? Lavender? Rose? I took a deep breath and slowly let it out. I didn't know. I was no expert on perfumes, but whatever it was it was delightful and subtle and not at all preceding her or leaving a trail.

"You look the same," she said, still smiling, turning to give me a closer look. There were about twelve inches between us.

"If that's a compliment, thank you."

Suddenly she kissed me. It was a quick kiss on the lips; one not intended to stir the emotions. Though brief, the kiss brought back good memories, memories of her lips and of her mouth and of a youthful erupting volcano of passion, but we were now in repose.

We stood there in the entryway.

"I'm sorry about your mother. I know this must be a very difficult time..."

"Thank you. We're coping as best we can."

There was an armchair by the window. I gestured toward it, saying, "Have a seat or would you rather go down right now for coffee?"

"Oh, no," she said, with lifted eyebrows. She was still very pretty. "Maybe later."

She was walking toward the armchair and she stopped and looked back at me then suddenly she sat on the side of the bed instead. It wasn't a coy move. She made it natural.

Somehow that gesture changed the whole meaning of her visit. The bed was still unmade but presentable enough to use as a thing to sit on.

She was holding a small pink and green cloth purse on her lap, holding it with both hands.

"I *brought* you something!" She reached into her purse and pulled out a photograph and handed it to me.

I held it. It was a photograph of Christy and me together at Rainbow Beach Park on 75th Street when we were students at Hyde Park High. We were about the same height. I was wearing green swimming trunks, and she was in a dark blue two-piece mesh swimsuit. Behind us high in the blue sky the sun was a blazing yellow disk.

I stared at the picture. I was hugging Christy around the waist and she had her arm around my shoulders.

Looking at our young selves, I remembered the last time we were together in Sweetman's old VW van. She was watching me gazing at the photograph.

I looked up at her face. Christy, the artist!

I said, "Are you still painting?"

"Not as much as I would like."

Again, I studied the photograph. "Wow, Christy, I remember that day."

"Do you remember what we promised each other that day?"

I didn't remember so I said, "No, I don't. What'd we promise?"

"We promised we would always be friends."

"Oh, yes," I said truly, "I do remember now."

I was standing in front of her, my knees almost touching hers. Christy threw her purse on the bed and with both hands reached for my hands, pulling me toward her.

Okay, I thought, this is it. I didn't know who she had become and yet we were about to embark upon the unknown, about to traipse boldly into, for me, an unknown ravine.

I sat down beside her. We kissed again, then again; the third time we kissed with more tongue interplay. Her lips were soft and warm. We kissed passionately for a long time. I was feeling pretty excited. I hadn't kissed a woman in a long while; I hadn't kissed a woman *that* passionately in a very, very long time. I felt hot all over. My ears were burning.

Soon we were lying across the bed, still kissing. It wasn't an appropriate time to have such a thought, but my mind went to Mother's dead body at the funeral home. I don't know how but I somehow managed to snuff the image out of my mind and concentrate on kissing.

I soon felt Christy's hands working at my clothes, tugging and unzipping. At the same time, I opened her blouse and sunk my face into her warm breasts. There was sweet comfort there. We undressed.

I kissed the mole inside her left thigh. She was now breathing heavily. I fell into a state of bliss. Together we walked a tightrope a long time without falling and when we fell, we fell together. Hitting the blessed net was pure triumphal ecstasy, and then we lay together in restful fatigue.

We made love again, then for an hour lay side by side in complete rapture, skin to skin, just holding each other. In a whisper, Christy said, "I should tell you I'm married. He's a dentist."

"Oh," I said in a pleasant voice. I had suspected as much but I was surprised to hear her say it at *that* moment, especially given the euphoria we had just shared.

"Did you marry anybody I know?"

"No, he grew up in Evanston. Todd Fontana. I met him after you left for California, met him at a party."

"Oh."

Christy said, "I'm one year older than he." She sighed. "We're going through a divorce right now but still living together. It's kind of messy. He's kind of crazy right now. I guess he's always been kind of crazy. He follows me around. He has guns."

"Guns?"

"Yes, guns! And he's violent."

"He hits you?"

"Yes. He has hit me with his fists; but mainly Todd uses verbal violence against me all the time."

"That's not good."

"And he goes through my purse. He checks my phone. I can't wait to be free of the whole situation, to just get my own place and be free of this marriage. You know the story 'The Emperor's New Clothes'?"

"Yes. Hans Christian Andersen."

"I always took the message of that story to be trust your own judgment and your own instincts. I had doubts about Todd from the beginning, but I ignored my doubts. I didn't trust my instincts. It was a mistake. I should have married *you* before you left for Berkeley."

I started to say something but changed my mind. I was thinking: would I've married her at the time? Probably. Mother would've pitched a fit; and I might not have gone to college.

Christy said, "I asked him if he was involved with other women and he said no. He lied. I don't like lies. He was having his way with a teenage girl in the neighborhood. I caught him in the act in *our* bed. He was also doing it to every woman at his office he could get his hands on and every woman in the neighborhood too. Not that I think people have to be sexually loyal, but people should at least be *honest* about it."

"I see," I said softly.

"I want him to move out."

We talked and talked till it was six-thirty; then we dressed and went down to the restaurant. Christy ate baked chicken with corn and cherry tomatoes. I ate meatballs and spaghetti in tomato sauce. Together we drank red wine.

During dinner we talked about things we did while we were high school kids, places we'd gone together, movies we had seen together, dances and parties we had gone to. I gave her my phone number. She gave me hers. With that exchange we were declaring a bond. Estranged from her husband or not, she was still a married woman.

With the rapture of the lovemaking behind us, I worried about her husband: he was crazy and he had guns. You never knew what a crazy or angry or jealous person might do. Yet I felt completely comfortable with Christy. I felt sorry she was suffering in her marriage.

Now I wanted to know how I might facilitate future contact with her without running the risk of a confrontation with her husband. It was a risk with a very real hazard.

Something was compelling me to persist. I had reconnected with my first love. Despite the precariousness of the whole situation how could I now turn back?

I might suffer a little anxiety in the process, but I didn't believe I was endangering Christy or placing myself in peril. I wanted so much for this to turn out to be more than just a seedy lovers' tryst. Christy and I were better than that.

In the lobby we kissed goodbye; then she left, saying, "I'll call you when I can."

I returned to my room and checked Facebook on my phone. Cliff had posted a picture of himself with a big steelhead he caught in the Sacramento River. Earl said he was happy to be spending a few weeks with his wife in the woods by a lake. Garth? He hadn't posted anything lately. His last post was a week ago and he said the terrorist problem was getting worse in Paris. Quickly I posted, "Still in Chicago ready to attend my mother's funeral." This post drew a lot of sympathetic responses. I said "thank you" many times.

Then I stood at the window looking down at the growing green darkness of Grant Park; its stretches of manicured lawns and its carefully trimmed trees and shrubbery were pleasant to see even in nightlight.

Sure, our bodies had changed, perhaps for the better. The lovemaking was better than it had been when we were teenagers; but I wondered why the image of Mother's body had crossed my mind during sex.

One thing was becoming clear: Mother's death gave me the courage to face my own certain death, hopefully at some distant point in the uncertain future.

It was similar to the way I used to think about the earth when I was in grade school. I knew it would perish because the sun was burning out, but that would happen at such a distant point in the future that it had no real meaning. The vast indifferent universe seemed to be giving me an indiscernible smirk.

17

At eight Marie called and asked me to meet her at O'Connor & Sons Funeral Home on East 78th Street at two o'clock the next day. She said she had a 12:30 appointment at the insurance company where Mother's house was insured. It was located near the funeral home.

She'd notified them of Mother's death and now needed to settle Mother's account. "They asked me to bring her policy in. I hope there won't be a hitch. Some of these insurance people can complicate things if you let them."

"Good thing you're a lawyer," I said.

"Yes, but sometimes it doesn't help."

I took a taxi from the hotel. The driver was an elderly white guy who sighed deeply when I told him where I wanted to go. He looked at me with the corners of his mouth turned up and said, "Okay."

We hit Lake Shore Drive and after some thick and slow going traffic by the Loop we picked up speed, sailing by Hyde Park. We got to East 78th Street in about thirty minutes.

Marie was waiting outside in front of the building. I paid the taxi and tipped him well. He didn't thank me. He was angry about having to come to this area of the city and not being able to pick up the fare as he might have, had my destination been O'Hare or Canal Street's Union Station or the Greyhound bus station.

Marie came across the sidewalk to meet me. Off to the left, I could see her Porsche in the funeral home's lot, parked way away from the other cars. Marie was trying her best not to get any door dents. She had had the Porsche only a few months.

Before the Porsche she drove a Mercedes, which she had bought used but in great condition. Mother often asked her why she wasted her money on such expensive cars and Marie would say, "I *deserve* the best. I do a lot of driving and I need comfort."

"Hi," I said. "Waiting long?"

"No. Our appointment is at two-thirty. It's ten after two now. I thought we'd use these few minutes to go over a few things before we talk with Mrs. Hunt."

"Okay," I said, "but I don't want to stand here. Let's go and sit in your car and talk."

In the car Marie said, "Mother had burial insurance but it's not going to cover the cost. She has two bank counts and I have access to both accounts. After she was unable to get around, she arranged with the banks for me to be able to have access to her money."

At five minutes to two we went inside the funeral home. With a gentle smile a little man in a black suit met us in the lobby. He said, "Hello, I'm Dale Kennedy. May I help you?"

"We've an appointment with Mrs. Hunt at 2:30."

"She's running a bit behind schedule," he said. "Please have a seat there outside her office. She will be with you in a few minutes." Then he turned to an elderly couple just entering the building and greeted them with the same gentle smile.

Marie and I sat side by side. She gave me a tight smile. I returned it. I was thinking about Mother's body. It was in this building somewhere. At what stage of preparation was it in? Would she look like herself? I didn't want to see her dead.

When Dad died and was laid out in his casket at the funeral home, then later at Manifest Memorial Gardens Cemetery in Thornton, he didn't look like himself. He was only thirty-six but dead he looked fifty with a scowl I had never seen on his face when he was alive.

I remembered all of us standing around his opened grave as his casket was being lowered into the ground and hearing the rollers squeaking as the ropes moved; and I remembered all of us crying as the minister quietly spoke the eulogy. It was a difficult time. I couldn't console myself.

Marie and I had known death before Dad's. Mother's parents died earlier. Grandfather Jake and Grandmother Muriel never accepted Mother's marriage to Dad. They never accepted us and we weren't comfortable around them. They seemed to merely tolerate our presence.

They always seemed rather stiff and silent, as if they were waiting for us to leave. It was understandable: they never forgave Mother for embracing the "blackness" in her ancestry. For her to have done so exposed her parents' secret. They were like two bugs squirming after the rock has been pulled back, exposing them to the light.

When Marie and I were small we went with Mother to Nebraska for her mother's funeral. None of Waverly seemed surprised to see the Bischoffs' olive-skinned relatives.

Grandfather Jake had died earlier. Mother went alone to his funeral. At the time she was pregnant with us. So, Marie and I were there too, but we were upside down with our eyes closed, presumably in a state of pre-birth bliss.

After our grandfather's death, we didn't see Grandmother Muriel very often. She rarely visited us, so when we saw her in her casket, I couldn't remember what she looked like before.

She looked like any number of elderly white women with white hair and sagging neck skin. They closed her eyes to make her look like she was sleeping; her pink skin had turned gray.

My phone rang. It was Christy. I stood and walked away from Marie and answered it. Christy said, "I can't talk but a minute. Todd followed me to your hotel. I don't think he knows why I was there, but just be careful. He's crazy. Talk soon." Then she hung up.

Great, I thought: one more thing to worry about.

Presently, Mrs. Hunt's office door opened and she came out smiling, with hand extended. She was a short portly woman in a blue no-nonsense suit and she wore her hair in a perm. "Call me, Gloria," she said, shaking my hand, then Marie's. "Come on in."

We followed her into her well-planned, well-lighted office. She motioned for us to sit in the two adjacent chairs facing her desk.

Marie said, "On the phone you kindly gave me so many options regarding the *type* of funeral, my head is swimming with indecision."

Mrs. Hunt said, "Nowadays Americans are becoming taller and taller and bigger and bigger and heavier and heavier, so those factors affect casket and grave size. There are lots of changes going on in the death business." She smiled. "I remember you said your mother is to be laid to rest alongside your father's grave?"

"Yes," Marie said, "out at Manifest, in Thornton. Our parents paid for the plots years ago."

"I see."

Marie said, "I'm not clear about the cost for the body preparation, the funeral, the headstone, the labor, the food and beverages for the reception."

"Sure," said Mrs. Hunt. And she spent the next ten minutes reciting those options in annoying verbal jabs. My eyes were glazing over. I was developing a headache. When she finished, she handed each of us a brochure outlining the options she had just spelled out. "This brochure will tell you everything you need to know."

"Well," I said, "we don't have a lot of time. I live in California and I'm here for a limited amount of time."

"I understand," she said. "If you both agree we can have the funeral this coming Saturday the twenty-second or Sunday the twenty-third or you can plan on Monday. I'll make arrangements for the limo. We've slots opened for all three days. We always have three or four funerals going at the same time." She paused. "Viewing can start tomorrow, Friday. She's ready. You brought her clothes, I believe, a couple of days ago. Right?"

"Yes," Marie said. "I want her arms covered and I want her to have on her white gloves; and I want a scarf around her neck."

"No problem," said Mrs. Hunt.

I said, "Have you worked with Manifest before?"

Mrs. Hunt said, "Yes, but for years they didn't want *us* out there but now they have no choice. In 1981 they got slapped with a lawsuit and had to stop discrimination on the basis of race."

"Our dad died the following year," said Marie. "Our mother had no trouble burying Dad there."

"Yes, now we're everywhere! We're no longer restricted to black cemeteries because so many of these cemetery companies were sued for racial discrimination."

Marie and I chose to have the reception *before* the funeral service in which people would stand up and speak about their memories of Adella.

We also fingered through a colorful brochure of caskets: a pink twenty-gauge steel casket with square corners, a blue casket with adjustable bed and mattress, a white casket with a locking mechanism and couch, a handmade oak casket with velvet lining, a casket of solid hardwood with velvet interior and swing bars.

There were caskets made of pine, oak, copper, stainless steel, bronze, maple, walnut, mahogany, and cherry wood. There were caskets for burial as well as for cremation; and the latter surprised. I'd thought the cremated remains had to go inside some kind of relatively small container, not a *casket* for ashes.

"I like this one," I said, pointing to a pink casket.

"That's the one I was going to select," Marie said.

Marie and I selected a casket titled, "Aiti." It was made in Finland. It had a bright pink exterior and was made of solid high gloss poplar hardwood and the interior was a light pink silk fabric. Mother's corpse would have an adjustable bed and soft mattress to lie on for a long time. The niceties, of course, were for us, not Mother. The casket had rounded corners and swing bars. It cost almost two thousand dollars and came with a product warranty.

We made an agreement with Mrs. Hunt that Mother's body would go on display that next day, Friday. The reception and funeral service and the burial would be that coming Sunday. I was sad and jubilant and nervous––sad we had to make such grim decisions, jubilant we were making progress, and nervous because something might go wrong. Marie and I had never had to do anything like this before.

Mrs. Hunt swiveled around and stopped at her adding machine on a table behind her. When she finished clicking at the machine, she pulled out the long narrow sheet, swiveled back to face us and handed it to me. It was a staggering amount.

I wrote a check and Marie wrote a check to cover the cost of everything we'd discussed with Mrs. Hunt, including the cost of the limousine picking us up Sunday at Mother's house and delivering us to O'Conner & Sons.

Then after the service Sunday afternoon the limousine would deliver us out to Thornton, Illinois, following the car transporting Mother's body on its last ride. After the funeral the limousine would take us back to Mother's house.

I checked my phone for the time. We'd spent a couple of hours with Mrs. Hunt, and I felt pretty good. We'd got a lot accomplished; and a lot of uncertainty in my mind cleared. I now knew what the next few days would bring.

Or so I thought.

18

The next day, Friday, Marie and Mary picked me up at the hotel at noon to return to O'Conner & Sons to see Mother's body on display. Marie wanted to make sure everything was just so; she didn't want to leave anything to chance.

I hopped into the backseat. Marie said, "Mark, Mother sure picked the right time to die. I've an easy caseload right now and Mary is on sabbatical. You're free of studying all that wonderful geological activity on earth."

I grunted and said, "That's not what I do. I'm *not* a geologist."

"I was just *kidding* you. Where is your sense of humor?"

Then Marie pulled out into traffic.

We were going to take a look at how Mother had been displayed in her casket; and to make sure the jewelry and clothing Marie had taken so much trouble selecting was arranged properly.

"My son and his girlfriend went to the Loop to do some shopping," said Mary, looking back at me.

I suspected they needed a break from the depressing business of tending to Mother's death. It could if you let it engulf you. You might feel inundated by demons dancing around you as if you were some sort of sacrificial creature.

One had to try to stay positive. I remembered words of Aristotle I'd memorized in my second year at UC Berkeley: "It's during our darkest moments that we must focus to see the light."

I was feeling fear—cold-blooded fear, fear of something I couldn't quite put my finger on. Would there be an expression on Mother's face I had never before seen?

I feared the embalmer had given her a brooding or a darkly coy expression. Or what if he or she made Mother look silly or even goofy? A preoccupied expression I could live with; even a beatific or doleful or inscrutable one but not a dejected or haunted or gloomy or a snarling or peeved or sour or sullen or tight expression. I simply didn't want an unbearable last expression placed on Mother's beautiful face. She deserved to leave this world with dignity and looking like Adella.

I remembered the gnomic Greek poet Pythagoras's words: "If there be light, then there is darkness, if cold, heat; if height, depth; if solid, fluid; if hard, soft; if rough, smooth; if calm, tempest; if prosperity, adversity; if life, death." I wanted life in Mother's death.

O'Conner and & Sons had five sedate parlors strung in a row along a neat hallway arranged with chairs—albeit uncomfortable chairs—by the doors and display easels with posters. The minute we entered the building, we could see a poster with a picture of Mother as a young woman propped on a display easel outside the second parlor. The door was open. I didn't look in. Instead, I read the little biography of Adella Smith placed beneath her photograph. It was the one Roswell, Celosa and I wrote in the hotel room.

Marie and Mary were in the doorway looking in. I knew they were looking at Mother in her casket. I wasn't ready to do that. I felt hot and nervous. My throat was dry and tight.

Mary said to Marie, "From here it looks like they did a fine job."

Marie said, "Let's go in." Then she turned to me. "Mark? Aren't you coming in?"

I didn't respond right away; then I managed to say, "I would rather remember Mother as I last saw her alive. If I see her dead, it will erase that image." At the same time, I didn't want to sound or seem unsympathetic. I needed to get on the bandwagon. There was no good excuse not to go in.

Marie looked puzzled; then she placed a hand on my shoulder. "Come on, it's going to be okay."

"Sure, it will," said Mary, touching my arm.

My heart was beating fast. Trepidation had me in its grip.

They were right. I realized how impractical I was being. I was going to have to look at Mother in her dead state. As much as I hated the idea, it had to happen. I had to be brave and not be derailed. Facing Mother's death *literally* might bring with it some much-needed reckoning. Mother's words: "Try to find something positive in whatever misfortune besets you."

Mary was looking directly at me, smiling faintly. Since my arrival, it was one of the few times I'd seen her smile. I thought: Mary is someone who lately has lived in the purple shadow of death. She *knows*, I thought. Mary knows!

I could see from the doorway nobody was in the room. Fluorescent lights emitted a low frequency white noise. All the seats were empty. On each was placed a folded sheet of paper containing Mother's biography and picture––a small replica of the poster propped outside the door.

And I could smell the flowers. The parlor reeked of them––white roses, calla lilies long-stemmed opulent orchids, carnations, chrysanthemums, hydrangeas, daffodils, and tulips. They were stacked and piled around Mother's casket.

Flowers were supposed to represent the deceased person's reclamation of innocence at the moment of death. Ironically, they gave death a euphoric sweetness it laid no claim to.

I joined Marie and Mary and the three of us entered the parlor. As we approached the front, I glanced at the casket, which was situated on a stand at the base of a stage with heavy purple curtains. Mother was propped up with her white face whiter than ever. Gray, it was drained of life. She was covered from the waist down as if she were sleeping in a warm comfortable room where she didn't need to pull the covers up to her neck. Her covered arms were folded across her stomach. Through the thin white gloves, I could see the backs of her bony frail hands.

But why were her teeth showing?

She looked like she was *grimacing!* She seemed to have grown smaller, but her teeth remained the same size, which left her looking like a malicious caricature of herself. This was the kind of thing I feared would happen: the embalmer would give her an unacceptable expression, one foreign to her personality. He or she hadn't known Mother so the finished product was at best a crapshoot.

I felt a heaviness in my chest. Marie walked up to the casket and kissed Mother's cheek. I had no idea *how* she managed that. It was the last thing in the world I would have thought to do. It was something I could *not* do and did not do.

Marie said, "They dressed her just as I wanted. They got the scarf right, too. They did her hair just right. Mother would have been pleased with the way they fixed her hair."

I looked at Mother's hair. She had always had lots of hair; straight, long, light brown hair.

I thought even in death we must keep up our proper and respectable and decorous and refined, and in Mother's case, ladylike appearance. That Mother had died relatively young made no difference. The quest for dignity and gentility had to be honored. Mother was brought up as a well-bred girl.

We heard someone enter. I looked back. It was the little man in a black suit, Mr. Kennedy, who greeted us the day before.

He came to us and stopped. With a smile, he said, "She's the prettiest one we've had in here in a while."

Marie said, "Thank you, sir. She *is* beautiful."

Mary looked at me. "You okay?"

I lied and said, "Yes."

Then we heard footfalls back by the entrance. We all turned. A short man dressed in a green cotton suit and red necktie approached. I recognized him. It was Viktor Weinberg, from the airplane. He approached grinning in his timorous way.

I was stunned. What intrigue was this?

The man in a black suit stepped up to the stage and disappeared behind the curtains.

Viktor joined us, still grinning, and said, "Hello, Mark, I came to pay my respects to your deceased mother."

I was still too stunned to speak, then I said, "Thank you."

"I apologize for my presence," Viktor said, holding his hand over his mount as he spoke. "I apologize. This morning, I saw your mother's obituary in the *Tribune*."

Marie and Mary looked puzzled. I could read their thoughts: Who is this person and why does he know Mark?

"I hope you don't mind," he said.

"Not at all," I said, and I told Marie and Mary how we'd met on the airplane. They looked surprised. Marie tried to smile, but her look was more of tentative suspicion.

Viktor walked over to Mother's casket and took a closer look. He gazed at her for a while, then turned back to us and nodded as if he was approving of her or of how she was presented or both. For all I knew he was nodding approval of death itself.

"I will go now," he said, smiling meekly. "And I won't bother you again. Goodbye, goodbye." He waved and kept waving as he walked back down the aisle and through the doorway.

"How strange," Mary said, clucking. "You met him on your flight here?"

I nodded yes.

"Strange," said my sister.

We stayed with Mother for another hour or so waiting in part to see if anybody would come. The reception and funeral and burial would be Sunday afternoon. They would pay their respects then. Mother knew many people from, as she used to say, different "walks of life."

Most I would not know. Friends and acquaintances from her neighborhood would come. A lot of folks from the History Department at Gerdts and others from across campus would also come. I doubted that any of Mother's old Hyde Park neighbors would. I also doubted anyone from Waverly or Lincoln would.

19

It was late afternoon when we left. Marie wanted me to eat dinner with her, Mary, Roswell and Celosa, but I said I was tired and wanted to get back to the hotel and turn in early and rest up for tomorrow.

In my room I noticed right away the phone was blinking green. I played the message. It was Christy. She said, "I was hoping to catch you. I'll try again later. I misplaced your number. I know it's somewhere in the jungle of my purse."

I undressed, took a shower, and put on the big fluffy white hotel robe, turned on the TV and stretched out on the bed to watch the news. In no time I was asleep.

I was dreaming. Marie and I were children, and at the same time we were grown. It was Christmas, time to buy presents for each other. For some reason she'd cut her brown hair short; maybe she was tired of wearing it long. For Christmas she bought me a carrying case for my Mac laptop.

I had sold my laptop and bought a Gibson Les Paul Standard guitar that in real life I would not have been able to afford; and I doubted that money from the sale of a Mac laptop would cover the cost of even ten percent of that guitar. I bought Marie a tiara. But Marie's hair was too short, and the tiara didn't fit.

We started fighting. Mother stopped us and Marie screamed at Mother, "Mark is your favorite! You always take *his* side!" Then in a soft voice Mother said, "That's not true, Marie. I've told both of you over and over I love you both *equally*."

I woke to a news anchor reciting the news, but I was groggy and not listening very closely. I got up and stumbled to the bathroom.

While I was in there, I heard the newsman say, "*Breaking news!* Police have arrested an Evanston man. Charges not yet made. His name is being withheld. Around five-thirty this evening police responded to a domestic disturbance. A next-door neighbor placed the call after hearing a woman scream several times, then a gunshot. The neighbor also said she often hears the couple fighting. The man was arrested and is being questioned. The women, whose name has not been released, is at Northwestern Memorial Hospital's Center for Trauma and Critical Care."

It could be anybody, I said to myself. Christy was going through a divorce, but I refused to believe the victim might be her.

Not calling me back, as she said she would, was probably due to lack of opportunity. I expected I'd hear from her later tonight.

I realized I was hungry. I had missed dinnertime and thought I'd have to hit the vending machines, get some pretzels, and call it a night. I went downstairs to check out the vending machine prospects and heard the excited hum of voices. I looked around and saw Herb N' Kitchen and Kitty O'Sheas still open. I walked into Kitty O'Sheas and was quickly seated.

A lot of people were still at the bar and at the tables. I ordered fish and chips. They were delicious, hot and crispy. I enjoyed a glass of white wine too. I rarely drank wine, I was a beer guy, but tonight I felt like having white wine. It went well with fish.

Back in my room, I saw my phone was again blinking. I played the message. It was Marie. She said, "Call me. It's important."

I called her phone and she answered. "Have you heard?"

"Heard what?"

"Do you remember Peggy from high school?"

"No, I don't."

"She was one of the fast girls. But I liked her. She called me just a little while ago and said Christy Werner is in the hospital. Peggy said Christy's husband shot her. Peggy didn't say her condition."

For a moment I was speechless. I said, "I saw a news report earlier tonight but––"

"I saw that too. That was about *her*, that was about Christy. They didn't give any names, but it was Christy for sure."

"Oh, my God," I said, truly astonished. It was entirely possible her visiting me might have had something to do with her being shot.

Was she going to die? Was she already dead?

Part Three

"Deep in their roots, all flowers keep the light."
—*Theodore Roethke*

20

I assumed Christy was still alive. Saturday morning, I got up with the notion of taking a taxi to Northwestern Memorial Hospital to visit Christy, but I quickly realized that trying to visit her in the hospital this soon wasn't such a good idea.

One had to go during certain visiting hours or make an appointment and I had no idea what those hours were. I didn't think to check online for the time. Wasn't it true that hospitals allowed only relatives to visit a person in critical condition? The hospital staff might not let me see her.

Her dangerous husband was probably in jail or out on bail; and Christy's parents, Walter and Sandra, might be at the hospital. Her mother and father would remember me. They didn't approve of me or of my relationship with their daughter. They would want to know why I was visiting her. It could be dicey, risky, and even perilous!

I was in a dilemma. I told myself nothing ventured nothing gained, dialed the hospital number, and asked if I could speak to Christine Debra Werner. I was put on hold. A different person picked up and said, "Are you a relative?"

I said no.

She said, "Sorry, only relatives are allowed to speak to patients in intensive care."

I said thank you and hung up thinking I should have said I was a relative. No, lying would not have worked. So much for a brilliant idea! At least I'd found out she was *alive*. Still, she might die. People in intensive care die all the time. I worried.

After a breakfast of sausage and eggs and biscuits, I hung out in the cool lobby while my room was being cleaned. I was too nervous to play video games or to check Facebook; I kept checking my phone. I was killing time.

I was trying desperately not to worry about Christy. There was still a chance she might recover; it depended on how bad the wound was. I had no information. I had no idea how badly she was hurt. So, I sat there monitoring my own sensations while trying to muster courage to forge a positive and optimistic outlook for her.

Saturday afternoon at three Marie and I walked into Attorney Berg's office. He greeted us in a low soft voice, offered condolences, and invited us to seat opposite him at a large dark oak desk. He was a tall well-constructed man with graying brown hair, wearing a white dress shirt and slacks. He was cross-eyed.

"We don't need to do anything right now," he said, brushing imaginary dust from the glass top of his large desk of dark oak wood, "but when the time comes, I will need the house deed, all of your mother's bank account information, insurance papers, investment records and so on."

"Of course," Marie and I said together.

I reminded him I lived in California and my dealings with him would have to be done long distance.

"Of course," he said. "No problem."

As we were leaving, Attorney Berg said he had grown up on the South

Side near Mother's house. It didn't surprise me. When Mother bought the house, the neighborhood was culturally and ethnically integrated. Now it was about ninety percent African American.

While Marie was driving me back to the hotel she said, "I think I told you Mother left the money in her bank accounts and her investments to me; but we are to share the profits from the house equally."

"Mother didn't leave a will. Show me where Mother said she's leaving all of her money and investments, stocks and bonds to you."

Marie snapped, "I know what she *told* me."

"Show me where she says that!" I demanded.

"I don't have to show you anything," she said emphatically.

I decided not to continue the discussion. Aside from the house, Mother had investments, stocks, and bonds, and two bank accounts loaded with money.

I would probably win a lawsuit, but what would be the consequences? My twin sister and I would become enemies. We would never speak to each other again. I didn't want that. It was unthinkable. The deck was stacked against a good, convenient, charitable, and fitting outcome.

Soon after Mother's retirement she was diagnosed with stomach cancer. Marie went with Mother to her doctor visits. As the cancer progressed and Mother grew weaker and thinner, Marie's attention to Mother's needs grew even stronger. I was in California feeling guilty for not being there to help.

"On a different subject," Marie said, "does Christy have a lawyer?"

"I don't know."

"I was thinking John Morrow in my office would be perfect for her. His specialty is domestic abuse."

As we approached the Hilton, Marie said, "You want to have dinner with us tonight, just Mary, Roswell, Celosa and me? We're going out, maybe to a pizza place, nothing fancy."

I didn't feel like it. I said, "No, thanks, Marie. It's been a long day, and we've a big day tomorrow."

Marie parked at the hotel's front door. I noticed the valets were watching to see if we needed any help. I waved to them and one smiled, perhaps remembering I was a guest at the hotel. We sat there for a few minutes.

"Let's not be angry with each other," Marie said.

"I'm not angry at you," I lied.

"Yes, you are angry. I know you like I know myself."

"I'm just focused on tomorrow."

"Okay," she said, resignedly. "If you can't admit you're mad at me then I guess we can't talk."

"I'm not going to bring up the subject again, at least not right now."

"Okay, okay. I'll pick you up tomorrow around noon. Okay?"

"Fine. See you tomorrow."

That said, I opened the door and got out.

Marie drove away.

As I approached one of the doors, a valet smiled and said, "I bet that girl is your sister. Right? You guys look just alike."

"Yep, we should: we're twins."

"Twins! Wow! Bet you guys are so close you can read each other's minds."

I just smiled and nodded and entered the building.

By the time I'd finished my dinner of Cajun shrimp and grits and gravy at nearby Jonny Joe's, on South Wabash Avenue, my anger had subsided. Later, I strode along Michigan Boulevard back to the hotel feeling nonchalant, enjoying the warm breeze off Lake Michigan.

In the room, I was glad to see the phone wasn't blinking. I turned on the TV and undressed, put on the big white fluffy hotel robe, and flopped down on the bed.

Resting against a stack of pillows, I was ready to watch anything silly or otherwise to try to sustain this carefree state of mind. I had the remote in my hand in case I needed to change the channel. So far, only commercials were playing.

Then the phone jingled. I picked up.

It was Christy. I was surprised to hear her voice.

"Mark, I can't talk long. The nurse won't let me."

"Okay."

"But I wanted to tell you Todd shot me. The bullet hit my shoulder, but I'm sure he was aiming for my heart. He tried to kill me."

Some utterance came out of my mouth.

"I'm not sure, but I think he may have followed me to your hotel. He picked an argument with me the minute I got home, and it escalated."

I said, "Yes, I thought so."

"He always goes for one of his stupid guns when he gets angry, and he starts waving it around."

"Did you call the police?"

"No, I didn't have a chance. He's already claiming the gun went off by accident. I think he's out on bail. He's very dangerous."

"I saw it on the news. How are you doing?"

She said, "I'm okay. I'm going to be all right. How are you?"

I said, "I'm better now knowing you're okay." I paused. "He could have *killed* you."

"Yes, but the bullet didn't do much damage. It went through the outer part of my shoulder. Thank goodness it didn't hit bone. I was in intensive care, but now they've moved me to a regular bed."

"I can't tell you how happy I am to *hear* your voice, and to know you're going to be okay. You *are* going to be okay, aren't you?"

"The doctor says I will recover. Now I've got to avoid getting an infection in the wound. Like I said, Todd was aiming for my heart, clearly. It was attempted *murder*. I lost some blood. I'm still on an IV."

"Have they operated?"

"Yes, they did that yesterday. They're now trying to get my blood pressure and temperature down; and they are still worried about infection. So am I. People die in hospitals from infections."

"How long will you need to stay there?"

"I've no idea." She paused. "Todd is losing his mind and he's dangerous. I don't want him anywhere near me or you either. I think he's been calling my parents trying to turn them against me."

"You should take out a restraining order."

"That's what I'm going to do. Daddy is coming to help me with that." She stopped. "I've got to hang up now, Mark."

"Can I call you or come to see you?"

"I don't know. The nurse says I got to hang up now."

"Okay, okay."

"Bye, Mark. I'll call when I can. I love you!" She hung up.

Although the battery was low, my phone rang the minute I hung up the hotel phone. "Hi, it's me," said Marie. "Another one of your old friends read about Mother in the *Tribune*. He wants to get in touch with you while you're in town."

"Who is it?"

"Tim Brownell—that boy who used to drive Mother crazy with those loud drums."

"Sweetman! Did you give him my number?"

"No, because I didn't know if you wanted to see him or not."

"Well, thanks for checking with me first. What'd you tell him?"

"That I would have *you* call him."

"Let me get a pen! Hold on!" I picked up the hotel pen. "Okay. What's his number?"

She gave me the number and I scribbled it on the hotel pad.

"Okay," said Marie. "See you tomorrow at noon."

I checked the time. It was ten to eight. Was it too late to call Sweetman? I last saw him a few days before I left Chicago to attend college. We sat on kitchen chairs on his back porch drinking 7 Up.

He was about to enter a program at a trade school to improve his electrician skills and to get certified. He had long worked with his father, a master electrician, and knew a lot about the trade. Sweetman was preparing himself to take over his father's company, Brownell Electrical Services. I had no doubt he was now a fulltime electrician, probably married, too, with kids.

It looked like a smartphone number. I dialed it. He answered and I said, "Sweetman, that you?"

"Hey, Mark! Hey, man, it's great to hear your voice! I'm sorry to hear about you mom!"

"Thanks, Sweetman. How are you doing?"

"Ah, man, just working and taking care of the family. You know how it is. You married?"

"Not yet, Sweetman. First got to find the right woman."

"Yeah. Listen, Marie said you're at the Hilton. Why don't we get together for a drink? I could come by there."

"You mean tonight?"

"Yeah, man. It's five after eight now. I could be there in an hour or so. We could have a drink at the bar. It would be great to see you."

"Sure. My mother's funeral is tomorrow afternoon. I can sleep late. Sure, come on by. I'll wait for you in the lobby."

"See you soon."

21

A half hour later I went downstairs to the lobby and I sat in one of the plush armchairs to wait for Sweetman. I wondered about him and James and Thomas. Where were they now and what were they doing?

Thirty minutes later a tall, handsome Black man with curly hair, dressed in a light blue dress shirt and kakis, approached me. He was grinning. This had to be Timothy "Sweetman" Brownell. I stood up.

We bumped fists then did a quick, awkward hug. "Wow," I said.

"Wow," Sweetman said. "Been a long time."

"How's your sister, Hazel?"

"Ah, she's fine, in more ways than one." He laughed. "We're close. We talk just about every day."

"Say hello to her for me."

It was a dimly-lighted room of oak walls, oak ceiling, and oak bar. The atmosphere was friendly and warm. The music was slow, soft, and mellow. I couldn't identify the type: it wasn't classical; it wasn't popular, more like elevator.

There were a few guys in suits and ties at the bar drinking and talking.

They looked like businessmen starting or closing deals. Casually dressed middle-aged couples were at tables eating, talking, and drinking.

Sweetman and I took seats side by side at the bar. The music switched to Pink Floyd then the Red Hot Chili Peppers.

I said, "So what've you been up to, Sweetman?"

"Mark, they call me Tim now. "

"Oh, okay. Tim it will be." I felt a little embarrassed.

"I now run my father's business and it's a big job. We get more work than we can handle. I've six electricians working for me, but I'm going to have to hire at least two more soon if the work keeps coming in like it's been doing."

"How is your dad?"

Tim's face changed. "He passed away last year."

"Sorry, man."

He chuckled. "We all got to go at some point." He looked at me. "You still out in California?"

"Sure am." I told him what kind of work I was doing, all the while watching his response.

He kept an expressionless face then said, "Good. Glad you're doing well."

The bartender arrived, smiling faintly. "What will it be, gentlemen?" He was an elderly and portly man with white hair. His moustache was turned up at the corners.

I ordered Budweiser Light and Tim ordered bourbon on the rocks. The drinks were quickly placed before us.

"Listen, man, sorry I won't be able to attend your mother's funeral tomorrow..."

I nodded, understanding. I sipped my beer. It was refreshingly cold and crispy and yeasty.

I asked about James and Thomas. Tim said James joined the National Guard and got sent to the Middle East. "He died over there, stepped on a landmine; and he was gone in seconds." That was shocking news. Thomas moved to Terre Haute, Indiana, and was teaching fifth grade in a public school. He had a wife and three kids.

Tim kept talking. He said three years ago he did some electrical rewiring at Mother's house. "At first she didn't know who I was." He laughed. "I told your mama my name and she *still* didn't know, then I told her my nickname, Sweetman, and her face lit up. She got a kick out of seeing me again. It was great to see her too. Teased me about my drums. I still got my drums." He was grinning.

"Say, Tim, what became of Eartha Murdoch?"

"Eartha Murdoch! Man, she's big time now. She's a TV anchor person in New York City; she also married big time, married a millionaire media mogul. I don't remember his name but he's big at CBS."

"Sounds like pretty little Eartha done well for herself."

"Absolutely."

We drank for a second or two in silence.

Then I said, "Hypoallergenic was hot." I was remembering our music of thunderclouds and expressive splendor, music edifying and sometimes turbulent. Those were our exhilarating days of invigorated youth!

Tim said he got married five years ago. His wife, Ruthie, was from the old neighborhood, but I didn't remember her. They had a son, Billy, three years old.

The music in the bar turned to mellow acoustics. Tim sipped his bourbon, smacked his lips, and said, "I know you remember your old girlfriend, Christy. Right? Guess what? Her husband shot her, just a couple of days ago. I saw it on the news. I don't think she died though."

I was speechless and then I said, "Yeah, I saw it too."

"Oh, so you knew. Christy was the coolest white chick at school. I always admired her. You were lucky she fell for you. A lot of guys wanted her." He laughed. "I even named my old VW van after her, once you guys christened it."

"Yeah, she was great."

Tim didn't respond. He kept his eyes averted. A few moments of awkward silence followed.

"I wasn't sure if I was going to tell you this," said Tim, "but, I've been diagnosed with lung cancer, aggressive lung cancer. I guess it's my payback for all those years of smoking, smoking since I was twelve years old."

"Oh, I'm sorry. You're getting treatment?"

"I'm scheduled for an operation in two weeks."

"You'll be fine, Tim. I know you will," I said, not knowing what else to say.

The conversation rambled on, awkwardly, till Tim looked at his phone. "It's getting late. I'm not going to keep you up, man. Maybe I'll catch you before you go back to California?"

"Yeah, let's try to do that," I said, knowing it wasn't likely to happen.

We finished our drinks. I paid the bartender and left a good tip and walked Tim through the lobby to the revolving doors.

Again, we did the bear hug.

Tim then got into one of the revolving doors and left.

I started dreaming the minute I fell asleep. I was at Mother's gravesite. It seemed like a hundred people were surrounding the grave. She was in her casket and it wasn't closed. It was suspended on props directly over the grave.

A Black preacher unknown to me was speaking but he wasn't delivering a eulogy. He was saying, "Many thousands gone, my fellow citizens! Many thousands gone! Many thousands gone, many, many thousands gone! The figures are not revealed..."

I woke in a sweat. I lay there with my eyes closed replaying the dream, trying to understand it. Was it, in some way, sparked by fear of what was coming tomorrow, the funeral and the burial?

22

Sunday morning! The big day! After a shower I put on a dark blue suit and blue tie, left a generous tip for the housekeeper, and took the elevator down to the restaurant. I ordered breakfast and started with a cup of coffee. I ate scrambled eggs with lots of pepper, crispy bacon, and a hot English muffin and I drank a glass of very cold orange juice.

After breakfast I hung out in the lobby; I again called the hospital and asked if I could speak to Christine Debra Werner. The woman said, "Are you a relative?" I said no. "Sorry," she said. "Only relatives." I said, "But she's out of intensive care." The woman said, "Doesn't matter, only relatives."

While my room was being cleaned, I continued to hang out in the lobby playing a video game. At ten, I called Marie, but her phone was on message. I left a message saying: "I'll be outside. That way you don't have to come in the lobby."

A short time later my phone played its little melody, indicating I had a call. It was Marie. She said, "Hi, Mark. I'm sending Roswell and Celosa to pick you up. They should be there right around noon. Okay?"

"Okay," I said. "Are you okay?"

"Sure, sure."

"Okay," I said, and didn't press any further.

I went back upstairs to brush my teeth. I checked myself in the mirror to make sure I was dressed properly for Mother's funeral. I thought I looked pretty good. Not flamboyant, not showy, not great, just pretty good.

At ten to twelve, I took the elevator back downstairs and continued on through the lobby and out through the revolving exit doors. I stood outside the entryway to wait for them.

They pulled up and stopped right in front of me. Celosa was driving her little black Honda Civic.

Roswell was wearing a dark blue suit and Celosa was wearing a black dress and black shoes. They both were properly suited for a funeral.

Roswell was sitting in the front passenger seat, but he hopped out, saying, "You sit in the front, Mark. Your legs are longer than mine."

"Okay," I said and climbed down into the passenger seat. With my long legs, it wasn't easy. I always had trouble with little cars. That was one of the reasons I owned a Subaru Forester wagon.

Celosa pulled out into traffic and headed for Lake Shore Drive. We were going out to Mother's house. The ceremony would begin there. In a way Mother's venerated house had, since her death, become a kind of sacred space, especially for Marie.

Soon we were speeding along parallel to the lake. It was sunny, and I loved looking out at the blue water and white sky. People were out running along the lake's cement promenade; some were jogging, and a few were pushing baby carriages or riding bicycles. One woman was running and pushing a baby carriage at the same time.

The sky was clear with only a few distant gray clouds over the lake. Out in the middle distance sailboats with white sails were floating along driven by a gentle breeze. It was all rather idyllic.

When we reached Wabash Avenue, I caught a glimpse of the rooftop of the Art Institute, and I thought of Christy. I remembered her writing to me the first year she started there; she was so excited. I was so happy for her when I heard she graduated from the School of the Art Institute of Chicago with an MFA in studio and art history. I shouted, "Bravo, Christy!"

My fingers were crossed for Christy, but Mother was dead, *very* dead. I kept looking out the window at people running along on the promenade. They were very much alive. I, too, was alive like the runners if not happily alive. I looked at Celosa. She was *vividly* alive and beautiful. She was talking to me and I wasn't paying attention. I said, "What did you say?"

"I said what have you been up to since we last saw you?"

I didn't really want to say so I said, "Planning for today."

Forty-five minutes later Celosa turned off Lockwood Avenue and parked on 83rd alongside Mother's house. I saw Marie in the dining room window waving to us.

She and Elsie and Mary met us at the front door. They were dressed in black dresses and black shoes. After greetings, Marie said, "The limousine isn't here yet; but I have the driver's cellphone number. He says just call him when we're ready. They aren't far from here."

Marie was speaking nervously in a twitchy voice. I knew my sister. She was feeling the weight of the occasion in her heart and anxious about the ceremony. The finality of Mother's death was hard to take. That she was no longer here to give advice or express an opinion was beginning to sink in. In life her presence loomed large. Ironically, her death loomed larger but with a great silence.

We were all restless. Nobody except Elsie and Mary sat down. Gathered in the living room, waiting, we paced back and forth.

When the time came, Marie called the limousine driver. When she was finished, she said, "He'll be here in ten minutes." I thought she was going to cry again. She was having difficulty breathing.

Mary stood and placed an arm around Marie's shoulder and pulled her to rest against her bosom. It was a touching moment. Mary was often the one doing the comforting and Marie was often the one needing the comfort.

They seemed perfect for each other. Their affinity, their sense of harmony and rapport was wonderful to watch. Their temperaments complimented each other. I saw this from the beginning of their relationship. Because Mary was more mature and had solved more day-by-day problems, she was a good match for Marie, because she could, in a sense, teach her how to avoid some of life's perils.

I stood at Mother's living room window and waited. Soon the limousine pulled up and parked under the big tree by the curb in front of the house. It was very long and very black and mysterious and it had gray tinted windows.

The driver got out and started toward the house. He was a big fat Black man in a black suit and a black chauffeur's cap.

We met him on the sidewalk. He said, "Hello folks, allow me to express my condolences." He tipped his cap. "I'm Lee. I'll be your driver today."

We thanked him and piled in. Celosa and Roswell sat facing back. Mary sat on the left facing the side. Elsie sat on the right facing Mary. Marie and I sat together in the back seat facing forward.

During the trip through the streets, we sat in silence. The day was turning darker. That morning I had heard that the weather forecast was for rain later in the day or evening. Now, with the gathering clouds, it looked like the rain might arrive earlier than predicted.

Because Sunday traffic was light the limousine arrived at O'Connor & Sons in less than an hour. I began to feel a familiar tightness in my throat and stomach. I didn't want to have to look at Mother again. Yet I knew I would have to.

Yes, I *had* to. It was compulsion propelled by duress. Something would *pull* me to look. My prowling grief and sorrow would again rush to the bubbling surface. Although I prided myself on fortitude and forbearance, I would not always be able to resort to stoicism.

Alighting on the sidewalk, I noticed across the street, *of all people*, Viktor Weinberg dressed in an unbuttoned oatmeal-colored overcoat, beneath which I could see a white shirt with green dots and red pants, and a funny-looking little homemade blue cap on his head. He was grinning generously and waving to me.

I waved back. His presence unsettled me even more than I was already. I quickly turned away and headed with the others to the entrance. I wanted to trust that he was harmless.

We walked into the lobby and stopped.

"The reception will be upstairs," Marie said. "I don't know if they are set up yet."

"Let's take a look in the parlor," said Mary.

As we walked toward the parlor where Mother was, Marie pulled a folded sheet of paper from her purse. "I don't know if we have time for all of these people to speak, but we will see how it goes. I just know there will be people not scheduled who will want to get up and say something. A lot of people from Mother's department will be here—some are already inside, and there is a drove of people from Mother's neighborhood coming."

With the corners of her mouth turned down, Elsie excused herself and went to the women's toilet.

We stopped in front of the opened parlor door. I glanced in at Mother propped up in her casket. Why did this have to be my last image of her? She didn't look peaceful. Then I noticed the people. I was surprised there were already so many. Two elderly women were standing by the casket looking at Mother's corpse. I had no idea who they were.

Roswell said, "Let's go upstairs."

Elsie returned, trying unsuccessfully to smile. You could see she was feeling a lot of grief and perhaps fear too.

Dale Kennedy entered the parlor and walked to the front by Mother's casket. He turned to the gathering and said in a loud voice, "Folks, the reception is upstairs! Starts in five minutes!"

People got up and started coming out. Kennedy joined them and stopped before us. "You folks can go on upstairs. The reception is starting."

We thanked him and headed for the stairway at the far end of the lobby.

There were about thirty people in the reception room, mostly women, dressed in their Sunday best. The caterers, all women, were busy unpacking the food and arranging it on a long table along the far wall.

People were coming in, in twos and threes and fours and more. Some were resettling in chairs at the tables spread around the room; others were milling about mingling, seeing old friends, and shaking hands or kissing cheeks. A few were at the tables to see the food. A line was forming there, with people picking up paper plates and plastic knives and spoons and forks.

Marie and I stood near the entryway shaking hands and greeting people as they entered. I wasn't in the mood for it, but Marie and I needed to express our gratitude and show decorum and politeness. It was necessary protocol and ceremony and ritual. Every time I glanced at Marie she seemed on the verge of tears.

The chair of Mother's department, Professor Laura Steinberg, came in, accompanied by her husband. She was tall, with gray hair and a no-nonsense expression. She shook hands with Marie and me and said, "We miss your mother very much. She was the backbone of the department. She kept everything running smoothly. It's going to be hard to replace her."

Her words meant a lot to me. I knew Mother had been dedicated to her job and confident in her ability. She took great pride in working at Gerdts.

Then there were the staff people who worked with and under Mother's direction: Lily Chang, Mona Channing, Tara Armstrong, and Joy Harrison. At home Mother talked about them. They had already come in and were variously in the food line or at tables. I remembered them all.

We greeted Mother's closest friends in the neighborhood––Anna Belle Johnson, Ruby Mae Williams, and Carla Ann Carter––and accepted their words of comfort. They had wonderful things to say about Mother.

My face was tired from holding a smile for so long. Some of Mother's neighbors sat at the table where Elsie had settled with her plate.

I shook a lot of hands of people I knew well and hands of people I hardly knew and hands of people I wished I knew and hands of people I had no interest in knowing. Mother's world had a diverse array.

But people from the old neighborhood, Greenwood Avenue at 55th Street in Hyde Park, weren't there. Mother apparently had lost contact with those friends and neighbors. It wasn't surprising. Many years had passed since we'd lived in Hyde Park.

I was sitting with Marie, Mary, Celosa, Roswell and a couple of others. I hadn't yet gotten any food. They were all eating and talking. I wasn't hungry. I excused myself to go downstairs to the men's room.

On the way down, I saw a young man about my own age standing at the bottom of the stairs. He was wearing a white shirt with blue slacks–– clearly not someone dressed for the funeral service. He was looking down at his phone.

He looked up at me as I descended the stairs and quickly put his phone in his back pocket. As I walked past him, I said, "Hello," but he didn't return the greeting. I saw him glaring at me with intense scrutiny.

A second after I entered the men's room he came in and stood at the door. He walked to the second sink and looked into the mirror. I was at the first sink, watching him out of the sides of my eyes. I could see he was watching me too.

I went to the urinal and when I finished, I headed back to the sink. As I was washing my hands, he turned to me and nervously said, "Are you Mark Smith?"

"I am, and who are you? Do I know you?"

"No, you don't know me, but I think you know my wife, Christy Werner."

"You're Todd Fontana?"

"That's my name." He gulped now holding one hand in his pocket. "I came here to warn you."

"Warn me of what?"

"To keep away from my wife. She's *my* wife!" he hissed. "If you don't· stay away from her, you're going to be very, very sorry."

"Christy and I've been friends since high school."

"*I don't give a damn! You hear me? I don't give a rat's ass! Leave her alone!*"

I had him figured out for a coward, but I couldn't be absolutely sure. I was a lot bigger and taller, and I knew he wasn't about to take me on. I said, "How is she?"

He didn't respond.

If he was going to get physical, I knew I could take him. If he had a gun in his pocket that would be a different story. Christy said he loved guns. Did he have a concealed weapon or was it a bluff? My hunch was he didn't come with one, not *after* being arrested. If he made a move, I was ready. He would go down.

Again, I said, "How is Christy?"

"That's none of your *goddamn* business!"

I kept a steady gaze on him. I could see he was fiendish but terrified of what he was doing, and afraid of me. It showed in his eyes. He was very unstable. But I wasn't going to turn my back to him. He was likely the kind of coward who would cut or shoot a man in the back or beat a woman unconscious. Careful not to take my eyes off him, I turned to leave, calmly walking out. He remained where he was.

Now I had a new worry. Even cowards could sometimes muster enough courage to strike. I needed to be alert and cautious and vigilant. I hadn't taken Christy's warning seriously, but I now had evidence that I needed to keep my eyes in the back of my head. This guy could be diabolical.

On the way up the steps, I thought Todd must have gone through Christy's phone to find out about me and where I might be found. He no doubt knew I was staying at the Hilton. What else did he know? He knew about the funeral. Hell, he probably knew everything about me. I knew for sure Christy hadn't mentioned me on her Facebook page. I'd looked.

Till a few days before, I hadn't had any recent contact with Christy, although I never stopped thinking about her. Given we were friends since high school she'd likely told him about me long ago. But what brought him to me at *this* moment?

Back upstairs in the reception room, people were in a festive mood. The chatter was intense. I shook a few more hands, received more condolences, and I still wasn't hungry. Marie said, "Aren't you going to eat anything?"

"What'd they have over there?"

"Greek salad, beef and pork skewers, hummus guacamole dip, Buffalo-styled fried chicken wings, potato salad, marinated vegetables, white bean dip, toasted pita chips, pigs-in-a-blanket, sliced ham, and a variety of snack-cheeses. There is going to be so much stuff left over, Elsie, Mary and I will be eating it for weeks." She laughed. "You can take some back to the hotel with you. You have a refrigerator in your room?"

"Yes, but I'm not taking any food back to the hotel, Marie."

"Okay, suit yourself," she snapped and wrinkled her nose.

I was still a bit rattled by my contact with Todd. I assumed he had left the building, but I wasn't sure. I sensed he was in the depths of despair, a place where skeletons often do a beckoning dance of death. But what a coward and a rat! I still had to remain wary and circumspect.

23

I settled in the first row of parlor number two for the funeral service with Marie, Mary, Roswell, Celosa, Elsie, and Laura Steinberg and her husband. We were like wooden ducks in a row. I looked back. No sign of Todd, yet he might still be somewhere in the building.

The minister, Dr. Julia Pallas, a woman with freckles and a perm and dressed like most of the other women in the room in black, stood before the gathering and said, "Brothers and sisters, we are gathered here together to honor the life of a beautiful soul gone to rest in eternity."

"*Amen!*" said the gathering.

"We applaud the strength and integrity of our friend, Adella Smith. She raised two magnificent children, twins, Marie and Mark. She loved and cherished them both. Both grew up to be successful and productive members of society."

"*Amen!*"

"And Adella was also the highly respected CEO of the History Department at Gerdts University. Her colleagues cherished her. God blessed her, and she will be greatly missed by her colleagues and friends."

"*Amen!*"

"But we must not be sad! Adella's life is exemplary! She was a model for her children and will long be a model for all of us, a model of integrity, intelligence, love, affection, joy, and compassion. She was a woman with a good heart."

"*Amen!*"

"We must not feel sadness and grief, for Adella has gone to rest in the comfort of eternity. May God bless her children and bless her friends and bless her colleagues."

"*Amen!*"

"Now, I will step aside so others can come up to celebrate Adella's life!"

Marie rose and walked over to the minister, who touched her shoulder, stood before the gathering. She said, "I loved my Mother. I will always love her. My mother was a singular woman. I loved her deeply. My brother and I grew up carefully guarded under her wing. Our father died young. He was only thirty-six when he was killed in a car accident on his way back from a job interview. After that our life was never the same, but Mother was strong. She did her best. She made the best with what she had. She raised us well. We never went hungry. We always had a roof over our heads. My relationship with Mother during my teenage years was most difficult, but we never lost touch with each other. I was young and had a lot to learn. We always loved each other. Now, I think I'm going to cry, but it's all right." She wiped away her tears. "I need to cry for my loss. Mother is gone forever, and I will need to get used to it."

"*Amen,*" said the crowd.

Marie rushed back to her seat, weeping.

Now it was Elsie's turn. She stood in front of Mother's casket briefly, then turned to us. She said,

"This woman, this woman you see here is not dead. Her spirit will live with me for as long as I can breathe. She took me in when I had no place to go. She made her home my home. I love her. I kept her house for her. I cooked her meals. We ate together. I wasn't so much a servant but a friend to this woman. We became best friends. She depended on me and

I depended on her. She trusted me. We spent many years together. I took care of her. I did the shopping. I picked up her prescriptions. After her diagnosis, three years ago, I became her nurse. I made sure she took her pills on schedule. Marie or I drove her to her doctor appointments, until they told her there was no use trying anymore; the cancer had advanced too far. Her pain grew worse. I nursed her through her radiation and chemotherapy treatments. As she got weaker, I became her backbone. When she could no longer bathe herself, I bathed her. When she could no longer walk, I held her up and walked her to the bathroom or to the kitchen table. I sat and watched TV with her. I changed the sheets on her bed when they needed changing. We became as close as any two people can become. I miss her. She was good to me. God bless her soul! Thank you."

"*Amen*," said the gathering.

Elsie wobbled back to her seat.

Now, it was my turn. I stood and faced the faces looking expectantly at me. I scanned the audience to see if Todd or Viktor was there. I was happy I saw neither one.

I said, "My mother was a great woman, a beautiful woman, a smart and courageous woman." I paused. "I loved her and will have a hard time living without her. We had many long conversations about everything under the sun. She raised Marie and me to be principled human beings, to respect others and to always have self-respect. She was a woman of great dignity, loyalty, and kindness. Hers was a positive presence in the world; and what greater achievement can a person claim? Thank you."

"*Amen.*"

Then there was a commotion at the back of the parlor. I looked back to see what was going on. A young woman with auburn hair was taking a seat in the back. She was looking down as she walked in so I couldn't see her face clearly. My heartbeat faster.

When she turned her face toward the light, I could see she wasn't Christy. Probably she was a staff or faculty person from Gerdts.

Mary stood and said, "Adella Bischoff Smith was my mother-in-law and I loved her dearly. She without hesitation accepted me and my marriage to her daughter. She did so at a time when most of the world was still grappling with same-sex marriages, when many people were still resistant to us, at a time when many hated us and would do us harm. My mother-in-law had an open mind. She was ahead of her times. Her example in the world should be a beacon. Thank you!"

After Mary spoke, others rose to speak kindly of Adella. Professor Laura Steinberg talked about Adella's "great service to the university."

When the ceremony ended, we headed for the cemetery.

24

We walked outside into a light rain and returned to the limousine for our trip to Thornton.

"This is very difficult," Marie said, dabbing at her tears with a tissue. Mary had an arm around her, rocking her gently, with almost religious reverence.

I was aware of the others in the car, although my gaze was fixed on the passing cityscape flowing by the tinted window. I was seeing it without seeing it. It was what I needed to do to hold myself together.

Roswell was sitting quietly, looking down at his hands folded on his lap. Celosa, next to him, sat with her eyes closed. What was she thinking?

I continued to gaze out the window. I was still worried about what Todd Fontana might try to do; but I was more worried about Christy's condition.

The drive to Manifest Memorial Gardens Cemetery took an hour and fifteen minutes. The limousine pulled into the cemetery road and parked behind the hearse carrying Mother's body and Reverend Pallas. The last time Marie and I were here was for Dad's burial. We were little and my memory of the event was hazy.

I remembered Mother weeping. I remembered Dad's casket going down into the ground, but I had no memory of the minister who must have been there speaking words of comfort and sonly the shallowest memory of the others around the grave.

I glanced at headstone names as we followed the four pallbearers from O'Connor & Sons. As irrational as it may have been, I wondered: do I know this name? Bowling, McCarty, Lankford, Maxwell, Ellis. But none rang a bell. Rain was still falling lightly, and the cemetery was swimming with the smells of nature, notably petrichor, the smell of dry soil suddenly turned wet. When we reached the opened grave, I glanced at Dad's headstone. I had long forgotten the epitaph: "*My love, gone far too soon from this world. My heart rests with you, Your Loving Wife, Adella.*" For some reason Mother's words shocked me. Below her words was a poem by John Keats titled, "On Death." Silently, I read it:

Can death be sleep, when life is but a dream,
And scenes of bliss pass as a phantom by?
The transient pleasures as a vision seem,
And yet we think the greatest pain's to die.

How strange it is that man on earth should roam,
And lead a life of woe, but not forsake
His rugged path; nor dare he view alone
His future doom, which is but to awake.

Seriously, Keats? Is life really a dream we at death wake from?

Reverend Pallas stood at the head of the grave, waiting for pallbearers to place the casket onto the straps of the lowering device. When they were done, she began. "As we say our last goodbyes to beloved Adella, let us remember that death can't be separated from life, that death is in all of us, and it's nothing to fear. Adella has gone back where she came from, as will we all. So, let us hold cheerful thoughts for Adella and for ourselves.

Think of it as an awakening rather than an ending..."

Seriously? You too, Dr. Reverend Pallas?

As she continued, Marie and I held each other and wept uncontrollably. My own weeping surprised me. I sobbed harshly and bitterly as I watched Mother's body being lowered into the ground.

Marie cried out. It was almost a scream, like some great and terrible pain coming up out of the earth and shaking the ground like an earthquake. It shook me.

A few others were also crying, but not nearly as loudly. I couldn't help it. Everything I had ever felt for and about Mother surged to the surface and burst forth in those tears. In retrospect, I think I was crying more for myself.

The rain continued to fall gently.

Then, suddenly, the rain came down in torrents, a tumultuous downpour that would end as quickly as it started.

Once the casket was resting at the bottom, my whole chest seemed to fill with grief. Poor Mother, poor Marie, poor me! We three had been a family. Now there was left only a family of two, just two. No, that wasn't true. Marie had Mary. I had only Marie.

Then it was over. The whole process had taken only ten or fifteen minutes. I was suddenly shocked back to reality but not rejuvenated. I became aware of the teeming mass of people around the gravesite.

Mother was truly dead and gone. Seeing her body lowered into the ground was an absolute ending and more of a scornful *shock* than I had anticipated it might be but what had I expected?

Again, I became aware of the dense smells of the freshly turned earth and once again the smells of the wet earth beyond and the smells of wet trees and wet grass and shrubbery all around.

This burial ritual said this was the end of Mother's physical presence; the end of being near her and hearing her voice; the end of seeing her in person or hearing her on the telephone. *The end, the end!*

An hour later the rain had stopped. The limousine pulled up in front of Mother's house, and Lee got out and held the door open for us. We thanked him for his services. He said, "My pleasure," and nodded and smiled.

I watched the limousine disappear in the distance. Its disappearance seemed to reinforce the *finality* of Mother's life. The ceremony of her death was over or almost over.

As we approached the stairway to the front porch, my phone chimed. It was Tim. I was surprised. I hadn't expected to hear from him again. He said, "Hey, Mark, me and Thomas were just sitting around at my place talking. What'd you say I bring him to see you, at your hotel, man? It's been a long time!"

"I'm not at the hotel, Tim. I'm at my mother's house. Hold on a minute."

I put my hand over the mouthpiece and told Marie that Tim and Tom wanted to come. She said, "Sure! They can help eat some of this food."

I gave Tim the address, but he said he already had it from the time he did electrical work for Mother.

We all seemed drained. I took off my jacket and necktie and hung both on Mother's coat rack in the hallway.

Mary sat on the couch and stared at the floor. Marie paced the floor. I sat next to Mary and looked around. The living room and the rest of the house were filled with Mother's life. In a crazy way for me her *life* was now more present than her death.

I got up and went to the dining room to look at Mother's antique dishes and bric-a-brac inherited from her mother, handed down from her grandmother, in her Hooker dining room cabinet. There was an eighty-piece set of Wallace Baroque gold-plated flatware, rare glassware, precious cutlery, fine china dinnerware, silver-plated coffee and tea pots and even things I could not identify.

Time and things were delicately shifting. This was a watershed moment. I knew these were Mother's highly valued things. Marie would take them and give them good care. They would now become hers and Mary's, as they should. I had no desire for any of it.

I looked at the dining room table. Elsie had already placed a stack of paper plates and lots of plastic knives, forks, and spoons on the table.

Marie said, "I'm glad we didn't have to bring any of that food from the reception."

Elsie, Roswell and Celosa were carrying all the food Elsie had prepared to the dining room. When they finished, the table was filled with an array of food: hot corn muffins, crispy fried chicken, ham hocks and steaming collard greens, hushpuppies, a baked dish of macaroni, a baked okra dish, and fluffy rice in a bowl, and a huge tossed Greek salad with three kinds of olives and big chunks of feta cheese. I wondered why so much food was always associated with death.

I went to the kitchen window and looked out at the backyard. The flowering cherry tree had no flowers and no cherries, and it was still early spring. It stood there in diffused light, a time-honored and a steadfast staple of the backyard, Mother's tree.

I returned to the dining room.

The doorbell chimed. I went and looked through the tiny round glass window at the top of the door to see who was there. As expected, it was Tim and Thomas. I opened the door and did the bear hug ritual with both of them.

Although I had just seen Tim, I hadn't seen Thomas since a few days before the first time I left Chicago for Berkeley. Thomas had not changed much: just a little heavier and obviously older.

I escorted my old friends into the living room. I orchestrated the introductions. Marie already knew the guys.

The doorbell chimed again, and Elsie went to the door. While talking to someone she held the door ajar.

I was looking to see whom she was talking to. It was Mrs. Tehrani, one of Mother's neighbors. She, her husband and four children were recent arrivals from Iran. I heard her say, "I brought a gift for you and

Mrs. Smith's two children." She handed Elsie a cake.

"Thank you, Mrs. Tehrani. I'll give it to them. Would you like to join us for dinner?"

"Oh, thank you, but I must decline. I am in the middle of cooking dinner for my husband. I just wanted to bring a gift in honor of Mrs. Smith. It's an orange cake. I made it myself. It's made without flour."

"It looks delicious. Thank you!"

With that Mrs. Tehrani was gone.

Elsie placed the cake on the dining room table. Marie said, "What a nice gift from Mrs. Tehrani!"

"Beautiful," said Mary, purring.

"Yummy!" said Roswell, smacking his lips.

"Maybe I'll skip to the cake," said Celosa.

Elsie gave her a dubious look.

"Just kidding," said Celosa.

Tim and I helped Elsie bring three more chairs from the kitchen so we could all have a place at the dining room table. We gathered around, took up paper plates and settled down to eat. The atmosphere was festive, and the room vibrated with excitement. It was a beehive of chatter and activity.

We all talked at the same time: Celosa, about the courses she was taking. Elsie, about Mother. Marie, about some new policy the mayor of Chicago was trying to establish. Somebody asked me about my work, and I talked about the water problems in northern California.

We were finished eating and were sitting around, still talking, when my phone chimed. I looked to see who was calling. It was Christy. I felt a rush of excitement.

25

I excused myself and went to the living room for some privacy. "Christy! How are you? *Where* are you?"

"I'm at my parents' house in Evanston. Where are *you?*"

"My mother's house." I paused. "*How* are you?"

"I'm better."

"When were you released?"

"This morning, but the bandages won't come off for a week or so. I have to keep changing them. I think I told you they operated on my shoulder. I still feel weak, but I'm okay. The doctor said I was lucky the bullet didn't break any bones or do any damage to vital organs; but it's going to take time to heal."

"Bet you're happy to be out of that place?"

"Oh, yes! I'm so happy to have those tubes out of me and to be able to eat *real* food."

"Can I see you? *When* can I see you?"

"That's why I called. I was wondering if you could come out to Evanston tonight. Can you meet me at The Howling Coyote? It's on

Davis Street near the fish market."

"Yes, I can. I know where it is. I was there years ago. What time?"

"It's six-thirty now. How about eight?"

"Eight is perfect."

"I'll call and make reservations for two and wait for you there."

I went back to the dining room. I was wondering what kind of excuse I could make to leave. To get to Evanston for eight, I would have to leave soon. If getting a taxi to come to Mother's neighborhood during daylight was difficult, it was impossible after dark. I decided to tell the truth. I said, "Listen, that was Christy! I'm going to see her. She's out of the hospital. I'm sorry to have to leave, but..."

Tim said, "Yeah, man, we understand."

Marie said, "You need a ride?"

"She's in Evanston," I said. "I was planning to call a taxi."

Tim said, "No problem, man. I'll take you out there."

Marie said, "That's all right, Tim. We live near Evanston. I can drop Mark off. What time do you need to be there, Mark?"

"By eight."

She checked her phone's time. "Then we had better get started soon. It's six-forty now. Where are you meeting her?"

"The Howling Coyote on Davis."

Elsie said, "You can eat a second dinner, Mark." She laughed.

"The Howling Coyote, that's easy," said Marie. "Mary and I eat there often. It's a good restaurant, nice and cozy. I love their shrimp fajitas, marinated in chipotle sauce."

"Marie, I'll ride back with Celosa and Roswell," said Mary.

Goodbyes were in order. I hugged Mary. I said goodbye to the guys and promised to stay in touch. I wished Roswell and Celosa a safe trip back to New York. Leaving, I hugged and thanked Elsie for everything and said, "I'll keep in touch, Elsie."

Marie and I left.

Sunday traffic was manageable. Taking the Outer Drive, we quickly got to the North Side. From there it was an easy drive to Evanston. There traffic was light, too.

Evanston was a quiet college town with street after street of stately mansions and homes flanked by well-kept lawns.

Marie stopped in front of The Howling Coyote. Under the name in blinking lights: *Fine Mexican Cuisine.* I checked the time: it was ten after eight. As I was getting out, Marie said, "How're you going to get back to the Hilton?"

"I'll take a taxi. I'll talk with you tomorrow. Don't worry. It's not far. Goodnight."

"Goodnight," she said.

I turned to face the café, and there was Christy sitting at a little table outside by the doorway, smiling at me as I approached. She was wearing a long-sleeve shirt and a windbreaker. I couldn't see her bandaged shoulder. A few couples were seated and eating at tables on both sides of the doorway.

With the blue darkness a cool breeze was coming in from Lake Michigan. After the spotty rain the air smelled fresh and invigorating with the beginning of a nighttime chill in the air.

As I walked toward her, Christy slowly got to her feet. I could tell by her slow movements she was still in pain being careful not to dislodge the shoulder bandages concealed beneath her gray windbreaker.

She was also wearing a yellow skirt that stopped just above her knees. Her legs were bare. Her sandals were also yellow. Her long auburn hair was pulled back in a ponytail, a way she rarely wore it.

We embraced and kissed. She gave me a faint smile. She looked tired and weary; and she had lost weight. She said, "You're wearing a suit?"

"Oh, yeah, the funeral."

"That's right! How did it go?"

"It was a fine funeral." I looked around. "Are we staying out here or going inside?"

"Let's go inside."

Inside we settled in one of the fake-leather booths. She looked at the big glossy menu and I watched her reading the options. A Mexican song was coming out of the jukebox: "Besame Mucho."

I said, "I've eaten so much today. I can't eat anymore. You go ahead. I'll just order a Dos Equis."

A woman in her forties wearing a brown uniform came to serve us. She looked tired and ready for the day to be over. I smiled at her, hoping to get a smile, but none came. She stood poised to write our order on her little pad and said nothing.

The background song changed. A Mexican guitar player started singing, "Cielito Lindo." I thought, how fitting: "my pretty sweetheart."

While reading the menu, Christy absentmindedly removed the clamp holding her ponytail, stuck it in her purse and fluffed out her hair.

She ordered chicken tacos and a soda, and I ordered a beer. The food arrived quickly. She said she hadn't eaten anything in ages. She had been fed intravenously for what seemed to her many days. This morning at her parents' house she'd had a glass of milk and some yogurt. I sipped beer and watched her eat.

"I think I told you, while I was in the hospital, I took out a restraining order on Todd?"

It was a question. "Good. Good thing you did. Have you seen him?"

"No, not up close, but I saw him parked for a while in front of my parents' house this morning. He sat there for about twenty minutes then drove away."

"Todd came to my mother's funeral."

"*What?*" Christy threw her fork down. It banged against her plate, bounced across the table, and hit the saltshaker.

"Yeah. He followed me into the men's room and threatened me. He had his hand in his pocket as though he had a weapon."

"*Oh, my God! What a fool!*" She glared at me, all the while running her fingers nervously through her hair. "What did he say to you?"

"He said I had better stay away from you or else."

"Yeah! He thinks he *owns* me. He's always been insanely jealous. He's very insecure! He's nuts! It sounds just like him but he's a coward, too. He would only attack a woman. I can assure you he didn't have a weapon. The police took his guns; and I don't think he will own another one any time soon. He's probably going to do some time. What did you say to him?"

"I listened to him rant. If I said something, I don't remember what I said. When someone is that worked up it's best not to stoke the fire. When did you marry?"

"We got married six years ago. I finished my MFA at the Institute a year later. Todd was having all kinds of trouble at the office. Hygienists and dental assistants kept quitting. His student loans were killing us financially. He'd come home and take out his frustration on me. I had a little studio in the back of the house, but he kept me so tense I couldn't work. He became very violent."

I wanted to say something but couldn't think of anything appropriate. A band was playing, "Siempre Te Voy A Querer."

"Then Todd started being *physically* abusive. I told you how he twisted my arm. I thought my arm would snap out of the socket. The first time he hit me was in response to my asking him a question. Another dental assistant, a girl named Hattie had just quit. I asked him why'd she quit. I was at the sink and he was at the refrigerator standing with it opened. He didn't say anything. He just drew his arm back as far as he could and slammed my face with the back of his hand. I was shocked. *Shocked!* My face was swollen for a whole week. I stopped what I was doing and drove to my parents' house five blocks away. You remember the red brick house at Foster Street and Lawndale Avenue where my parents live?"

I said, "Sure do," as "La Cucaracha," filled the restaurant with its rhythms.

"My house is a wood-framed house on Dempster Street near Crawford Avenue. It's not paid for but there is good equity in it and the house was another source of constant problems. I took a job downtown at an advertising agency, Freedenberg & Strolls, to help pay off the house.

I was making the house payments and he was paying off his student loans. It was a nightmare. Still is! Now, I don't know what's going to happen to the house, but I know one thing––I'm done. I'm finished with him. There is no going back this time."

"So, after he hit you the first time, you went back?"

"Sure, like a fool! He begged me to forgive him; promised it would never happen again."

"And it did."

"It got worse. I hadn't been back from my parents but two weeks before he hit me again. This time we were in the car. He was driving. The light was turning yellow and he sped up to get through it but it turned red before he could get there and he went through anyway. A cop was right there and saw the whole thing. In no time he was right behind us with lights flashing. He pulled us over and came up to the driver's side and said, 'Mister you just went through a red light.' Instead of saying, 'Sorry, officer, I had poor judgment,' or something to that effect, Todd got smart with the cop and ended up getting a ticket."

"And...?"

"When we were on our way, I told him if he'd been respectful to the cop, he might not have gotten a ticket. Todd once again slammed me in the face with the back of his hand. I shouted at him to stop the car and let me out."

"He wouldn't let you out?"

"No, he wouldn't. I didn't care where I was: I wanted out. I didn't want to spend another minute in the car with him, but he wouldn't pull over. He drove home. This time I didn't run home to my parents. I stayed up all night sulking, trying to figure out what to do. As time wore on, I began to lose self-respect, to feel something was wrong with me, that I somehow deserved this treatment. The abuse continued, and I kept taking it. When I realized he might kill me, I came to my senses, but it was too late. I didn't get out in time."

"He was aiming for your heart."

"Yes, he was. He missed but he was trying to *kill* me. I told the cops he was trying to kill me. I've no doubt he was trying to kill me; but I bet you anything he's not going to be charged with attempted murder. He's claiming the gun went off by accident and I think the DA is buying his story. He's probably not going to prison."

"People get off with good lawyers."

"That's true. The legal system stinks!" She sighed. "But the good news is I no longer think of myself as a *victim*. I'm a *survivor*! That's how I see myself now. I'm going to survive for *myself*."

"That's the spirit."

"I'm not the fresh young thing you knew years ago in high school. I have baggage now, but that baggage is part of who I am. Do you want me, Mark? I'm available." She laughed and her cheeks turned red.

"Yes, I want you."

"Do you *really* mean it?"

"Of course, I mean it."

I reached across the table for both of her hands. She placed them in mine. I held her hands for a few seconds before I spoke. Then I said, "Baggage or no baggage, I still love you."

"Do you want me to move to California?"

"Yes, I would like that," I said, without knowing for sure that I meant it. Then I thought it would be a dream come true.

She sighed. "I think about my mommy and daddy. They've had this kind of relationship, and it's lasted all these years. She plays the dependent role, the supportive role, so daddy can feel strong and in charge, but the truth is mommy is a stronger person than daddy. I would hate to be so far away from them, but I am willing to move to be with you, Mark."

"After I stopped hearing from you, I kind of gave up on the idea of us being together."

"Although I married Todd and believed I *could* love him and I did in a way love him, I never stopped loving you. You were my first love. I came to think of it as romantic and probably not realistic. After you left for Berkeley, I told myself you would be surrounded by hundreds of beautiful girls and you would have your pick. You would forget all about me.

I told myself I would be foolish to go on hoping for a relationship with you. Then I met Todd. I got pregnant, and Todd and I got married; and at first, despite all the problems, it looked for a while like we were going to be okay; then I had a miscarriage! Todd blamed me. He said I deliberately lost the baby; and that wasn't true. My womb is *tilted,* and I can't carry a pregnancy. Is that going to be a problem for us?"

"No," I said, without knowing if I really meant it.

As "Solamente una Vez" played, I thought what she had been through was heartbreaking. Was the impossible about to become true? Christy belonged to my heart. How strangely ironic and tragic life could be. But the more I thought about the idea of Christy being with me in California, the more I liked it. Could Christy and I become one indivisible? There was much she had yet to deal with.

"I guess you'll have to go to court?"

"I don't know. I think Todd has a hearing coming up this week. Right now, he's out on bail. I'm sure he has a lawyer, but I bet you his lawyer doesn't know, despite the restraining order, he's following me around; and I bet you any money the lawyer doesn't know Todd confronted *you.* That's a crime."

I took another sip of beer. "How about coming back to the hotel with me?"

She hesitated. "I'd have to call Mommy and tell her I'm spending the night with a friend. She'll be concerned but I'm an adult."

"I know they were happy when I left Chicago for Berkeley."

"That's true. They're really good people, Mark, but they grew up in a community when prejudice was as common as breathing."

"They don't know I'm in town?"

"They probably do. They know your mother died. They saw it in the *Tribune.* Mommy pointed it out to me. Listen, I don't care if they know I'm spending the night with you. It's none of their business. If they don't like it, they will just have to get used to it again."

"Okay," I said. "Great! I'll call a taxi." I took out my phone and asked for a taxi to come to The Howling Coyote.

26

I held her close when we were in bed, careful with her shoulder. She rested her head on my chest as we watched a TV show about two guys searching for "treasures" in piles of junk. Christy took her pain medication. We fell asleep around midnight.

While Christy and I were downstairs eating breakfast, my phone rang. It was Marie. She said, "Are you leaving tomorrow or Wednesday?"

"My return ticket is for Wednesday." When I said that Christy looked up from her English muffin and scrambled eggs, her eyes widening.

Marie said, "I want to go easy on Elsie. You understand that, don't you?"

"Of course."

"I know we have to sell the house, but let's not be in such a big hurry that it looks like we are kicking her out. I want to give her time to decide what she's going to do. She may go back down south to live with one of her relatives in Atlanta."

"I understand."

"I know there are things of Mother's you want, such as family photographs, but you will have to be patient, Mark. I don't think we should start moving things out of the house right away, not even photographs. Mother's home is also Elsie's home. I just don't want her to feel violated."

"I understand."

"So, you're leaving Wednesday, for sure?"

"My ticket says Wednesday."

"You and Christy getting back together?"

"We *are* together."

"I'm glad to hear she's okay. I always did like her. I think she is good for you."

"I agree."

"Anyway," Marie said, "I just wanted to touch base with you. Will I see you before you leave?"

"Of course. Hold on," I said. I asked Christy if she would be able to have dinner with my sister and Mary and me tonight.

She said, "Sure! I'll just have to go to my parents' house first and change clothes."

I said to Marie, "Why don't you and Mary and Celosa and Roswell have dinner with Christy and me tonight?" I was watching Christy as I spoke. A faint smile crossed her lips.

"Roswell and Celosa left for New York this morning."

"Oh, I see; then you and Mary?"

"Great! It'll be nice. I think Mary will like her." Marie paused. "There is so much we are going to have to deal with in the coming months, and not just regarding the house."

"I know, but let's not talk about it right now," I said.

"I'm glad to hear you say that. Is Christy moving to California?"

"I hope so, but she has some issues here she needs to tend to."

"I would imagine."

Later that morning, Christy and I stopped at the front desk and arranged for her to share my room and get her own key before helping her into a taxi. She was careful because of the hypoallergenic bandages on her shoulder. These she would change before returning from her parents' house. She would get back to the Hilton by five.

In the afternoon, I took a walk along Michigan Boulevard looking in the shops, I stopped at a sidewalk café and sat for a while sipping herb tea and eating a slice of carrot cake.

Marie and Mary agreed to meet Christy and me in the lobby of the Hilton at six. I made reservations at La Cocina de Mama, a Spanish restaurant on Wabash Avenue not far from the hotel. Christy arrived by taxi at five. Marie and Mary drove up at five to six. The attendant took Marie's car to the garage.

Marie already knew Christy. They shook hands in a slightly unsure way. Mary smiled dubiously as she was introduced. Her handshake with Christy was tentative and hesitant.

At the restaurant, we got a booth near the front. Marie sat next to Christy. Mary and I sat side-by-side facing them. A platter of tapas and a bottle of red wine were placed at the center of the table. Both were delicious. The three women relaxed and seemed friendly toward each other.

They wanted to know about the work I was doing with water resources. I told them about the benefits and the problems. They talked about shops along Michigan Boulevard, QVC and online shopping and social media. It was interesting to see Christy interact with my sister and Mary.

"What'd you do, Christy?" said Mary.

"I'm a painter. I paint." Her smile was hesitant.

"Oh," Mary said, "You're an *artist*. That's nice."

When we finished dinner, Marie said to Christy with a forced smile, "I hear you're planning to move out to California?"

"As soon as I can," Christy replied. Under the table, she touched my leg with her foot.

Mary said, "I think of California as the land of milk and honey."

I laughed, and said, "And earthquakes and drought and––"

"Mark when are you leaving?" said Mary.

Before I could answer, I saw from the corner of my eye a man outside with his hands cupped around his face trying to peer into the restaurant. It was Todd Fontana. I touched Christy's arm, motioning for her to look. She had time to see him before he quickly walked away.

"That was Todd, my husband, at the window," she said. "He's giving me the creeps. I have a restraining order against him. He's not supposed to be doing this sort of thing. I could have him rearrested."

"Why don't you?" said Marie.

Christy said, "The restraining order says as long as he stays three hundred feet away from me, I've no grounds for accusing him of physical abuse or harassment or intimidation or stalking."

"Although he was outside and standing at the window, he was less than three hundred feet away," I said.

Marie said, "You filed an order of protection, right?"

"I guess that's what they call it," said Christy. "My father drove me down to West Harrison Street and he helped me. At the time I was too weak to do it on my own."

"Of course," said Marie. "Your husband is not supposed to call you or text you or email you or follow you and he's not supposed to attack you or disturb you in any way. He's not obeying those orders. Is he still living in the house?"

"No, nobody is. I'm staying with my parents."

Marie said, "Christy, you need to call the police."

"I know that's what I should do."

"How are you feeling now?" said Mary.

"I'm better. Each day I feel better."

Marie said, "You do have a lawyer, don't you?"

"No, not yet. I'm not sure I need one."

Marie touched Christy's shoulder. "Christy, you *always* need a lawyer. I don't handle this kind of case, but my firm can represent you; that is, if you want us to."

"Are you sure it's not a bother?"

"Listen, call me tomorrow at the office and I will set up an appointment for you to talk with John Morrow. He handles domestic abuse cases, and he's one of the best." Marie reached in her purse and pulled out her business card and handed it to Christy.

Tuesday morning, Christy woke me getting out of bed. When she came back from the bathroom she placed a hand on my chest and said, "Why don't we go to the Art Institute? Have you been there recently?"

"Not since I was in high school on a field trip."

"I'd love to show you around the galleries; then I'd love it if you'd go with me out to Evanston to say hello to my parents. You're leaving tomorrow. I know they weren't very nice to you when we were kids, but they've matured a lot. My mother even voted for Obama, and both my parents have been dyed-in-the-wool Republicans forever."

The first idea excited me and the second one gave me pause; but if Christy and I were going to live together in California, then her parents would have to adjust to our relationship. I said, "All right! Let's do it. After breakfast, I'll rent a car at the Magnificent Mile for the day so we can get around."

Christy said, "But we can walk to the Institute from here. That way we don't have to worry about finding a parking place."

"Okay. Then we'll use the car to get out to Evanston. I can even keep it overnight to get to the airport in the morning and turn it in there."

Christy leaned over and kissed me on the mouth. "*Ouch!*" she said. "I moved my arm a little too fast. Got a sharp pain!"

"Be careful."

At the Art Institute, Christy said we should start upstairs and work our way down. In gallery after gallery of Impressionism, she explained painting after painting. Cézanne's *Madam Cézanne* and works by Cassatt, Morisot, Monet, Degas, and Lautrec. I began to develop a headache.

We went up to the Art Institute restaurant, Terzo Piano, for lunch. We got a seat by the long window. Both of us ate pasta and salad. I remembered Fad telling me he came to one of the Institute's restaurants, possibly this one, and the old waiters seated him behind a pillar near the kitchen. When he asked for a different table, one by the window--and there were about a dozen available--they said no, those were spoken for. Dad said there were only four other customers in the restaurant of over a hundred tables. The waiters then moved Dad to a table behind another pillar, still close to the kitchen. He got up and walked out.

After lunch, Christy and I returned to the galleries. She explained several large paintings by Seurat, Caillebotte, Hopper, Matisse, and Seurat. I learned about Seurat's pointillism, Matisse's fauvism, and Hopper's painting of "silence."

She also explained how paintings are made and the function of foreground, background, composition, harmony and how various colors and impasto work. I was beginning to understand. Her lecture was good because I wanted to know more about the things that interested her.

Holding hands, we walked back to the hotel. A good breeze from Lake Michigan swept along Michigan Boulevard and the warm sunlight felt good. I was sure the colorful paintings inspired my happy mood.

27

Although Christy had a key, she pressed the door buzzer. Mrs. Werner came to the door to let us in. I sensed the tension in both her parents when we entered the house. Mrs. Werner's mouth smiled but her eyes showed fear. Mr. Werner stood behind her, also trying to smile but his face showed stress.

He reached around his wife and shook my hand. "Hello, Mark."

"Hello, Mr. and Mrs. Werner. Nice to see you again after all these years." I was thinking: *guess who is not coming to dinner?*

"Come on in," he said. Walter Warner had aged quite a bit since I last saw him. His hair was snow white and he had gained a lot of weight and now he used a walking cane. "Todd came by here yesterday and the day before."

"Todd called here too, I don't know how many times," said Sandra Werner. She squinted as if to gauge our reaction. She hadn't gained much weight and her hair was now dyed blond. It had been auburn.

Christy and I followed them into their living room where the sectional sofa and chairs were brown and the oak coffee table on casters was trunk-style with storage drawers. Lying on the table was a copy of *Evanston Now*, a local newspaper, and two half-empty cups of coffee.

Christy and I sat side by side on the sectional with our backs to the front window. "*Why* is he bothering you guys?" Christy said, her voice rising in anger.

Her father said, "He's been trying to get us to talk to you on his behalf. He says he's sorry."

"Sorry," Christy said sharply, "won't cut it this time. It's finished, and he's finished."

Her mother said, "I understand how you feel, dear. He does sound unstable."

"Unstable is an under-statement. He's *insane* and *dangerous*. He tried to *kill* me. From the beginning he's waved those guns around at me; then he shot me."

As they talked about Todd, I remembered the day Christy's parent left Hyde Park. I was walking our dog, Toby, by then an old dog. Mr. Werner was taking things from their house to the U-Haul truck. I spoke to him and he mumbled something in return. The big van with the bulk of their furniture had already gone to Evanston where Mrs. Werner was waiting.

This was the first time I had been inside *this* house. I had driven here in my first car, a little VW bug, to pick up Christy during our senior year in high school. After the family moved to Evanston, I rarely saw her parents.

Once her father came out to my car as Christy was getting in. He wanted me to know he wasn't prejudiced, but he felt "an interracial relationship is just too hard on everybody because of the way the world is."

He kept saying it wasn't *his* feeling. "The problem," he said, "is the world. The world is just not ready for it." As I listened, I knew he was wrong. The evidence was the opposite. The country by then had adjusted to all kinds of so-called "interracial" marriages. It was clear to me *he* wasn't ready for it.

Now here we were again. Did he still feel the world wasn't yet ready?

The latest research said one in seven American marriages was between people of different so-called "races" or ethnicities; but I wasn't ready to argue with Mr. Werner.

Christy said, "Mark's mother died last Monday."

Mrs. Werner said, "We're sorry for your loss, Mark."

I said, "Thank you."

"Todd went to the funeral and confronted Mark," said Christy.

"*He what?*" said Mr. Werner.

"He followed Mark into the men's room and threatened him," Christy said.

"Mark, Todd threatened you with a gun?" said Mr. Werner.

"Not with a gun *necessarily*," I said. "Although he had his hand in his pocket in a threatening way. He *may* have had a gun. I don't know."

Both Christy's parents wanted to know what he said so I described the event in detail as best I could. As I talked, Mr. Werner paced back and forth with his cane. He was breathing heavily. Then he abruptly stopped at the front window and looked out. "*Christy, come here!*" he said. "Isn't that Todd's car out there on the other side?"

Christy leapt up and rushed to her father's side. With him, she peered through the slightly parted white curtains. "That's him! *See! See* what I told you? He's still following me around. This is *illegal!* I'm going to call the police right now!"

"Wait a minute," Mr. Werner said. "Just hold on. Think about what you're doing."

"But Daddy, Todd is supposed to keep three hundred feet away from me and he's *not* doing that."

"Just calm down, Christy!" said her father, touching her shoulder. "He might actually be three hundred feet away. He's on the other side of the street."

Christy's voice was getting louder. "Daddy, surely you can't approve of what Todd is doing, not after what he has done to me. My *life* is in danger!"

Her mother rose and stood at Christy's side. "Todd said he is sorry, and he just wants to talk to you."

"Well, he can't and if you guys are on *his* side, I want nothing to do with it."

"You want nothing to do with *us?*" said Mr. Werner.

"That's *not* what I said!" Christy shouted angrily.

Her mother snapped, "It sounded like that."

"Come on, Mark, let's go!" said Christy.

I stood up, ready to go.

"Wait," said Mr. Werner. "Don't leave like this. Both of you *please* sit down."

Christy hesitated. She looked furiously at her father, then took my hand and we returned to your seats.

"Christy," Mr. Werner said, "we recognize you are a grown woman. You make your own decisions, but *think,* so you don't make a mistake."

"Thank you, Daddy, for saying that. As soon as I am no longer required to be here for legal reasons concerning what Todd did to me, I plan to move to California to be with Mark."

"Move to California?" said Mrs. Werner, alarmed. She stood slightly behind her husband.

"Yes!" Christy was emphatic.

"I understand why you would want to get away," said her father.

Mrs. Werner said, "Do as you please, Christy, but you must admit this is all *so sudden.*"

"Would you suggest I return to Todd?"

"Oh, no, no, I'm not saying that at all."

"Then *what* are you saying?"

"I don't know what I'm trying to say, dear." Tears came to Mrs. Werner's eyes. "Everything has been *so* unfortunate. I'm just grateful you and Todd didn't have children."

"Are you coming back home tonight?" Mr. Werner said.

Christy said, "No, I'm spending the night with Mark at the Hilton. He's leaving first thing in the morning. I want to be there to see him off."

"I see," said her father.

"I'm coming back after Mark leaves."

"What's going to happen to the house you shared with Todd?"

"I don't know. I made the payments on the house; but I don't want to live there anymore. That's why I brought my things here. I still have a lot of stuff I need to get out of that house. It will have to go on the market and be sold; that is, if Todd goes to prison."

"He's not going to prison, dear," said her mother.

"How do you know that?"

"He told us the DA is calling it an accidental discharging of a firearm. They're saying it was *unintentional.*"

Christy said, "After five years of verbal and physical abuse they have the nerve to call his shooting me *accidental?*"

"Todd will be on probation for five years, and he can't own a firearm," said Mr. Werner, "and, like you said, he won't be able to go anywhere near you."

Her parents gave her a sheepish look. Then her mother said, "I'm just glad you weren't hurt more seriously."

"I was hurt worse than you know." Christy was indignant.

Her father said, "Even in the worst of situations, there are things we can be grateful for."

"You be grateful *alone,* daddy. I'm not ready to forgive and forget."

"I understand, dear," Mrs. Werner said.

"Let's go, Mark." Christy stood and walked to the window. "Todd's car has gone. Come on, Mark, let's go."

"I don't know why you're *annoyed* with us," said Mrs. Werner.

Christy didn't respond. She took my hand and we walked toward the front door, her parents following.

Christy turned around, hugged her father and mother, then quickly opened the door.

"Nice seeing you both, Mr. and Mrs. Werner," I said, trying to sound as sincere as I could

Mr. Werner said, "Yes, Mark, it was nice seeing you too. Safe trip home!" His tone was flat and unenthusiastic.

After dinner, when Christy and I were back in my hotel room, I called my sister. "Marie, I'll call you when I get home."

"Okay. You know, I've never been able to adjust to your living so far away. It just seems strange. It bothers me. Is it because we are twins?"

"I don't know."

"You don't feel that way? You don't feel *separated* from me?"

"Not especially."

"People say twins always stay together, but I guess we defy the rule."

"I didn't know that *that* was a rule."

"Maybe it's not. After Dad's passing and now Mother is no longer with us, I feel we *should* be closer together. You obviously don't feel that way."

I didn't say anything because I wasn't feeling what she was feeling, and I didn't want to hurt her or get into another argument.

"Okay, Mark. Call me when you get to California."

"I love you," I said.

She hung up without responding.

"I want to go out to the airport with you," Christy said next morning. It was eight-fifteen. My United Airlines flight to Sacramento was slated for eleven-twenty.

I hugged her. I had finished packing and my luggage was on the hotel four-wheeler ready to go. "It's not necessary, sweetheart. I have to turn the rental car in. It's going to be hectic out there. How would you get back home?"

"There's an airport shuttle between O'Hare and Evanston."

"Okay!"

After I had checked in at the airport and got my boarding pass, we sat down together outside security on a bench by the wall. We kissed and hugged. "It won't be long," I said.

Tears were in her eyes. "Please send for me! Mark, let's make it happen, okay?"

"It's going to happen. Don't worry." I meant it too. I had long wanted a serious and lasting relationship but had no idea it would ever be possible with Christy, my high school sweetheart. "I'll call you as soon as I get home."

We kissed goodbye. Her lips were soft and giving. Unmindful of the public, we kissed a long time.

Part Four

"Nothing is old, nothing is new, save the light of grace, underneath which beats a human heart."

—George Rouault

28

Once I was settled in my aisle seat, I closed my eyes and thought about my time in Chicago, which had gone so quickly. Though I felt great sadness about Mother's death and reflected on my father's, my mind traveled to Christy.

I felt good about our prospects. The galleries in Sacramento would probably be receptive to her work. Perhaps we could get an apartment big enough for her to have a studio before her birthday, which was December 31, same as Matisse's—she'd once told me. I was excited thinking about our future with her doing what she loved: painting. Christy and I were essentially forging a new, *unified* identity, and it felt splendid; but it was also scary.

I thought about Christy's parents. No matter how troubled her relationship with them was, she was deeply attached to them. Their bond was formidable, and I respected it.

I remembered their move from Hyde Park. Christy told me her parents' official reason for moving was "a change of jobs," but they moved to Evanston without any prospects for work. After two months there,

Mr. Werner found work in an established certified public accountant's office, Larsen & Crane, where, for the first few years, he worked on consignment.

As for Mrs. Werner, she worked as a substitute teacher at Oakton Middle School, then for a brief time at Dewey High, then she was hired on at Dawes Elementary for a couple of weeks, while a teacher was on vacation. It was a full year before she found a permanent position. It was at Stuckey Elementary where she remained until she retired.

I was hopeful they were coming around or at least becoming kindly resigned to the inevitable. As unpromising as meeting them was this time, it gave me new but cautious hope.

I thought of Marie. Time had done its work. In our early years I thought of Marie and me as two halves of a whole, sharing a deep bond. We weren't rivals, as were so many sisters and brothers.

Later, in college, I thought of Marie as my doppelgänger. I took a mythology class and learned some tribal people often thought of twins as "godlike." They fascinated me: Castor and Pollux, Artemis and Apollo, Yami and Yama. Some West African tribes believed twins represented a form of higher being. Twins in Zuni culture were also very special, even magical.

Not all twins in mythology were harmonious and mutually support- ive. I remembered the rivalry of the ancient Persian deities, Ahriman and Ahura Mazda, one good, one evil. Perhaps Marie and I were now mirror- ing those two?

But my thoughts kept coming back to Christy. She was an artist and I a scientist. Would living together be like oil and water? I was water and she was oil. Under the right conditions the two mixed quite successfully.

Christy would have to finish her medical treatments for the shoul- der wound. She might also have to appear in court when Todd's case was decided. Christy or Todd would have to make some arrangements for the house she and he shared. They were equal owners.

I was exhausted when the plane landed, and I went to pick up my large suitcase. It felt good to be on the ground again, to be back in California.

I took a taxi home from the airport. When the taxi driver pulled to a stop at my address, I said, "Well, the house is still here. That's a good sign."

He laughed.

I called my next-door neighbors, Ralph and Sid. Ralph answered. I thanked him for keeping an eye on my apartment while I was gone. Ralph said, "Anytime, Mark!"

I looked around. Everything was as I had left it. Only a bit of daylight was entering the room at the edges of the curtains. It was depressing. Being home was somehow both good and unsettling; and I didn't know why I had such mixed feelings.

Part of the problem was that I had to adjust to being home again. Change was difficult. In those few days I had adjusted to *living* at Hilton Chicago. A new adjustment was now before me.

I left my luggage by the front door and went to the kitchen to check the nearest telephone for messages. It was blinking twenty-eight messages. Twenty-eight were too many to deal with at that moment, so I made a mental note to check them later. I opened windows to let in fresh air or what passed for fresh air.

I changed my mind and played the first message: "Mark? You there, Mark? It's Clifford. It's been a while since we've talked. Call me."

I was exhausted and frazzled, but I promised Christy and Marie I would call. Because the conversation was likely to be shorter, I decided to call my sister first. Since I was tired of sitting, I stood with my back against the kitchen island, and made the call. An automatic voice said she was unavailable.

I hung up and called Christy's number. It was only two-thirty Pacific Time in the afternoon and four-thirty in Chicago. I had gained time flying west. Christy said, "Hello?"

"Hi, sweetheart."

"Mark! You're home?"

"I'm home. How are you?"

"I've been on pins and needles waiting for you to call. I'm at the gym right now on the treadmill trying keep myself in shape. You sound tired."

"I *am* tired. Careful with your shoulder."

"I'm being careful. I know you didn't sleep well last night. I was restless too. I guess I'll crash soon. I miss you."

"I miss you too. As soon as you get things finalized there you can come out here. When do you see the doctor to take off those bandages?"

"He said the bandages can come off in twelve days, but I would still have to continue taking Amoxicillin to make sure there is no infection and to keep the pain under control with prescription Tylenol."

"Sounds good. Anything from you-know-who?"

"Nothing; and I hope he keeps it that way." She paused then said, "Oh! I started painting again! I'm working on one I'm calling 'Self Portrait with Bandaged Shoulder.' Get it?"

"I get it. Glad to hear it."

We continued to talk for another twenty minutes, saying over and over how much we missed each other, then I said, "It won't be long, sweetheart. I think I'll take a nap. What time should I call you tomorrow?"

"I promised to help Mommy do the grocery shopping at Whole Foods; and we should be done by eleven. We will probably have lunch downtown. How about two o'clock my time?"

"Okay, that's twelve o'clock my time. I'll call then. You go ahead and hang up first."

"No, you hang up first," Christy said.

"Okay." And I hung up.

That night I slept well, but toward morning, with a rapid pulse, I woke with a jolt, remembering my dream. I was outside a building in which a large conference was taking place. I could hear the voices of the participants. They were like swarming bees. I knew I was supposed to be inside but for some reason I was not. I had arrived late and found the doors locked. I couldn't find the entrance.

I kept walking around the building. I found a side door. I turned the knob. The door opened. I entered the building into a long, dark hallway.

As I walked the hallway my footfalls echoed; then I came to a lighted room full of conference participants. I saw my old college friend, Clifford, and my old band buddy, Timothy, together, sitting at a table.

These were two people who had never met. But in the dream, they were apparently the best of friends. They were laughing and talking together.

Happy to see them, I walked over to them but when I spoke, they stopped laughing and talking and looked at me with cold eyes. When I said, "What's going on, guys?" They looked at each other with puzzled expressions.

Tim said, "Do we know you?" and Cliff said, "I don't believe we've met before." At this point I awoke, my memory of the dream at first fuzzy, then clearer.

I sat there in bed thinking there were only five days left in the month of April. I'd have to get back to work and start counting the days.

29

Thursday morning at six-fifteen my phone chimed; I picked it up from my bedside table. I recognized the number and sat up. It was Christy.

"Mark! *Todd killed himself!*"

"What?"

"Todd *hung* himself!" she said.

"Slow down, slow down, he—*what?*" I held my breath then let it out. "Hung himself? When? How? Where?"

"The police came here this morning, waking us before daylight. Mommy and Daddy and I let them in. They said they went to the house looking for Todd. No answer. This was the third time they had gone there looking for him since yesterday. They went and got a search warrant and broke down the door. They found his body hanging from the light fixture in the bedroom closet. We're all shocked. Stunned! Speechless! They said since I am still legally his next of kin, I've got to claim his body."

"What about his parents?"

"They've contacted his parents, too. I talked with his mother this morning, and she said they are going to take care of the funeral expenses.

It's such a great shock for them. I'm shocked too, I guess I knew he would do *something*."

I, too, was stunned.

Christy said, "I thought he'd kill *me*. He tried! I thought he'd try again; and I worried that he would succeed."

"The police took his guns?"

"Yes, they took all the guns. I knew he wanted to kill *somebody*. I knew it! In the end, since he no longer had a gun, he hung himself. *Oh, God*, I feel so sorry for him. He was *so* sick and just never got help."

I was too shocked to know what to say.

"Daddy is going to drive me to the police station this morning. I got to sign some papers. To say the least this has not been a normal morning." She paused. "Mark, Daddy's ready to go. I'll call you later today. Got to go! Love you! Bye!"

I was at loose ends. I played the landline messages. Most were scam calls or calls from somebody trying to pitch something I didn't want or need. Several were political messages trying to get me to vote a certain way.

One legit call was from my friend Ashley in New York, "just to say hello." Another was from my sister, Marie, the day I left California, a call placed while I was on my way to Chicago. She said, "Have a safe flight. See you soon."

I showered, dressed in a T-shirt and jeans, and walked down to Lee's Café, a little amiable breakfast and lunch diner a block from my apartment. I took my laptop with me.

Half the people there were already peering seriously into laptops or some other electronic device. The Wi-Fi there was exceptionally good. I sat outside at one of the tables under the canopy. The daylight was clear and good, and the breeze felt refreshing.

I ordered toasted bagel and fresh cream cheese and I ate while checking my Facebook page. Then I ordered a cappuccino and sipped it while catching up on my Facebook friends from Berkeley days.

Garth had posted a picture of his French wife, Lyna, and him on a sailboat on the French Riviera. Above it he wrote: *We had to get the hell out of Paris. We needed a break from all the bad news, the suicide bombings and terrorist threats. This is Muriel's father's boat. Pretty nice, huh? He retired here in Antibes. Old Town here has 16th-century ramparts. The bay is full of luxury yachts. But things are pretty scary down here too.*

Then I checked Clifford's page. He hadn't posted anything in a while. He was living and working in Davis. I scrolled down to look again at his photographs: Cliff with his dog Cody and Cliff fishing in the Sacramento River.

Looking at Ashley's Facebook page, I knew what to expect: details about vacations with his wife, Stormy, a woman he'd met since moving to New York City; pictures of their two cats and complaints about politicians in Washington. He and Stormy had an apartment from which, if you looked to the extreme left out of the bathroom window, you could see the Empire State Building.

I went to work the next day. My boss, Herb, came into my office. "Mark, I see you're back from your mother's funeral: my sympathy again for your loss."

"Thank you, Herb."

"I hate to throw work at you so soon," he said, "but I need you to go up to the Jansen Power Plant and check out the situation involving the reservoirs and the facilities. It's been a crazy morning. I've been on the phone all morning with FEMA about that emergency in Yolo County. I know you've been to the Jensen before but David Young is more familiar with it so he will go with you. He's very familiar with the site. Seems the salmon and steelheads aren't returning to spawn at the Brymner River Fish Hatchery, the way they are supposed to. Might be a problem with the water flow from the Klinkhoff. You know that's how the Jensen gets its electricity."

"Sure, Herb. No problem. Is the Jeep available?"

"No, take the red Bronco."

And I was truly back at work.

May Day, the first day of May came. The days quickly passed and then we were at the end of a month of warm dry tricky erratic weather. Memorial Day passed and I was already getting antsy because I was daydreaming of marrying Christy.

I told myself to take it slowly; there is no need to hurry; *if* marriage is coming let it come naturally. I wanted stability in my life, and I thought if Christy and I got married rather than just living together I might feel more secure.

I felt badly about Todd's death. To have killed himself suggested that he was suffering greatly.

With me, Christy's life would be without restrictions. I wasn't the controlling type.

I kept going over various scenarios, ending up where I started: coming to no conclusions except I was excited that we would soon be together. I was on a joyous quest. In those days of waiting, I woke feeling triumphant and exhilarated and blissful. I rejoiced at the slightest accomplishment: sealing an envelope without getting a papercut, making a drinkable cup of coffee, getting through the day without a headache, not having road rage while driving to or coming from work. Some drivers carried guns, and they were ready to use them at the slightest perceived provocation. I didn't own a gun and never wanted one.

It was the first Saturday in June and a beautiful day. I remembered Nina-Momo Ishikawa reciting words by Pablo Neruda: "Green was the silence, wet was the light, the month of June trembled like a butterfly." The sky was bright powdery blue with no clouds.

I was sitting at a table outside Lee's Café enjoying a cappuccino when Marie called and said, "I have those two photo albums from Mother's house you want. I'm going to send them to you by UPS."

"I thought you were concerned about Elsie seeing things leaving the house."

"It was actually *her* idea. She suggested I send them to you."

"Don't you want any of them?"

"You can make copies and send them to me." Marie sounded indifferent.

"Okay, I'll do that."

"You're more the family archivist than I am. The originals belong with you."

Christy and I were talking now two and sometimes three times a day. She would be coming out soon.

In early June, the drought had ended, but there was no rain in the valley. On weekends I went with guys from the job to root for one of our favorite teams. We went to cheer for Sacramento's baseball teams or for the butt-kicking River Cats. We also played tennis; and on Wednesday nights bowled and drank beer. Keeping busy helped to keep me from thinking too much.

When I couldn't sleep, I watched old black and white movies of the 1920s and 1930s on cable TV. I found solace in them; I liked slower pace and the absence of loud music. All of the characters in those movies seemed to live in a more serene and sympathetic world. It was an illusion, but they consoled me as I waited for Christy's arrival.

30

Christy arrived on a day that held some unmistakable personal symbolism--July 4, Independence Day.

She had put her house on the market and Todd's dental business had been sold; the paperwork was being finalized. Christy was his next of kin and entitled to the proceeds. Call it destiny, call it prosperity, call it fate or call it karma: the prevailing winds were blowing in her favor.

Her doctor had removed her bandages and she was well on her way to using her left arm more freely.

I was waiting at the baggage carousel luggage at the Sacramento Airport, pacing back and forth when my phone chimed with her message: "We're on the ground! We got in early! I'm so excited!"

A half hour later there was Christy, pulling her carry-on. She was in a green jersey and blue jeans and black flats coming toward me in all of her casual elegance. I walked quickly to meet her, taking her in my arms and lifting her off the floor. We hugged and kissed a long time. Her ears turned red with excitement.

While we waited for her luggage to appear, she said her easel, paintings, drawings, drawing table, supply cart and her other studio things would arrive by UPS. "They said in about a week."

Christy and I collected her luggage and piled it into my Subaru and headed for 19th and J. I wished I'd been able to get a bigger place before her arrival, but my lease would not be up for renewal for a few months.

We arrived at my two-bedroom apartment. I used one for my home office. We needed to find a suitable place for Christy to paint.

She looked around at the apartment. "Not bad."

"Yes, but we need more room." I was trying to see the place as I imagined she saw it.

"I'm going to try to find work out here," Christy said. "Mr. Freedenberg, at the ad agency, says he'll be happy to recommend me."

"That should help." I hadn't thought of her working. I'd imagined she would paint full time; but if working at an ad agency was what she wanted to do, I was in full support.

"There are a lot of art galleries in Sacramento," I said.

"I know. I looked online a few days ago and saw some interesting ones. I'd love to check them out. It would be great if I could be represented by one of them. A gallery in Evanston represented me but they went out of business last year. Would you go with me?"

"Sure, of course."

Sacramento was very hot during July and August, conditions varying from dry to steamy. For a couple of days the weather was unusually mild and we were grateful for them. We held hands, walked in the park and around the neighborhood, window-shopping, happy to be outside rather than in my small, hot apartment.

That first week we made love a lot. It was better than ever before. For the first time we weren't in a hurry. Christy was more experimental than I ever knew her to be. This was refreshingly new. We were in our own bed and not in the back of a VW van or on a couch or standing up somewhere for a quickie.

We ate most of our meals at Lee's Café or we ordered Chinese or Thai food from nearby restaurants. We didn't cook.

In the days that followed, mostly in the cool evenings after I was off work, we went apartment shopping. Our real estate broker was Kim Rooney. She was in her forties or early fifties, pleasantly heavyset, dressed in beautifully tailored business suits with skirts. She was from Liverpool, England, and had lived in the States for many years. She had two grown daughters, one married and the youngest still in college. Her husband had died from a heart attack at age forty-five.

She had a sweet smile and wore her hair dyed blond. "Why don't you guys buy a house?" she said. "Why keep wasting money renting an apartment?"

Christy and I looked at each other. "That's a great idea!" I thought of buying a house but put it out of mind because the process seemed so complicated. I didn't need that much space; but now that we were a couple, living in a house was a perfect idea. It would give Christy a big studio; I would have my home office and maybe there would be a guest room, too.

Christy and I went with Kim in her car to look at houses. We looked at seven but none seemed quite right for us. Either I didn't like something, or Christy didn't.

One night after work, Kim drove us to look at a house in Elk Grove. We liked the look of the area. The first house we saw, a Tudor style, had four bedrooms and two bathrooms. It had a two-car garage and a newly paved driveway. The house was three thousand square feet large. We liked it and thought we might take it, but Kim said, "Let me show you one more."

She drove us to Roan Ranch Circle and stopped in front of a house with immediate curb appeal. It was an appealing Cape Cod gray, two-story, four thousand square feet, with four bedrooms and three bathrooms. This one, too, had a newly paved driveway, and garage big enough for three cars and a big front and backyard. It was listed at $550,000.

We went inside. The living room was big, bright, and comfortable, with a high ceiling and recessed lighting. The kitchen, with an island and granite counters, was large as was the dining room. The master bedroom with a big walk-in closet. There were three other smaller bedrooms.

From what I'd heard on the news and read in the newspapers, Elk Grove, with a population of about 168,000, was one of the most politically conservative suburbs of Sacramento. It was sixty-two percent white, eighteen percent Asian, ten percent Black and ten percent "other." Incomes were above average, and the crime rate was low. Mother's words came back to me: "People are just people." On some subterranean level, I believed there was some truth in her seemingly simple-minded statement.

Kim said, "I'll wait outside in the car so you two can talk privately."

While Christy looked around the kitchen, I went to the garage to check the hot water heater and the fans for the heating and cooling units in the attic.

"What'd you think of the house?" I asked Christy when I returned to the kitchen.

"I love it," she said. "But it's expensive. Can we afford it?"

"We'll have to see. We'll need a bank loan. We'll have to see if we qualify." I had saved a lot by then and probably had enough for a good down payment. I had some investments I could tap, if necessary. We would have to act quickly before somebody with deeper pockets grabbed the house.

We got back into the car with Kim and told her we liked the house and wanted to try to buy it. "Great!" she said. "I'll see if I can get the price down a bit, too."

31

Christy and I did some late-night calculating. Once her Evanston house sold, she would have a sizable amount of money. She was soon to receive money from the sale of the dental business. Once my mother's house sold, I would also have a lot more money than I had at present.

Given the revenue from those sales, if we managed to buy the Roan Ranch Circle house, we could pay it off in a relatively short time.

The shipment of Christy's things for her studio came and we piled them in the living room. We had to walk around the boxes for a while, which reminded me of the temporary way I lived during my college days.

Christy could start painting again. I remembered her drawings and paintings and how much I liked them. She was her only model. She did variations of self-portrait, painting images of herself as many different women with dynamic immediacy. Sometimes the figures were foreshortened, sometimes blurred and indefinite or ephemeral and outraged. They were de Kooning-like women, some smiling, others wincing or scornful or looking soulful or dreamy.

She painted them among Spanish jasmine and reefs and shoals. She painted them against backgrounds of polished limestone and against backgrounds of opaque farmhouses.

She painted them in shimmering textures and in shifting contours. She painted them with a natural simplicity and in bold warm colors. Was she searching for a definition of self or searching for the perfect parallel to herself?

I remembered her theory of chromatic harmony and spatial compression and visual metaphor. She loved the melancholy blur. She knew how to make a picture dance with life. Rarely did they baffle.

Christy kept in touch with her parents by phone and by Skype. They were still concerned about her move to California. They constantly wanted to know if everything was going okay for her. She assured them she was happy, but they kept asking if she was all right, if she was happy. "Are you going to get a job?" She assured them she was planning to get a job. They were worried about us *not* being married. They were also worried their daughter *might* marry me.

"When I tell them you're a scientist and an engineer, it seems to calm them a bit; but they still have this image of you as that high school boy I was running around with."

I laughed. "That's a funny image." Was there some other unspoken issue? Did I have halitosis? Dandruff?

After Christy and I lived together a month, I began to understand things about her I had never known. She was excessively neat; she spent a lot of time grooming herself, and she kept her surroundings in perfect order. She wasn't exactly what people called a "neat freak," but she was close to it. I, too, tried to be tidy, so her orderliness didn't bother me except when she scolded me for some minor irregularity such as leaving the bathroom towel on the edge of the bathtub. She never had to scold me for leaving the toilet seat up. Mother had trained me well.

Christy loved reading, especially at night in bed. I was delighted she had ways to occupy herself; she had great inner resources and didn't always need my attention.

She set up her easel in the middle of the living room. She worked at her painting and drawing methodically; and she photographed and dated each painting when she finished it. She kept systematic and businesslike records of her artwork. These were habits she said her art teachers had instilled in her.

For a smock, she wore an old paint-stained man's dress shirt with red and blue stripes and one pocket on the left breast. I suspected it once belonged to Todd. That bothered me, but I refrained from saying anything because I thought doing so would sound petty. Then one day she said, "This is one of my Dad's old shirts." I was relieved, but I wondered if she had read my thoughts.

I loved the magical figurative work she was doing. The canvases were about thirty by forty inches, occasionally larger, and they were piling up.

She sometimes photographed herself in the nude and worked from the photograph You often had to look for a long time before you could see the figures emerge in the composition.

She called herself an Expressionist. Before long she would have enough new work for an exhibition. The next step would be to find a gallery owner interested enough to give her a show.

Her house in Evanston hadn't yet sold. The longer it remained unsold the worse the chances. Prospective buyers might begin to think something was wrong with it. I wondered if people had gotten wind that a man hung himself in it.

Our bank loan came through; rather, *my* bank loan came through. Because we weren't married, the bank refused to give us a loan in both names. I had been on the job long enough to please them and my salary of $ 90,000 was suitable; I also had a few other assets: the Subaru, my savings, and I was part owner of a house in Chicago. They were satisfied I was a good risk.

Kim managed to get the Roan Ranch Circle house's price down to

$400,000. Since the owners were moving to Panama, they wanted a quick settlement. There were no loopholes: the deal went through smoothly; but there was an unbelievable amount of tedious paperwork to be read and signed.

By the autumn equinox, we had moved into the Roan Ranch Circle house. There was a lot to do to make the house fully our own, but I felt more comfortable there than I had anywhere before, including the house Marie and I grew up in, in Hyde Park.

It was because the house was my own. I didn't have to tiptoe around Mother's rules about every little thing, including how many times a day the refrigerator door can be opened. I could leave a light on in a room I had left. Not that I *would* do that on purpose, but I could if I wanted to.

We hired a local cleaning service, Quentin Janitorial Services, which sent someone in every other Thursday to clean. The housekeeper who came most frequently was Charlene Lopez, a short heavyset woman with dark-brown skin and a big smile. She had four small children. If someone came from the service in Charlene's place, we knew it was likely one of her kids was sick.

One morning on my way to work I stopped at a red light. A young man with blond hair in a pickup truck adjacent me looked at me and frowned; he raised his fist and shouted, "*White power! White power forever!*" and spat out the window toward my car.

The time to fly to Washington D.C., for the demonstration was now upon us. Herb and some of the other people at the office had already gone ahead to help with organizing.

People on the national committee had floated and knocked around many possible names. None completely feckless: Save The Planet, Protect Our Environment, We Are Running Out of Time, Climate Change Is Real, March for Your Life, The Time Is Now. The one selected was: Give Earth and Climate a Chance, echoing John Lennon's "Give Peace A Chance."

I invited Christy, but she declined. She needed to keep working at her painting to get ready for an exhibition. She wanted to be ready if and when luck came.

We were all going to fly the same airline and stay in the same hotel. In that way we got a group discount.

I arrived the day before the march. It was night by the time I checked into the Kempton Carlyle at Dupont Circle. The march would start early the next morning. I got a good night's sleep and was up bright and early. After a hot shower, I went down for a breakfast of orange juice, pancakes and sausage, then left for the march.

On the way out, I saw several people I knew from our office. We were all excited. We would march from Washington Circle down Pennsylvania Avenue past James Monroe Park and the White House to the Capitol grounds. It was a clear day with only a few small clouds off to the north.

Sharing the cost with three others from the office, I took a taxi from the hotel, but because of heavy traffic the driver had to go in an indirect way to get to Washington Circle. We got there just as the march was about to begin.

We didn't see Herb or the others at first. I spotted them after we started marching. Organizers and helpers were passing out signs with various messages to carry. Mine said: "It's Up to Us to Save Our Planet!"

I fell in step with a coterie of marchers walking down the middle of Pennsylvania Avenue that quickly became a pressing multitude. Police wearing sunglasses and helmets on horseback and on motorcycles escorted us.

Being part of this robust mass movement of people was empowering. Most people along the sidewalks waved to us in a supportive manner. A few rabble-rousers jeered and jostled. A few others held signs saying climate change was a lie of liberals. Others were more insulting. Many more shouted words of encouragement. This was tremendous. I felt superb. I was in good physical shape and the other marchers and the crowds along the sidewalks were magnificent in their support.

Would we make a difference? Who knew? We were people from all over the country. Motley crew that we were, we believed that the effects of climate change were imminent.

Later, news reports estimated the number of participants in the march at fifteen thousand; but we thought it felt more like twenty or thirty thousand.

We stopped at the Capitol grounds. There we listened to twenty-one speeches on various environmental issues. The speakers were famous environmental activists. One they said was a movie star. I'd never heard of him. He spoke on the paralysis of big business regarding climate change.

At the end of his speech the famous environmental activist Dr. Lynn Yeslin, quoted historian Howard Mumford Jones: "Persecution is the first law of society because it's always easier to suppress criticism than to meet it."

Then this: "Ours is the age which is proud of machines that think but suspicious of men who try to." Yeslin said: "It's time to think boldly!" Jones's words and his own got Yeslin great applause.

By the end of the day I was exhausted, but I felt sensational. Later that night all of us from the Sacramento office met at the restaurant in our hotel, in one of the private rooms, and had a great celebratory discussion and feast: pizza! Dozens of pizzas moved up and down the table.

The organizers stood and made toasts. One said, "Here's hoping the governmental officials were paying attention!" and we each touched our glasses one to the other in celebration and with hope.

The dinner conversation was lively. After a couple of hours, I stood and shook hands with a few nearby people I knew and walked out into the lobby and to the elevator. I was glad I had come.

September went by quickly. Marie and I talked about twice a week. She kept me informed on Mary, Roswell and Celosa's doings as well as on Elsie's.

Every time I talked with her it became clear that she wasn't yet ready to sell Mother's house. Selling seemed to her to be blasphemy. It disturbed and agitated her. I had never lived there, so I didn't feel the way Marie felt about putting the house on the market. I felt that a respectable amount of time had passed since Mother's death, but I didn't press the issue. The tension between Marie and me persisted. Even when we talked about other matters the house loomed offstage.

Strong feelings lingered from my experience at Mother's funeral and burial. I was now in grief's depression stage. I was sure that part of what I was feeling had to do with my growing awareness of my own mortality, which came with a level of disbelief and anxiety and apprehension.

Now I daydreamed about asking Christy to marry me, then I would think of the tragic marriage she had just emerged from. Despite my enthusiasm for the idea, I thought it was unlikely she would want to get married again so soon.

We had known each other for many years, but we really didn't know each other very well *as adults*. We'd been together just a little over three months. I thought she might be thinking these things; but I was wrong.

One day early in October Christy said, "I think we should get married."

I tried not to show too much enthusiasm or surprise, but as calmly as I could I quickly said, "I agree. We should do it. It actually might make a lot of things easier. Had we been married we could have bought the house together."

"With *your* money," she said, smiling.

I nodded.

She said, "I had the money I got from the sale of the dental business transferred to my account out here."

I nodded approval.

32

One Saturday, Christy and I went to De Vons in Sacramento and selected matching gold wedding bands; rings with lots of *bling*.

We would skip engagement and go directly to wedding. One day on the way home from work, I stopped in Sacramento's Old Town. At a well-known jewelry store I bought Christy a six-prong classic Solitaire diamond-studded engagement ring. It was more expensive than I could afford, but I told myself to go for it.

Though Christy had finished fifteen paintings, this wasn't enough for a one-person exhibition. She needed twenty-five or thirty. But she wanted to start inquiring around Sacramento galleries to see if any dealers might be interested in representing her.

One Saturday afternoon we packed five of her best and most colorful canvases in the back of the Subaru to show as examples of her work. The first three dealers said they weren't taking on any new artists. One said, "Come back around the first of the year." That was a nibble.

Then we drove to Gallery Brombo in the 1800 block on P Street.

Under the gallery sign was the name of the owner: Mario Amedeo Brombo.

It was the grandest gallery we'd seen that day. The ceiling was high and there was lots of white wall space. The floor was highly polished tile with a black and white design pattern. There were three linked brightly lighted showrooms connected shotgun-style.

The minute we stepped inside a young woman stood from the desk at the back. Smiling, she said, "Hello! Welcome! First time here?"

Christy and I said, "Yes."

The young woman extended her hand. "I'm Leslie Corn, the gallery secretary." She was small and thin; she was wearing a white blouse with a ribbon at the neck and a brown skirt; her movements were quick and decisive. She was still smiling. "Are you collectors?"

"Not really," Christy said. "I'm an artist, a painter."

"Oh, an *artist!*" She was polite but also obviously slightly disappointed we weren't collectors.

Christy said, "I was wondering if you're taking on any new artists?"

"Mario isn't here at the moment. He's the owner. He would be the one who could answer that question."

"Oh, I see," said Christy. "Well, should we come back another time?"

"Of course. He was supposed to be back by now."

"Well," I said, "should we come back in a couple of hours?"

"That would be fine." But as she said those words a stocky little man came in. He had a big head, thick black hair, and he walked with a quick no-nonsense stride, as if he were ten feet tall and proud of it. I guessed him to be about forty-five years old.

He was wearing a white shirt, dark blue slacks, and pointy-toed black shoes. I imagined he was a Napoleon type, with a limited amount of time to give to any one thing. Impatience would be his hallmark. If he had any patience, no one would know the password for connecting to it. He sniffed a lot like somebody whose nose lining had been destroyed by sniffing cocaine for many years.

"Here is Mario now," said Leslie Corn.

He walked up to the three of us and with a nervous tick, and a critical and sallow face quickly looked Christy and me over.

Leslie said, "Mario, this young lady is a painter. She wants to know if you're taking on any new artists."

Mario looked Christy over again, checking out her breasts and her legs then her face. "Maybe," he said. "You have any examples of your work with you?"

"Yes, out in the car."

"Go ahead," he said with an impatient wave toward the doorway, "bring your paintings in."

Christy and I scrambled out to the car. I brought in three and she brought in two. We stood them on the floor against a wall below the paintings on display.

The paintings were done with impasto strokes and in bright colors of blues, reds, and yellows. In some, the paint seemed to be skidding across the canvas. In others the paint seemed to quiver and dance and squirm. Still, you could see that they were all based on the same model: Christy herself.

Mario gazed steadily at the paintings looking back and forth all the while stroking his chin, as if in deep thought, and sniffing. After about five minutes he said, "Sure. I'd be happy to show your work. Do you have enough for an exhibition--say, about thirty or thirty-five?"

"I'm working toward it every day."

"Good, keep working. When do you think you'll have enough for a show?"

"Oh, gosh! Maybe in six or seven months?" The tone of Christy's response sounded like a question, but it was her answer.

"That would be perfect timing. I won't have an opening for at least a year, so take your time; but I can show a few of your paintings in a group figurative show I have coming up this fall. What's your name?"

She told him her name.

Then Mario reached for my hand and we shook. I said, "I'm Mark Smith."

"Good to meet you, Mark. You folks live in Sacramento?"

"Elk Grove," I said.

"Actually, I think I've seen *you* on the evening news. Have you been on the news?"

I smiled. "Yes, I'm an engineer; we get interviewed a lot regarding the problems at the Klinkhoff Dam and the Jansen Power plant and Lake Tahoe." I laughed, "I'm all over the place."

"That's *it*—the flooding, the *snow*melt and the spillway!" said Mario.

"That's right," I said.

Then to Christy, Mario said, "If you want to leave three of them here, I can plan to put them in my November figurative group show. It's from November 6th till November 29th. The reception will be November 8th. Do you have frames?"

"No, I never frame my work."

"No problem. We can hang them without frames if you like or I can slap some frames on them. I've a storeroom of hundreds of frames."

"Which three do you want to keep?" said Christy.

"Let's see. I'll keep this one, this one, and this one." Mario walked along the line, touching each of the three he wanted for his November show.

"The titles are on the back," said Christy.

"Good. We need titles."

Christy and I left elated, she for herself and me for her.

Still using herself as motif, Christy worked furiously at her painting. She didn't put much time into looking for an ad agency job, but she did fill out a few online applications, but so far had gotten no responses.

Then one night Marie called and said, "Sweetman died."

"*Timothy died?*"

"Yes, I just read about it in the *Defender*; it was in the obit section, with a picture of him. I might have missed it had they not put his picture in there."

"This is shocking! He was so young! Did they say the cause of death?

I know he had lung cancer, but he was in remission."

"His sister Hazel called me to get your phone number and I asked her. She said it wasn't lung cancer. He died from a blood clot starting in his leg that travelled up to his heart. It killed him."

"A blood clot at his age?"

"She said he met some girl online. She lives in Houston. Tim communicated with this girl, I guess, on Facebook or on Instagram or on Skype or maybe on all three for about a month or two then he flew down to Houston to meet her."

"What about his wife, Ruthie?"

"What about her? Sweetman was trying to have an affair with this Houston girl without his wife knowing anything about it. He told her he was going to Houston to a conference on the practical uses of electricity.'"

"Hazel told you this was the lie he told Ruthie?"

"That's right," said Marie.

"How did Hazel know?"

"Sweetman told his sister everything. They were close."

"I think I know where this is going."

"Coming back, he started feeling sick with an upset stomach and chest pains and a headache. He thought he was coming down with a cold or the flu."

"Chest pains aren't a sign of a cold or influenza. It would be time to get quickly to an emergency room."

"Be that as it may, he thought the chest pains were gas. He didn't go to the emergency room. His wife treated him for a cold. Ruthie made chicken soup and he ate it and she rubbed his chest with Bengay and tucked him in."

"And that was it?"

"And that was it," Marie said. "In the morning Ruthie couldn't wake him. She kept shaking him and shaking him, but he wouldn't wake up. He'd died in his sleep while she was sleeping alongside him."

"That's tragic and ironic; very sad, very sad! It's heartbreaking!"

"Yes, it's heartbreaking," said Marie, "but I thought you would want to know. Hazel and Ruthie both might call you."

The next day Hazel called and said, "I guess Marie told you what happened?" We talked for about twenty minutes. She wanted to know if I was coming to the funeral. I told her I wouldn't. I apologized but I gave her the best words of comfort I could think of, words to be repeated at the funeral.

Ruthie called the next day. Same thing. She wanted to know if I was coming to the funeral. Same answer, different words of comfort.

I felt badly about my decision not to fly back to Chicago for Tim's funeral; but I also felt I couldn't comfortably take off again so soon. I had stored vacation time, but I wasn't willing to use it. I also didn't have the *will* to go through yet another funeral ceremony so soon.

33

Christy and I decided to marry on October 6th, a Friday. One night while we were sitting up in bed, she wrote the opening words for the justice of the peace to say at the private ceremony. I read the statement and edited it, adding and subtracting a few words; then she revised it again.

The next morning at breakfast, she said, "Marksie, can we have a honeymoon?"

I think it was the first time she'd called me by a pet name.

"Where would you like to go?"

"I'd love to go to New England and see the October colors; see the trees exploding with brilliant colors. I've never been there. Then we could end up in Boston and visit the art museum there. I've longed to go there."

"I've never been to New England either."

We would leave on October ninth and return on October sixteenth.

We decided we'd start in a little town called Brattleboro, Vermont. Before Christy married Todd, she had a friend and fellow student artist at the Art Institute of Chicago, Fiona, who was from Brattleboro. Fiona told Christy many wonderful things about her hometown. As a result,

Christy long imagined the town to be an idyllic place especially in October.

We would fly into Burlington, rent a car, and drive to Brattleboro and stay at the landmark Latchis Hotel; then spend a couple of days in Brattleboro before driving the scenic route to Boston. October would be a perfect time. With luck if there was sunshine, the leaves of reds and yellows and purples would explode with brightness.

The next day at work, I said to Herb, "I'd like to take some of my vacation time, maybe ten days off early next month. I'm getting married and going on my honeymoon. Okay?"

"Congratulations, Mark, glad to hear the good news. A local girl?"

"No, she's from the Chicago area."

"Ah, so you fell in love while at your mother's funeral?" He laughed.

"I guess you could say that."

"You can take off, but at some point, over the next few days or so, I want you to go up to Tahoe and do some testing at Lake Tahoe, the Tahoe Dam and Truckee River. WETLAB, over in Nevada, is doing a great job, but we need our own results. It would be a pity if we lose yet another alpine lake to pollution."

"Sure," I said.

"As a state agency we have a responsibility to monitor what's going on up there. Plus, I'd promised the secretary of Natural Resources a report next month. I know you haven't done work there very often so now is a good time for you to get more familiar with the lake; and meet the people up at the basin. You'll be looking for sediment levels, phosphorous and nitrogen levels. I've gone up there every summer for my vacation and I don't want to see the lake get any worse. Okay?"

"Happy to do it, Herb. I'm excited about the assignment."

"Good."

At home I told Christy I had to go up to Tahoe to do some testing. She said, "Fine. I've got so much work to do here, I can use the solitude."

The next day, I got in the red Bronco and drove Interstate 80 through Echo Pass taking the cutoff route to Tahoe. I checked into the Duncan Motor Lodge, ate dinner, then I called Christy. We talked for about an hour. I turned in early and got a good night's sleep and got up early the next morning, ready to work.

While I was in the field, I met Randy Walker, from one of the Nevada testing divisions, and Joe Scully, from one of the California testing divisions, and we worked together all day at the lake then at the dam. I got a lot done in one day. I was pleased I would be able to report back to Herb that the sediment levels were no worse than they were last year: not good but not getting worse.

There were certain people I needed to update. I called Marie and told her Christy was now living with me and we would soon get married. Marie said, "I'm not surprised! Speaking of marriage, Roswell and Celosa just got engaged! They plan to marry next year."

Online, Christy found a justice of the peace, Rosetta Darby, on Branigan Lake Way in Rancho Cordova who agreed to marry us in her home.

I wore the same dark blue suit I wore to Mother's funeral. It was my best suit. It fitted me perfectly.

Christy wore a light blue dress, having decided against white or yellow or pink, all colors she considered and rejected. I bought her a pink corsage to wear on her left wrist. It matched her pink earrings and shoes.

I drove. As I was parking in front of the modest, well-kept house--white stucco with brown wooden shutters--a woman I assumed to be Mrs. Darby came out to meet us. She had a blonde Gibson girl hairdo piled high on her head and she was wearing a green cotton sweater.

She waved to us and said after I'd rolled down the car window: "You can park up here in the driveway. It's safer!" She was a pleasant-looking middle-aged woman with blue-gray eyes and a kindly smile.

We shook hands with Mrs. Darby when we got out of the car. She said, "Call me Rosetta. I didn't know you guys were an *interracial* couple.

You're my first!" Her smile was wide as her face. "Come on in."

We followed her into the house, all the while she chattered about her two grown kids and her husband who was upstairs and about the high price of everything; about the danger of living in California because of earthquakes. She told us how she broke her leg skiing two years before at Squaw Valley Ski Resort. She never stopped talking. Her house smelled of freshly baked brownies.

The living room was comfortable with couch, love seat, armchair, and throw rugs over highly polished wood floors, and two paintings of happy Red Skelton clowns over the couch.

She invited us to sit down while she got some tea and brownies. Christy and I sat side by side on the couch.

When Rosetta returned, Christy said, "As I told you on the phone, we wrote our own opening words. Okay?"

"Absolutely," said Rosetta, taking an armchair across from us.

The three of us sipped tea, while Rosetta continued her rambling narrative about everything in her universe; then she said, "Shall we get started?"

We stood and faced her together. Christy took the sheet of paper containing the statement from her purse and handed it to Rosetta.

"Thanks, Christine."

"Call me Christy."

"Okay, Christy." Rosetta read the text. When she finished she said, "This is perfect!"

"Thanks," said Christy.

"I've asked my husband to be a witness. We do need a witness, you know." She looked toward the stairway to the upstairs and shouted, "*Elwin!*"

A man about her age came slowly down the steps. Elwin was balding on top and had gray around the ears. His eyebrows were black and wild.

Rosetta introduced us to her husband, and we shook hands. Christy took out her phone and handed it to Elwin. "Would you please record the ceremony for us?"

"Of course," he said, with a smile.

Christy showed him how to record.

Then he took the phone and sat down in the nearby armchair. He aimed the phone at us.

"Face me, Mark and Christine," said Rosetta. Clearing her throat, she read:

"We are gathered here to announce the wedding of Mark Smith and Christine Debra Werner. As Justice of the Peace, I have the special privilege of joining them in marriage. Mark and Christy have been friends since high school. They now wish to legalize their friendship and love in a monogamous, committed relationship. They want the protections of a legal union as a couple. They are well aware marriage means sometimes compromising, and they are ready to fully commit themselves to each other with patience and courage. On the strength of those words, I pronounce you husband and wife. Mark, you may now kiss Christy."

I kissed her.

Christy placed my ring on my finger then I placed hers on her finger.

I placed on her ring finger the diamond ring I had been carrying in my pocket. She was shocked to see it and her face bloomed with happiness.

We held hands and we quickly kissed again.

"How did the video turn out?" Christy said to Elwin.

"I think it turned out fine. You look and see what you think." He handed her the phone.

She replayed the video and I watched over her shoulder. It was clear and well-focused. Elwin did a good job.

We stayed a while longer for more tea and brownies. Before we left, Rosetta signed the documents we needed her to sign and I put them back in the envelope. She walked us to the car and took a picture of us with her cellphone. She said she would send us a copy by email, saying what a nice fall afternoon it had turned out to be.

We spent the next day shopping for more things for the house. Delivery services pulled up frequently in front of our house to deliver the packages.

I told Marie what Christy and I were doing. Marie said, "You could use Mother's things. You've been so anxious to move stuff out of the house. Why not move some of it to *your* house?"

"I don't want Mother's things. Even if I wanted them, it would be impractical moving stuff two thousand miles across country."

"People do it all the time."

A few days later we received word from Christy's real estate broker: her house sold. It was good news that would be transformative in more ways than one. Christy grabbed my hands and waltzed me around the living room.

I was delighted to see her so jocular, so gleeful, so untroubled after all she had gone through.

On the same day Christy's father, Walter, called to tell her a collection agency was trying to find her. That was bad news.

They wanted her to pay off Todd's student loans. Walter told her he called his lawyer and the lawyer said since the student loans were incurred *before* Todd was married to Christy, she wasn't liable. "They're bluffing, hoping to scare you into paying. They *know* they don't have a legal leg to stand on."

When she hung up, I could see by her expression she was already starting to worry and fret, despite her father's reassurance. I took her in my arms. I said, "Your father's lawyer is right. You aren't liable, so don't worry."

I hadn't lately been in touch with my old friend, Clifford, except on Facebook where he would occasionally send me a message.

One day, soon after Christy and I married, he sent me an email saying, "Mark, why don't you come over to Davis and have lunch with me? We can get caught up."

I told Christy about Cliff. "Would you like to go with me to Davis and meet one my old friends Cliff from college?"

"Sure," she said.

And so, it was arranged.

34

He wanted us to meet him at a popular restaurant in Davis called Crepeville in the 300 block on 3rd Street, near the campus. It was packed when we arrived. Christy and I found a table outside and waited for Cliff. I thought he might bring a girlfriend with him, but he was often between girlfriends, so it was just as likely he would show up alone.

When Cliff was coming across the street, I recognized him right away. He was a short, stocky guy with bright red hair and dimples and a twinkle in his gray-green eyes and a loping walk.

He spotted us right away, too. In a sea of pink faces my face was easy to spot: the seeker had only to look for the copper-colored face in the crowd.

I stood up as Cliff approached and we did the rough manly hug. He said, "So, wow! You're married, now! *This* beautiful woman is your wife?"

"Yes."

I introduced Christy to Cliff. Cliff, being Cliff, took her hand and kissed the backside. He was treating her like she was Venus rising from the sea; yet there was a bit of mockery in his courtly gesture. Christy was amused; she smirked in a playful way.

In the line to order café style, Cliff pulled from his pocket a folded sheet of newspaper from *The Davis Enterprise*. He unfolded it and handed it to me. "Look!" he said. "Look what I caught!"

It was a news story with a picture of Cliff proudly holding up a large fish. Part of the caption read: "A seventy-eight pounder, one of the largest king salmon ever caught in the Sacramento River."

"Wow," said Christy.

"Congratulations," I said, handing back the article.

We managed to find a table inside just in time for our food to be delivered. The server, a tall, good-looking girl, brought Christy's combo Greek salad and bowl of split pea soup; Cliff's tuna salad sandwich with home fries; and my ham and cheese on rye. Christy drank carrot juice. Cliff and I drank beer.

I said, "Good seeing you, Cliff. How're things going?"

"Aside from my car leaking oil like crazy, everything's going well."

"Aside from your car leaking what else is going on?"

"I'm buying a house and still paying off my student loans. They're killing me. How did *you* manage?"

"I didn't get many student loans. I worked. Mother helped some. I didn't qualify for affirmative action. You must remember. I worked on campus where I assisted for two years at the science lab and I worked for a while at the library. I waited tables one year. After I finished college for the first year I practically lived on bread and water and paid off the few student loans I had."

Cliff turned to Christy. "How about you, Christy?"

"I worked and paid my way."

Cliff said, "What kind of work?"

"I was a model," said Christy. "For a while, I also worked as a waitress. My parents helped, too."

Then Cliff told us about the interesting software he was developing at Winik Technologies. It would allow the user to do shopping across the internet at *one* site, to pay for an array of merchandise at that same site, as well as to arrange for delivery, from all the various sites, to your home address or office. Sounded like a miracle of commerce!

I said, "You're going to become a tech celebrity. You won't be able to stand the constant spectacle around you."

"Don't make fun of me, Mark." His tone was brusque.

"I'm *not* making fun of you. I'm *serious*. When did you become paranoid? I wasn't making fun of you." I was dead serious. Celebrity could be hell.

Cliff didn't respond. As he talked and chewed, chewed and talked, I was carried back to our days at Berkeley when we were all so ambitious and making plans. "We have to take the world by storm," Cliff used to say. It was now great seeing him again and knowing he was doing marvelous things.

When lunch was over, Cliff walked us to our car. As we approached, I clicked the Subaru opened, Cliff again kissed Christy's hand and again she was amused. This time she was also a bit embarrassed. She was blushing.

The next day, October 9th, we were on our way to Burlington, nonstop on American Airlines. In flight I read Chester Himes's detective novel, *Blind Man with a Pistol*. Christy spent the time surfing the web.

We both felt groggy when we landed, but we recovered by the time we picked up our rental car, a Honda Accord, and got onto the highway for Brattleboro, about a two-and-a-half-hour drive away. We drove past the exits for Montpelier, Woodstock, Lebanon, Keene, and other places. Unlike northern California the landscape was plush green. I was enjoying it.

Christy looked out the window and she kept saying, "Wow! Look at the radiant colors!"

The tree leaves in the sunlight glowed bright red and dark red. There were brilliant yellows, amber, and citrine and dense purples, violet and lavender. All along the route the thick cluster of trees and their leaves gently waved and turned, turned, turned in the brisk wind, reflecting the light.

We were late arriving at the Latchis Hotel and worried they might have given our room away. We knew the hotel were fully booked because there was a literary festival in town. A lot of people were wandering up and down Main Street.

We parked alongside the hotel, which faced Main Street, and went inside to the small lobby to arrange for our room. I'd read that the hotel was built by a Greek family in 1938; the lobby was in the Art Deco style and it was quaint and charming. The hotel was attached to the Latchis Theater next door; both the hotel and theater had been popular in the 1940s and 1950s.

We got our luggage into the tiny ancient elevator. Christy said, "This is an adventure! I *love* it!"

We got our things into the room, which had a stone floor, a renovated shower, and a flat screen TV. While unpacking, I asked Christy if her friend from art school still lived here.

She said, "No, she married a guy from Florida, and last I heard they live in Fort Lauderdale. I got a postcard from her a few years ago with a picture of a beach on the front. They spend a lot of time on the beaches and boating. He owns some kind of shop on the promenade along A1A."

An hour later, sitting on the bed looking at our maps, guidebooks and notes for the trip, Christy said suddenly, "I don't feel well."

"You think you might be pregnant?"

Her eyes widened. "No, no way. My womb is *tilted*. I was X-rayed back when I was eighteen—a short time after we had that pregnancy scare. The doctor said I might never have children. I've had two miscarriages, both with Todd."

I decided not to say any more about pregnancy although I kept thinking she might be. On the other hand, she probably was just exhausted from traveling.

We left our things there and went out in search of a restaurant. We walked up Main Street, past Sam's Outdoor Outfitters store, stopping at restaurant after restaurant, looking at menus posted on street-side windows.

I wanted steak and Christy wanted a dinner without meat. "I've been eating too much meat lately," she said. We considered Fireworks, Duo, Katy's Great Food, Turquoise Grille, and Kebab Heaven.

We agreed on the menu at Kebab Heaven. The place emitted warmth and enticing aromas of delicious cuisine and it was crowded with people happily eating Indian food. We had a bit of a wait; about fifteen minutes, but then the maître d' led us to a seat by the window.

As we approached one of the two elderly women at the next table grabbed her purse from the back of her chair and nervously dropped it on the floor between her ankles.

Christy and I sat down. The purse woman glared fearfully at me. That look said, please reassure me with a grin or a smile that you are not a dangerous purse snatcher. In response, I gave her a friendly smile.

Through the window we could see the literary festival people still milling about on the street. I suspected most of the diners in Kebab Heaven were also from the festival.

Our server was a girl with dimples and short honey-colored hair; she was wearing purple earrings. She gave us menus, then went away to give us time to study them.

Christy ordered their special vegetable kebabs. I ordered the filet mignon shish kebabs. With our kebabs we got Turkish style rice pilaf, which was delicious, and ezme salads. We dined first with our eyes.

Of ambrosia-quality, the food looked delicious and smelled good. It tasted even better! We also drank tea.

We finished dinner and left a big tip, feeling we had chosen well. Our honeymoon was progressing without a hitch.

The next morning, while still in bed, the question was: what should we do? What do people do on a honeymoon?

We got up.

Christy made coffee with the in-room coffee maker.

I turned on the news and watched while sipping my coffee.

"So, what should we do today?"

"We don't have to do what other people have done on honeymoons," Christy said. "Let's be original."

"Okay," I said, "I'll try to think of something original."

While Christy was in the shower, I checked my email. There was a message from Thomas: "Mark Anthony, I was just looking at one of those websites where women show *all*; there were a lot of pictures of a certain girl, in all kinds of poses; she sure looks a lot like Christy. She couldn't be Christy, but she sure *looks* like her! If you want to take a look, here is the link."

I was so sure it wasn't Christy I was in no hurry to look. I hadn't told Thomas that Christy and I got married. I doubt he knew she had moved to California. He might have known had he met Marie by accident and she told him. That was unlikely. She lived on the North Side and Thomas lived on the South Side.

I had rarely gone to such websites. I knew about them and in passing I had seen a few. I opened the link into my phone and the pictures popped up.

I looked closely at the girl's face. She was a lot younger than Christy. I kept looking. The first frame was a face and bosom shot. In the second the bush and what a bush it was. Dark red! It looked a lot like Christy's, but I knew it wasn't. The color of the hair was different, or could that simply be the lighting?

I clicked to the next frame. She was sitting down with her legs apart. Then I saw it: the *mole* inside her left thigh.

It *was* Christy! Her web name was "Candy." Worse than the pictures were the captions under each picture. They described her with words like "lustful" and "wench" and "vixen" and "juicy" and worse. These captions were directed to men, inviting them to "use" Candy in any way they pleased.

She was a piece of licorice anyone might enjoy. All the caller had to do was *click* and use his or her imagination; but what I saw were teasers. You'd have to sign up, pay, and become a member of the website, to see more.

35

My heartbeat faster, and my stomach muscles grew tight. My throat felt dry. *When* did she pose for these pictures? She looked *so* young; she was eighteen or nineteen or maybe twenty or twenty-one. She was now thirty-four.

I started to rush into the bathroom and confront her, but I stopped. Think! Be calm! I walked over to the armchair and sat down, waiting for my heart to stop racing and for my temples to stop throbbing and my hands to stop sweating.

I sent Thomas a reply: "Thomas, I checked out the photos. She's a hot-looking girl, but it's *not* Christy! Take care, M."

From that moment I knew it would be hard to make love with my wife without erotic images of Candy crowding my imagination. Or should I say *clouding* my imagination? They would be like pockmarks on the skin of my fantasy life.

No matter how hard I tried to forget the images, I couldn't. They appalled me, and yet I found them erotic.

When Christy came out of the shower with the towel around her body, she said, "Would you put some cream on my back?" She had a jar of Clinique body moisturizer in her hand. Rubbing each other's backs with cream was a habit we'd recently developed. As I spread the cream across her back my hand was shaking, and I couldn't stop it.

This was not the first time I noticed Christy never shaved; but this time I fully reflected on the fine auburn hair under her arms and on her legs.

"What's the matter?" she said. "Your hand is shaking."

"Oh, I don't know. Too much coffee, I guess."

An hour later, I said, "I saw the pictures of Candy on that porno website."

She didn't look surprised as she said, "So? I thought you'd seen them a long time ago."

"Why would you think that?"

"I don't know. It's just what I assumed."

She continued, "I think the human body is beautiful. I'm not ashamed of my body. I also used to pose for other artists at the Institute to help pay expenses. At first it was kind of difficult being the only naked person in the room, but I soon began to feel a sense of power in it. Everybody was looking at me. They were admiring my body because it was their motif, their point of reference. I came to love doing it. Then for a brief time, I did some erotic dancing in a club on the Near North Side, too."

"You mean you were a *stripper?*"

"I call it erotic dancing. That's how I paid my way through art school. I posed and I danced. I see nothing wrong with it. I wasn't selling my body or anything like that."

"But those photographs weren't erotica. They were something else."

"I disagree."

Hearing this, I tried to have an open mind, but it wasn't easy. Was I being prudish? I worried I wasn't open-minded enough.

Again, Christy said, "I think the human body is beautiful."

I, too, believed the human body was beautiful. Was it simply that I didn't want other men looking at pictures of Christy's body? Thousands had already seen it. Why worry about it? I didn't want to believe I was becoming possessive.

I wasn't going to let this discovery ruin our honeymoon or our marriage, even though Christy was turning out to be somebody other than who I thought she was. Was I now seeing her in a brighter light? She was clearly more complex and unpredictable than I thought.

On the way out we stopped in the downstairs breakfast nook, sat in the window seat, and ate breakfast. I had a toasted English muffin with a glass of orange juice; Christy made herself a bowl of oatmeal.

Beyond the window on the sloping street, people were going about their morning activities. Except for the literary festival it was apparently a normal Brattleboro morning. The sky was clear, and the sun was moving toward the top of the sky.

We walked around town doing nothing in particular, stopping at interesting places to take selfies. In front of a bookstore a girl in a bomber jacket offered to take our picture.

As we walked, I reflected: six months have passed since Mother's death. I could still hear her voice in my head. I was resigned to the fact that our relationship had been imperfect. Nothing could be fixed or changed, except in my mind; and I would continue to work at what seemed like the unattainable.

The rites of the funeral and the burial had helped in the healing process but selling Mother's house remained an issue. Marie still wasn't ready to let go. For her, holding onto the house was her way of holding onto Mother. It annoyed me but I respected her need to do so.

Much had happened in six months. I reconnected with my old high school girlfriend; and we rekindled our relationship. Then her husband shot her. A short time later her husband hung himself. Christy then moved to California. We got married.

Now I'd discovered pornographic pictures of my wife on the internet for the whole world to see. I couldn't stop seeing that mole inside Christy's thigh; I mean inside *Candy's* thigh. I thought: shouldn't I just make a distinction between Christy and Candy?

After lunch by the river, we got in the car and drove around town to get a more complete sense of Brattleboro. It was a rustic friendly town. People said hippies had come here in the sixties and changed the personality of the place. I liked the effect they had on the look of the town.

"What's wrong, Mark?"

"Nothing," I said defensively. "I guess I'm a ready to move on."

"We can leave for Boston a day early. We can leave tomorrow, if you like."

"Sure, let's do that."

Early the next morning, a Saturday, we got started, taking back roads through small towns. Though it was a bit out of the way, we decided to stop at Amherst where a friend of Christy's from the Art Institute once lived. At lunch near the UMass campus, the waiter suggested we visit Emily Dickinson's house when we told him we were looking for interesting things to do. I knew she was a nineteenth-century poet who never married. I'd probably read some of her poetry in school. Christy got excited, saying, "Dickinson is my favorite poet! Let's go find her house!"

I wasn't excited about going to the Dickinson House; it turned out to be *two* houses, both in the Federal style. One was a museum with a shop and the other was the homestead Emily's father built for her brother as a wedding present.

We got to the museum in time for a tour. I could see Christy was totally absorbed by the tour guide's words. I was listening but not retaining much because I found the antique Federal and Chippendale furniture and antique books in antiques bookcases with locked glass doors and Emily's little writing desk and bureau so fascinating--though I suspected many of these things were reproductions of the originals.

I imagined Emily and her father and mother, sister and brother moving through these rooms. If there was a chambermaid and a scullery maid, I could hear the swish of their long dresses and the clump and skidding of heavy shoes up and down the squeaky wooden hallways and stairways front and back. I didn't know why, but I also imagined the smell of buckwheat pancakes or johnnycakes coming from the kitchen. I'd just eaten. Was I still hungry?

When we came out into the yard, Christy said, "That was delightful! What a lovely and enjoyable interlude! Imagine! We'll always be able to say on our honeymoon we went to visit Emily Dickinson."

I put my arm around her as we walked around the house and down the slope back to the car parked alongside the road. Her interest in Emily Dickinson showed me yet another aspect of the woman who was now my wife.

"What do people do on honeymoons?" she said.

"Go to the beach and lay on the sand and go to a club at night."

"Then what?" she said.

"Then they do the same thing the next day and the next."

Slowly finding our way along the back roads to Boston we started talking. Christy began by saying, "You've never told me anything about *your life* after you left Chicago."

I thought about the question. What was there to tell: four years of undergraduate work and three years of graduate work, all seven years at UC Berkeley?

I told Christy most of the time my head was stuck in books.

She said, "I meant *girlfriends*. Did you fall in love with anybody after?"

"I don't think so, but it wasn't for lack of trying." I didn't know if I wanted to tell her about my three failed relationships.

"You must have had girlfriends?"

"Sure, I had a couple of dates while I was in college."

"Did you ever meet anybody online?"

"Oh, sure but not to date. How about you?"

"Me? I thought I was in love with Todd. We met the year I graduated from the Art Institute, at a dinner party given by a mutual friend from the neighborhood. Evanston is a small town."

"Nobody before Todd?"

"You," she said.

"I meant *other* than me."

"Hmm, maybe. At the Institute, I had a crush on one of my teachers, a terrific artist. I learned a lot from him."

"What was his name?"

"José de la Garcia. Ever hear of him?"

"Nope!" We were driving through a town and I slowed down to twenty-five miles per hour. "I remember when we first started going together, at Hyde Park, you said I wasn't your first."

"First what?" she said with a startled look.

"First person you'd been with?"

"I said that?"

"That's what I remember."

Christy said, "I don't think I said that. You must be *mis*remembering."

And I knew I wasn't *mis*remembering, but I didn't argue with her memory. I knew what she had said.

"The first man I had sex with was a friend of my father." Like a schoolgirl, she giggled. "It happened while Daddy was sleeping in the next room. This friend of his had stopped by. I don't remember why. I was at the kitchen table doing my homework. He felt me up here and down there and I suddenly got hot all over. In no time we were on the floor doing it very quietly."

"How old were you?"

"Fifteen. I knew about sex and I was curious about it. I guess I was receptive when it came along. I didn't want the first time to be with a boy. I wanted the first time to be with a grown man. I felt safer with a grown man rather than a boy at school. I also knew it was illegal and he could have gone to prison for it. That made it all the more exciting. It happened with him just one time. Then you and I got together a few months before

I turned eighteen."

"Did you and José de la Garcia get involved?"

"Noooo, no way! He was my *teacher!*" She seemed insulted. "How about you?"

"You *know* you were my first. I always told you that."

"I know."

"Then why did you ask?"

"No reason."

As we moved along a two-lane road we stopped talking for a while. A car drew up behind us, eager to pass. The driver honked his horn and, to avoid potential road rage, I pulled over to the side to let him by.

He sped past us, blasting his horn, spewing a cloud of blue exhaust fumes, filling our car with fumes. Too late, I quickly rolled up the windows. As he passed, I heard him shout the "N-word".

Christy said, "Just another moron."

We checked into Hotel Marley at 3:30. It was across from the regal Charles Hotel. We parked the car in our hotel's underground parking garage, where we would leave it till we were ready to drive to the airport.

The Marley was a small hotel with a small lobby. The style was Japanese. Once we were settled in the room, I turned on the TV. President Obama was being interviewed about American advisors to troops in the Middle East.

As the only food in our hotel was in vending machines we walked across the street Sunday morning for breakfast at Henrietta's Table, a restaurant in the Charles Hotel.

The restaurant was crowded with well-to-do-looking people. We were escorted to a table, and we were given water and bread in a basket. I ordered bacon and eggs sunny side up and toast and orange juice. Christy requested pancakes and orange juice. It was a busy but comfortable place.

At the table across from us was a group of six men and three women all wearing nametags. Two of the men were African American. I always noticed names, especially unusual names on nametags. One of the African

Americans was named John Canoe.

On the way back to the Marley, we stopped at a nearby supermarket. Christy grabbed a shopping cart, and I followed her down the aisles. She put her purse in the shopping cart and started picking up things from the shelves: a roll of paper towels, a gallon of spring water, cookies, a package of walnuts and a tube of toothpaste.

I stepped away to look for aspirin, so we'd have some on hand. As she was reading a label, Christy had her back to the shopping cart.

At that moment, I turned back just in time to see a well-dressed middle-aged woman calmly lifting Christy's purse out of our shopping cart.

"*Hey!*" I shouted.

Christy turned to see the woman release the purse back into the shopping cart.

The woman fled down the aisle and out of the supermarket.

"What *nerve!*" said Christy under her breath and with furious anger: "*Obnoxious thieving bitch!*"

In front of the hotel, we hailed a taxi and within a few minutes shot out of Cambridge into Boston, getting out at the Museum of Fine Arts, Boston. Christy said it was going to be a treat and the furthering of my education in art history.

Christy led me quickly to the nineteenth-century art, her favorite period. We stood before Sargent's *The Daughters of Edward Darley Boit*: Four sisters placed strategically in a half-lit room: two standing together by a giant vase, one standing alone and the youngest on the floor playing with a doll.

All except one girl looked toward the artist painting them. I was intrigued. Besides being a great painting, it was a statement about the various temperaments and moods and personalities in a family––and family was something I had been dealing with lately.

Christy explained works by Monet, Cassatt, Cezanne, and van Gogh. She talked about their color schemes, their compositional schemes, and their narrative schemes. I had always been one to keep an open mind to new ideas and new information.

It had never occurred to me a painting could have a narrative. Once the idea entered my head it was so obvious, and I was embarrassed not to have known it before. After lunch at the museum, I learned about complementary and clashing colors and muted colors and I learned why foregrounds are often dark and backgrounds light.

Christy also explained the effects and meanings of brushwork: criss-crossing brushwork, agitated brushwork, impasto brushwork, transparent brushwork, wet-on-wet brushwork, wet-on-dry brushwork, and delicate brushwork. "You never put dry on wet," she said.

The museum wasn't crowded that day, and it was pleasant to stroll through leisurely. I became more familiar with the things that interested Christy. Cezanne, Monet, Degas, Pissarro, and Renoir were no longer just names; they now took on complexity. I began to better understand art movements such as impressionism, expressionism, cubism, abstract expressionism, and American abstract art. Christy talked about the French artists who had influenced Americans such as William H. Johnson, Glackens, Henry O. Tanner, and Mark Rothko.

I remembered Carl Jung's comment: "As far as we can discern, the sole purpose of human existence is to kindle a light in the darkness of mere being." Christy had kindled a light in me. As we walked, I was thinking what a complex and interesting and intelligent and gifted person my wife was.

We hung out a few more days in Cambridge and Boston. The next afternoon, after lunch, at a sidewalk café in Harvard Square we drank Fundador Solera Reserva Spanish brandy. I didn't care much for it, but Christy wanted to try it. She liked the name. "We have to do classy things on our honeymoon," she said.

Later, we stood in a crowd in Harvard Square watching some kids break dancing, displaying amazing acrobatics. The crowd's enthusiasm was electric.

Another time we stood in a larger crowd listening to a terrific saxo-phone player obviously influenced by the great John Coltrane. I watched his incredibly dexterous fingers. The fluidity of the music was so magical it could make birds cockeyed.

We sampled ethnic food in interesting restaurants. We visited the Harvard Museum of Natural History, the Peabody Museum of Archaeology, and the Fogg Museum. We were honeymooners becoming connoisseurs of Cambridge and Boston culture. We would fly back to California taking with us an abundance of it.

36

Back in California, Christy got busy again with her painting, preparing for her exhibition sometime the following year. I went back to the problems of managing water and monitoring water quality.

The weather had turned cold. The figurative group exhibition at Brombo Gallery opened November 6. It would be up till the end of November. The reception was scheduled for Saturday, November 8.

With Christy's three paintings in the show there was no way we were going to skip the reception. Mario said the receptions tended to be informal, so we didn't dress up. I wore a Polo sport jacket and jeans. Christy, one of the stars of the exhibition, wore a form-fitting navy-blue sheath with crocheted ivory white lace trimmings down both sides and slightly opened at the collar and capped sleeves. She had bought it when she was working at Freedenberg & Strolls Advertising Agency. Over it she wore her trench coat.

The reception started at five; we got there early. In the brightly lit main gallery, only a few people were milling about, sipping wine, while classical music played in the background. Mario, in a brown sport jacket with white stripes, rushed to meet us at the door, surprising Christy and me by kissing her on the cheek. She wasn't expecting a kiss from somebody she had seen only once before. She jumped.

Mario smiled and backed off. "It's just my European heritage. Sorry!"

She relaxed and said, "Oh, you just surprised me. I wasn't expecting such a warm greeting." Christy's comment reminded me of the line often incorrectly attributed to Mae West in her 1933 film, *Done Him Wrong*: "Is that a gun in your pocket, or are you just glad to see me?" (Mae West did use that line in a later movie, long after the myth had become part of popular culture.)

Mario said, "Come on in and get some wine. The show is great. Go look at your paintings. They're among the best in the show." He spoke quickly; his eyes constantly blinked; his nose twitched and sniffed, and his hands continually moved as he spoke, emphasizing his words.

Leslie Corn, who was mingling among the guests, introduced us to several collectors and artists and people there just to look around. Then we moved to the paintings. Christy's three were in substantial frames and they looked resplendent. Each was priced at a thousand dollars, which surprised me. She had no reputation here in Sacramento and only a slight one back in Evanston.

Would they sell at that price? I looked around at the other paintings and soon realized a thousand dollars was about the average price.

The hors d'oeuvres were not of the best quality nor was the jug wine. There was some sort of spam-like paste on Ritz crackers and tiny grayish shrimp with a toothpick stuck in each and breaded, deep-fried chicken fingers, which were over-cooked; yet people seemed to enjoy all of it.

When I turned to say something to Christy, I realized she wasn't there. Looking around, I spotted her standing off to the side talking with Mario. When I finished looking at the paintings, I wandered over.

"Beautiful work," I said to Mario.

"Only the best, only the best," he said, in his quick way. His voice crackled like wildfire.

Christy wore a frozen smile.

Mario said to Christy, "You like the frames I put on your paintings?"

"Yes! Nice frames."

"When we do your solo show, maybe sometime after the first of the year, we don't have to use frames. If you paint the sides of the canvases that would be just fine; but people do tend to buy quicker if a painting is already framed. So, you can decide. I know it's a big expense to buy so many frames; but think about it. Sometimes you have to spend money to make money, and I'm all about making money."

On the way home Christy said, "Mario was telling me if I sell a painting the gallery will get fifty percent. That surprised me. He said that is the going rate. The gallery I was with in Evanston proposed twenty-five percent of any sale, but I never sold anything."

Only two paintings in the "New Figurative Paintings" exhibition sold. Christy's three paintings got a lot of praise but didn't sell. After the show closed, we brought them home minus the frames.

November went by quickly. Christy now had more money in the bank from the sale of the house in Evanston and from the sale of Todd's dental business. We had by now worked out a couple's division of labor: she would pay the bills for the utilities and groceries, and I would pay the mortgage and taxes.

We would share a bank account at Bank of America which meant, I put her name on my bank account, but she kept the money from her house in a separate account. Where there was no trust there was no relationship.

One night in early December as I was getting ready to go to bed, I found several small strands of red hair in the bed on my side. Although they seemed too light, I thought they were probably Christy's, though her hair was much darker. On second thought, the strands probably weren't hair at all, just lint.

Still, they puzzled me, but I didn't say anything to Christy I wondered if some of her auburn hair contained stands of lighter hair. That seemed possible. If they were hairs and not lint, I concluded they had to be from Christy's head.

It was the second week of December. Christy and I were in the kitchen eating breakfast. She said, "Daddy and Mommy want us to come spend Christmas with them."

"Are you sure?" I was surprised. I was thinking: was seeing me the price they had to pay to see their daughter?

"Yes, I'm serious. They like *you*."

I didn't say anything, but I was sure I looked incredulous.

She said, "Come on, Mark. Give them a chance. Okay?"

"Sure." I paused. "I want to, believe me."

Christy didn't say anything, but she made a face. I knew what that meant.

A couple of weeks later, middle of December, Christy purchased tickets online on our shared American Express credit card. Then, three days before we were to fly, she wasn't feeling well, so I drove her to the clinic to see her doctor, Adriane White.

When she came out, she said, "I was diagnosed with influenza. Dr. White said I shouldn't travel at this time. It would be a mistake and a danger to others. Oh, my God, Mommy and Daddy are going to be *so* disappointed. I don't know if we can get a refund on our tickets."

"I'm sorry, sweetheart." I hugged her.

I was sad she was sick but relieved we didn't have to go to Evanston. I knew it was selfish and harsh, but I also didn't care for the process of getting there. Flying had become a chore not easily borne.

In the car she said, "We have to stop at CVS and pick up a prescription."

Later, Christy called the airline; they wouldn't refund the money but said we could apply it to tickets to be used within a year or we lose it.

In the New Year, in the mid-February, one of the coldest times in Sacramento, I returned to Tahoe to do some testing at Lake Tahoe, the

Tahoe Dam and the Truckee River. Some locals suspected E. coli in the lake, possibly from animal feces, though it struck me as unlikely that E. coli was thriving in water as cold as it was in February.

This time of year, we didn't have to worry about releasing water from Lake Tahoe to make room for snowmelt that came down from the mountains. That release normally was done in spring or early summer.

I enjoyed going to Lake Tahoe, especially in the winter, because often a high wind was blowing and the air was cold and refreshingly clean compared to Sacramento's poor-quality air.

"I'll be gone two nights," I told Christy, as I packed a few things and my heavy parka for subzero weather. "You'll be okay?" It was the first time I would be away from her overnight since the trip to Washington.

"I'll be fine. I still have a lot of work to do for my upcoming exhibition."

Tuesday, I left the Subaru for Christy and had her drop me off at work, so I could pick up the red Bronco. Then I hit the road. It was eight in the morning and raining and traffic was heavy. Car and truck lights glowed and sparkled on the wet pavement.

I drove very carefully, passing at least three accidents along the way. It was slow going mostly because drivers were rubbernecking as they drove past the crashes. The atmosphere was thick with smoke from a forest fire in the hills outside the city, and visibility was low.

Just off the highway at Roseville, I stopped at a gas station–convenience store and bought a box of powdered doughnuts. I enjoyed powdered doughnuts. I would have my own private doughnut-party in my motel room.

I parked at Duncan Motor Lodge, and to see what the snow was like, I walked to the edge of the parking lot where the snow was piled high. I stooped and dug my hand into it. In the motel light the snow was blindingly blue-white and to the touch, the snow was cold and crisp and flakey.

It was already dark. After I checked in, I washed my face and called

Christy to say goodnight. Then outside I heard loud scratching noises. I looked out, and in the light of the parking lot, I saw a giant bear standing on his hind legs and scratching on the window of the passenger side of the Bronco. What the hell!

Then it hit me: he smelled the powdered doughnuts. I'd forgotten them on the passenger seat. The bear started shaking the truck. He then licked the window. Crazy bear! It was freezing, cold enough for his tongue to stick to the glass. But it didn't. He gave up and lumbered away.

Around ten-thirty, I got a call from Herb. "I need you to come back tomorrow, Wednesday, not Thursday as we planned. There is an emergency situation at Lake Berryessa that needs attention, and I don't have anybody else to send there."

"Okay," I said, feeling relieved because it was already close to zero degrees at Tahoe.

While I was getting ready for bed my phone did its musical number. It was Marie. "What's up?"

She said, "Was that guy you met on the flight here Viktor Weinberg?"

"Sure was."

"Well, guess what?"

"What?"

"His picture is in the obituary section of the *Tribune* today."

"Are you sure?"

"According to this, he was not so young. He was retired from teaching. He was in his sixties. You want me to read it to you?"

"Sure. Read it."

"Viktor Eric Weinberg, sixty-three, died peacefully in his sleep Tuesday night. Viktor was born in Hattiesburg, Mississippi. He earned a master's degree from the University of Indiana at Bloomington, and he taught high school math for twenty years at Wendell Phillips in Chicago. His friend and mentor, retired Professor Pierre Rothschild, of Roseville, California, said Viktor often quoted Albert Einstein: 'Pure mathematics is, in its way, the poetry of logical ideas.' Viktor requested in his will that the following words be placed on his gravestone: 'The true spirit of delight, the exaltation, the sense of being more than Man, which is the touchstone of the highest excellence, is to be found in mathematics as surely as poetry.'—Bertrand Russell. Due to an undisclosed illness Viktor retired early. He was in the care of Dr. Peter R. Fiske-Urdang of Shultz's Mental Health Clinic of Chicago. His sister, Mrs. Kama-Keziah Chilton, of Hattiesburg, Mississippi, survives Viktor."

"That's it?"

"That's it."

"Thanks, Marie. Strange. I don't know what else to say."

Wednesday, I got an early start and I finished my work at the lake by noon. It was a cold morning. I stopped once for lunch and twice briefly at rest stops. It was beginning to turn dark when I drove into Elk Grove.

Although Christy hadn't been worried that I was going to be away for two nights, I knew she would be happy to see me. I decided to surprise her. I had been worried about leaving her alone in a house. The crime rate in Elk Grove was relatively low, but the crime rate in the Sacramento area was relatively high: especially home break-ins.

When I opened the door, I heard scuffling and scrambling and hushed urgent voices. I called out, "*Christy? You okay?*"

The scuffling continued and so did the muffled voices. The sounds seemed to be coming from the bedroom. Instantly my heart started beating faster and I tensed with fear and an urgency to act. My instinct was to protect Christy.

I rushed to the bedroom and flung open the door. I saw Mario completely naked, a stocky silhouette in the bedside light, struggling to get into his trousers, his stubby penis dangling beneath the overhang of his gut. He was shaking and looking at me with terror in his eyes.

A half empty bottle of Chablis and a glass sat on my bedside table. Another glass was on Christy's bedside table. Both had a bit of wine left in them.

Christy was sitting in bed with the covers pulled up to her neck glaring at me. She said one word: "*Mark!*"

I didn't think. I reacted from my gut. I shot over to Mario and grabbed him by his thick head of black hair. He swung at me. He struggled, fighting me as best as he could, kicking and punching.

I had an ironclad grip on his hair and forced him downward. I could smell his sweat and hair lotion and the wine on his breath.

Christy kept shouting for me to stop, but I ignored her.

As calmly as I could, I said, "Take your car keys out of your pocket!"

"There're on the table," Mario groaned.

Still holding him by his hair, I walked him on his knees to the table and picked up his wallet and car keys. I stuck both in my pocket.

I was twice his size, taller, stronger, younger, and fully able to handle a stocky little man like Mario. He looked up at me with confusion, saying over and over, "What're you doing?"

His pants were only halfway up his legs. Still gripping his hair, I twisted him down to the floor. His butt hit it with a thud.

"*Mark, don't do that!*" shouted Christy.

With my free hand, I grabbed his pants by the cuffs and yanked them off. I then pulled him to his feet and walked him to the bedroom door as he continued shouting, "*What're you doing? My clothes! I want my clothes!*"

I marched him up the hallway to the front door, opened it, took his car keys and wallet from my pocket, and threw them out onto the walkway. Still holding him by his hair I pushed him out, slammed the door and locked it.

At the window, I watched him pick up his keys and wallet and scamper off down the street, looking every bit like one of those naked medieval forest dwarfs. A pair of tail lights flicked on. Presumably, he had parked down the street to throw off any suspicion from our neighbors.

I went to the kitchen, got a trash bag, and returned to the bedroom. Christy was seated in the armchair in her bathrobe. She was looking at me with disgust.

Mario's clothes were still on the floor. I picked them up, stuffed them in the trash bag and dropped it at the side of the road where the trash was picked up.

37

I found Christy in the kitchen, making herself a cup of instant coffee. She said nothing. I guess she was waiting for me to say something. But where could the conversation go?

I got a can of beer out of the refrigerator and I sat down at the kitchen table. My head was buzzing. My face was hot and my arms were trembling from tension.

I felt deeply hurt and deeply disappointed. It was like I had never really known this woman and was a fool for marrying her. I was too angry to cry.

Christy said, "What I did was wrong, I know, but what you just did wasn't right either."

I looked up. I didn't say anything. I sipped the beer and looked at her. She was beautiful. No wonder Mario wanted her. Many men would want her.

I said, "How long has this been going on?"

"Only two or three times."

I thought about the strands of red hair I found in the bed. Mario's hair was black. I knew I wouldn't be able to sleep in that bed tonight, not on my side where Mario had wallowed with my wife. I would sleep on the couch. I might not be able to ever sleep in that bed again.

"What I did was for my career, but it wasn't the right way to go about it. I don't know what this means for our marriage."

"I don't either," I said, standing and walking out.

She followed me into the living room where I stretched out on the couch.

She sat down in the armchair facing me. "I love you, Mark. You may find that hard to believe right now, but I love you with all my heart. There are things about the way I look at life I don't think you understand."

"Well, *how* do you look at life?"

"I don't believe love has anything to do with sex."

"So why did you get married? You don't believe the statement you yourself wrote and read at our wedding?"

"I think there was something in it about faithfulness or loyalty, but loyalty is not the same thing as asking someone to be sexually *restricted*." She paused, then said: "It's *unnatural*."

"We didn't talk about these things *before* we married, and we should have. I assume then it's all right with you if I have sex with other women."

"No, it would *not* be all right."

"Then you have a double standard?"

"No, I don't have a double standard," she said.

I said nothing. I was bewildered.

"I say it again: one thing you should understand about me is I don't associate *sex* with love."

"What about being sexually faithful to your husband?"

"You're talking in circles. I just told you I don't associate sex with love and marriage."

I turned and looked over at her. What an amazingly evasive, complex, and self-contradictory woman!

She said, "I think you must know that little man means nothing to me, except he has the *power* to make my career."

"I think you have too much confidence in his power to help you."

"That's probably true."

"But you're willing to screw your way to the top of the art world?"

"You don't need to be cynical and vulgar."

"What you did was cynical and vulgar," I said angrily.

"Maybe so, maybe so. *Touché!*"

"So, you don't associate sex with marriage, right? Well, to come back to my question: I guess you then won't mind if I have sex with other women?"

She didn't answer this time; instead, she gazed at the hardwood floor.

"What was the point of marrying and declaring loyalty and trust and faithfulness?"

"I just told you we never declared *any* of those things to each other."

"Yes, we did. *Faithfulness* was in the document. *You* wrote it. So, answer my question. It will be okay with you if I see other women?"

"No, I already answered that question: I can't say that it would be all right."

"But it's okay for *you* to go to bed with other men? Is that the way you see it?"

She didn't respond.

We were now talking in circles, but I feared we would soon enter a period of prolonged unhappiness, of silence, secrecy and more deception. Rather than separating and releasing each other from pain and anguish, I worried we would be one of those couples that stayed together and tortured each other with abuse. I felt Christy and I were now at that threshold.

I wasn't willing to live that way.

Again, Christy said, "I *said* what I did was wrong."

"How could it be wrong if you believe that it wasn't wrong?"

"I don't understand what you mean," she said.

"You say you don't associate sex with love and marriage, that having sex outside marriage is okay and in the same breath you say what you did was wrong. How can it be both okay and wrong?"

"I don't understand your point."

"Forget it. So, what are we supposed to do *now*?"

"Mark, you could forgive me. That would be a start."

"By your standards what is there to forgive? Anyway, I don't know how I *can* forgive you. At least I'm not ready now to forgive you. I don't know how I will *ever* be able to forgive you."

"Maybe it's not so much a matter of forgiving me as it's trying to *understand* me. I understand *you* and accept you as you are. I don't believe you *need* other women. I believe I am plenty woman for you, but the same is not true for *me*."

"So, this is something you've always done?"

"I'm not going to lie to you. I want to be completely honest with you, Mark. I wasn't honest with Todd. I should have been."

"So, Todd didn't know you had affairs?"

"I didn't say I had affairs while I was married to Todd." She nickered. "He suspected it, though." The snicker again! "We once hired a neighborhood boy––he must have been about fifteen––to paint a raw wood rocking chair we'd picked up at a woodshop. That day while Todd was at his office, in one steamy afternoon, I taught that boy everything he will ever need to know about women."

She sounded proud of what she said. I thought she could have been arrested and sent to prison for seducing a fifteen-year-old boy. Then I remembered when she was fifteen *she* was seduced by a grown man.

"Another time," Christy said, with a chuckle, "Todd went to the annual dental convention and one of my fellow students from the Institute came over while he was gone. I knew Todd expected me to call him that night in his hotel room. So, while my visitor had his way with my body, I talked with Todd." She giggled. "My speech was punctuated with whines, groans and grunts, because my visitor was treating my poor body like I was a piece of wood and he was a nail-gun."

I was amazed by the ease with which she was telling me these things. I said, "Did you love, Todd?"

"I *thought* I did. I thought I did."

"I wish I'd known all of this *before* we got married."

"You knew I was cheating on Todd when I came to your hotel room at the Hilton."

"That's true. I don't know what to think or to say." I paused. "I thought when you and I got back together, I trusted we would be together for life. How naïve I was!"

"I didn't fool you! You have my loyalty and you always will have it just as you will always have my love; but I can't imagine spending the rest of my life having sex with just *one* man."

Again, I said, "Why didn't you tell me *before* we got married?"

She was silent a moment then said, "I *thought* about it, but I didn't see an opportunity. I guess I didn't think it was *that* important."

I didn't know if it was pure animal response or possessiveness but a man in my bed doing *it* with my wife bothered me.

I remembered TV documentaries in which bulls fought for dominance over a herd of cows and gorillas fought over females. But I was supposed to be a civilized adult *human* male with a certain amount of refinement and civility. I wondered if it was my responsibility as a civilized *being* to overcome primitive emotion. If so, I was failing.

The silence between us was heavy and promised to become a permanent part of our relationship--if our marriage continued. I was beginning to think of ending it, though I was determined not to make any decisions that night, even though I could see no light out of the darkness.

This Christy wasn't the Christy I thought I knew in high school. Back then maybe I didn't know her well enough. Maybe we were too busy lustfully enjoying each other, too busy covering our tracks and plotting ways to be together to get to *know* each other; or maybe we were too young. Secrecy and deception started back then, and I was part of it. Now, at this point, how could I be so surprised, so innocent, so naïve?

Christy was *driven* to be sexually adventurous. In high school, some girls had a reputation of being "easy," but Christy wasn't one of them; yet girls gossiped about her. She *did* have a mixed reputation

From the beginning, the clues were there: sex with her father's best friend; sex with me in high school, mostly during our senior year; the pornographic pictures online made shortly after I left for Berkeley; cheating on Todd and now cheating on me with Mario. Who knows how many other adventures she had had? Probably more than she would ever admit to.

She and I had never talked about what our married lives would be and we had never said what we expected of each other.

I felt trapped in a web of my own making, a web spun blindly and thoughtlessly. I had given myself too much credit for forethought and intelligence. I thought of myself as a person of integrity and kindness and, yes, trustworthiness, ambition, faithfulness, strength, and courage. Now, I wasn't sure of anything, least of all Christy, my *wife*.

If I now had contempt for Christy, I had as much contempt for myself. This was the truth I needed to face; and I didn't need a metaphor to make the point stick. It was a horrid and dreadful fact. No conventional gestures of affection would now save us. There was no return to happy harmony.

That night I slept on the couch. It was a restless night for me with gruesome dreams. In the single one I remembered on waking, I was chased by a pack of repugnant wild dogs trying to tear off my clothes. They didn't catch me because I climbed a tree, but the tree turned into a castle in which dreadful things were happening. On the upper floor, arisen from the dead, Mother stopped me and shook her head in despair. She said, "I told you, I told you *that* girl was no good."

In the morning, I got up and looked out the living room window. The bag containing Mario's clothes was gone. Either Mario came back and picked up his clothes, or a dog dragged the bag off or somebody walking by picked it up. I didn't spend any time puzzling over it.

Part Five

"We have all had the experience of finding that our reactions and perhaps even our deeds have denied beliefs we thought were ours."

—*James Baldwin*

38

A month later, in early March, I was eating a cheeseburger and drinking a malted milkshake at Byrd's Diner on the west edge of downtown Sacramento when Françoise walked in. *Françoise Levant Germaine!*

She was just as I remembered her: very tall and a natural blond with blue eyes. She looked more German than French; and I remembered she'd once said, "If you go far enough back in my family, *il y a une connexion allemande*, there is a German connection. Think about the name *Germaine* and the French word for German is 'alle*mande*.'"

I knew Françoise worked at an insurance company in the downtown area near Byrd's Diner, so I wasn't surprised to see her. She had her green card and was hoping to become an American citizen so she could have dual French and American citizenship. That way she could live as she chose in either country. She loved California.

She didn't want the fact that her father, Maurice-Henri Germaine, was a famous filmmaker to give her an advantage. She wanted to succeed on her own. She was trying to become a fiction writer.

When she saw me, I stood up and we did the French greeting: a quick kiss on both cheeks––one cheek if you didn't know the person well, two cheeks if you were close.

She said, "I'll order, then may I join you?"

There were two chairs at my table. I'm a big guy but I was occupying only one. "It would be my pleasure."

"I must grab something quick and get back to the office, but it's so good to see you, Mark."

I thought about how she now spoke: "grab something quick." Her speech was becoming more and more Americanized, but she still had a strong French accent. The two made interesting verbal and tonal bedfellows.

I could hear her ordering a Greek salad; and she came back and sat facing me, waiting for Bev, the server, to bring the salad.

"So what've you been up to lately?" she asked after Bev brought her the salad.

Her American lingo was so quick and so natural: "Been up to" hadn't been part of her speech earlier.

"I've been going up to Tahoe a lot, to do testing, and I've had to take the trusty snow-survey-pole to the Donner Lake area a few times lately. How about you?"

"*Déborde de travail!* Overwhelmed at the office with paperwork, but I'd love to get together with you for dinner or something sometime. I'm so delighted we ran into each other. I've been thinking about you a lot. I had a dream we got back together, but just before I woke, the CIA started investigating us." She laughed. "Isn't that silly?" Then she added, "You want to get together for lunch?"

"Yes. It would be nice to get caught up," I said.

"How about Saturday after next?"

"Sure. You still at the same address?"

"Yes, same address."

"I'll stop by and pick you up at say around noon?"

"*Bon! Bien! D'accord! Bonjour*, Mark!"

Françoise lived on West Curtis Drive, off 10th Avenue, in the Curtis Park area. Seeing her cheered me a bit. I had been pretty much in the dumps since catching Mario in my bed. Since then I hadn't touched my wife.

It was the first week of April, a year since Mother died, and I was reliving my grief and loss. I was too far away from Manifest to visit her grave; but I wanted to pay my respects and to express my grief while kneeling there. In the back of my mind, I was planning at some point to do just that.

Marie still wasn't ready to sell Mother's house. Not putting the house on the market was costing us money and time: taxes and upkeep and utilities and heating and air conditioning to be paid and monitored.

I occasionally talked with Elsie to see how things were going and to find out if she needed anything. She usually said, "I can always use a little extra money, Mark," and I sent it. Marie was also giving her a regular paycheck for housesitting paid out of one of Mother's bank accounts.

These things--coupled with imperceptible anger, mild despair, and sadness brought on by the mistake of marrying Christy, discovering that she was "Candy", the porn queen, hearing her confessions of her early passionate escapades and her "erotic" dancing, and her secret illicit "business" dalliance with Mario--left me in a bleak state. A period of bitter silence between us had ensued. We tiptoed around each other. For me--and perhaps for her--the seeming tranquility was a mask for anger and deep disappointment. We were mute combatants.

I concluded that Christy, despite her abundance of inner resources, was restless and impulsive and at times even silly. She clearly loved novelty. She giggled at things I didn't think were amusing, such as having sex with her father's best friend and her sexual conquest of an underage boy.

Since Christy and I were now barely talking, I no longer needed to tell her when I was leaving the house or why. Our life was now divided into two parts: before Mario and after Mario.

I took no interest in what she was doing or why. She left the house and returned, and I never asked her anything about her activities. One minute I was thinking this period of silence might end and Christy and I would return to the happy romantic moments we knew when we bought the house, and the next minute I thought we were finished and there is no going back.

We were living in hell.

But the fact that we were still living together meant something. We weren't ready to let go. We did have very elementary conversations, such as the following:

"Would you take out the garbage?" she would say, and I would say, "Yes, when I have time," or, I would say to her, "Did you pay the utility bill?" and her answer would be, "Yes," or, "No, not yet, I haven't had time." Such was the extent of our verbal contact.

I was still not sleeping with her. We had the three other smaller bedrooms. Christy used one for her studio. I used one for my home office. I was now sleeping in the third one, the guest bedroom that had yet to accommodate a guest.

I avoided even touching her. I no longer put cream on her back, and she no longer did the same for me. If she accidentally touched me, I made it clear to her I didn't approve. I knew I was going too far. I felt it. I also knew I was hurting myself more than her.

I avoided using the bathroom off the master bedroom. I showered in the bathroom off the guestroom. I tried to avoid looking at Christy naked and fresh out of the shower.

I had no idea if Christy was still seeing Mario or had met someone else. I suspected she couldn't go long without intimacy with a man. I tried not to think about her finding a new lover although I suspected she might do so if she hadn't already done.

One night I said, "Christy I think we should separate and get an annulment or a divorce."

"Fine with me."

"Are you willing to move out?"

"No, I'm not going anywhere."

"Then, *I* will have to move. I'll start looking for an apartment."

"Suit yourself," she said.

A few days later she said, "Mark, sex is no big deal. Why do you have to get all bent out of shape about it? I love *you*. Isn't that enough? I don't want a divorce. What I wish you could do is have a threesome; you, me, and another man, *any* man, maybe your friend Cliff. That's an experience I've never had. How about it?"

Was this a joke? I wasn't sure if she was sincere or just plain sadistic or both sadistic *and* sincere. The idea repulsed me. I looked at her hard for a long time and said nothing. I was thinking: this woman is a candle burning at both ends. Apparently, she was drunk with the need to use her body in countless ways to experiment sexually.

Thomas left a private message for me on Facebook: "What's up, Mark Anthony? I'm back in school, tech school, trying to learn more about computer programming. What are you up to?"

I responded: "Christy and I got married. Biggest mistake of my life! I caught her in bed with her art dealer. I'm done."

Thomas responded: "I don't know if I should tell you this. Tim and James made me swear to never tell you, but they are both now gone to heaven. Maybe I'm released from the promise. While we were at Hyde Park, she did *both* James and Tim. James twice. Tim once. That's what James told me."

I didn't respond.

Thomas's words ended my romantic illusions about Christy. My idyllic sense of our high school romance was shot to pieces like a cardboard silhouette of a medieval knight on a shooting range.

Anything I could say about Christy's waywardness also easily applied to me. Who was the writer who said our illusions are the last to go? There were limits to my own self-torture. If marriage was a critical error, I hoped I was no longer unconsciously looking for further ways to torture her or myself.

39

I was asleep in the guestroom. I awoke in the dark with Christy having her way with my body. So much for my efforts at distance! In the half-light she seemed unreal. The moment dazzled with unreality.

I smelled her, felt her, hated her, loved her, and longed for her to stop and to never stop. I didn't have the will to stop her. The animal sounds she was making were violent and passionate.

She finished me in an explosion of painful ecstasy and left the room having said nothing, which made the experience all the more unreal, strange, enigmatic, and furtive. All that was left was the whiff of her jasmine perfume.

Christy never asked to use the Subaru. If she wanted to go somewhere, she called a taxi, grabbed her purse, and left the house. Then one day she drove up in a new blue Toyota Camry and parked it in the driveway alongside the Subaru.

It took me no time to realize she had bought herself a car. The one she'd left in Evanston had been sold. Her parents sent her the check. It was an old car and she got only eight hundred dollars for it.

At eleven –thirty-one, on a cloudless Saturday morning, I found myself parked in front of Françoise's Curtis Park apartment building with a sense of an awakening. I felt like I had come through something gruesome and death-like and was alive again, about to enter a new phase. I felt dazzled and charmed and somehow victorious, though I was debating with myself about the wisdom of what I was doing.

I thought about Françoise. On the recommendation of one of her professors at the Sorbonne, she had come to the University of California at Davis as an exchange student for one quarter in the creative writing program.

Her ambition was to write a novel and to make a career of writing and she felt a creative writing workshop would help to give her the foundation she needed. Because of its temperate climate, northern California was the place she wanted to be.

When the exchange agreement ended, Françoise decided to transfer from the Sorbonne to UC Davis and earn a master's degree in English and creative writing.

She said it was widely believed in Europe that creative writing couldn't be taught so there was little or no effort to teach it. People said she was *crazy* to give up a Sorbonne degree for a UC Davis degree. Her answer was: "*Chacun a son proper programme*," or "Each to her own agenda."

During her first year on the Davis campus she met Jarvis Ingram, a fellow UCD student, originally from a small farming town in the Midwest. He was also in the creative writing program and he wrote poetry. Françoise and Jarvis fell in love, and they started living together in his cramped Sacramento apartment.

By the time Jarvis graduated and returned to the Midwest, Françoise had made up her mind to remain in California, though not necessarily Sacramento. She kept her small apartment in a cheap part of town. That was then.

She was now in a better apartment building and in a better part of town, though when I talked with her in the past about where she would live, she was daydreaming about moving to San Francisco. She frequently visited there. She said San Francisco reminded her of a European city. She loved the culture and the climate and the parks and the bridges and the hilly streets and the variety of people and cultures, the museums and the food, the coffee and the wine, the Fillmore and the Mission and the Bay. She frequently visited but moving there had yet to happen.

I sat there a while and thought of driving away; then I changed my mind, got out of the car, walked into the lobby, and pressed her door-buzzer. She buzzed me in. Her apartment was on the second floor.

When I climbed the stairs to the landing, she was standing in her doorway waiting with her ironic smile. She was a moody girl and at the same time very pleasant, and I liked her a lot.

The place was as I remembered it: a small studio apartment with an open plan, an island counter separating the living room and the kitchen. Françoise's bedroom, which looked out onto the park, was off the living room.

"*Bonjour!* So, here we are again. Come on in, Mark."

"*Bonjour!* Thanks! Yes, here we are again."

After she closed the door she said, "And why did we break up? I don't even remember. Do you?"

"I think you went back home to France for a visit and..."

"Yes, that's it! I went back to France. Please have a seat, Mark. I was thinking perhaps I would make lunch for us here rather than bothering to go out. What do you think?"

"Sounds good."

"*D'accord!*"

I sat on the couch and she brought me a glass of good dry French Chardonnay. I noticed she had poured herself a glass; it was on the island where she returned to continue tossing a salad.

We sat across from each other at her small dining room table, the bottle of wine between us. She had made an impressive lunch: *salade Lyonnaise* with boiled eggs and croutons, paté on hard bread, *gratin dauphinois* and pan-fried *foie gras*. Everything was delicious.

While we ate, she reminded me that she was from Nantes, a town in western France, about three hours by car from Paris. "None of the things for lunch today are necessarily typical of my region. Because of Papa's work, I kind of grew up everywhere. I'm not really the *fille provinciale* I like to believe I am. Nantes just happens to be where I was born. When it comes to food, I simply make what strikes my fancy."

She smiled. There was always something a bit sad in her face. As I watched her and listened to her talk, I knew I liked Françoise, but I sensed I needed a more reified sense of who she was.

"Papa, as you know, was so famous in France his fame cast a large *ombre*, I mean shadow, over our lives."

"A shadow is usually a negative symbol."

"*Cela a compliqué mes années de croissance*. I mean it complicated my growing-up years. You know what I mean?"

"Yes, I do."

I had seen some of her father's films and liked them. As a director he was in a category with Jean-Luc Godard and René Clair, François Truffaut, and Robert Bresson. I was no scholar of French films, but while a student at Berkeley, I saw quite a few of them; and I like to think I developed an aesthetic ability to judge foreign cinema. French films were at the time all the rage.

"I grew up," Françoise said, "struggling to keep a hold on reality. *Quand j'étais enfant, j'avais une imagination très actif.* What I mean is my imagination was always running away from me. You know what I mean?"

Sometimes she had to say things in French before she could find the words to say them in English. I understood the need and was patient with it. I enjoyed her strong French accent.

"No, I don't quite know what you mean," I said in order to get her to elaborate.

"*D'accord!* Papa's world was a world of fantasy and make-believe: *Un monde de fantaisie et de créativité.* It took me a long time to learn his world wasn't the *real* world and the day-to-day world we lived in wasn't a *fantasy*. I kept confusing them. *Voilà!*"

"Yes, okay, *now* I understand."

"I know I've talked with you about these things before. You being a scientist fascinated me and still does. Science was a world of *facts* and mathematics and hardcore reality. I needed to gravitate to that world. That is one of the reasons I was attracted to you."

"What were the other reasons?"

"Well," she put her fork down. "You're very decisive and handsome and smart and gentle too. I like those qualities in a man. I've always gone for the dark and tall and handsome type. My boyfriend at the *lycée* was a dark-complexioned Italian boy, born in Paris but Italian." She gave me her ironic smile. "So, Mark, are you happy? What is *your* life like nowadays?"

"I'm not happy," I said. I thought of telling her my mother died and I foolishly married a few months ago a girl I had been involved with in high school. I thought of telling her the whole rotten sordid truth, but it all seemed too unpleasant to bring up. I didn't want to spoil the moment with the train wreck that was my life.

"Do you care to talk about it?"

"Not right now."

"*Bon!* That's fine." She reached across the table and took my hand into hers. "Do you want to go lie down with me for a while?"

I didn't answer right away; then I said, "I'd like that."

"Come!" she said, standing up. "I want to hold you in my arms like a baby."

Naked, in bed, we lay close. Françoise shifted, turning on her side, and looked at me. With the fingers of her left hand she gently traced an invisible design on my face, starting from the temple and down my cheek. "You have such beautiful skin," she said. "I love your skin." She kissed my chest. I was aroused.

At the start, she pleasured herself and her knuckles bumping against my stomach threw my rhythm off. When she stopped, it was smooth sailing: we got into the same rhythm. I felt her climbing, climbing, climbing to the summit. Then she reached it, it felt like she'd leapt triumphantly into the sky, then descended into a fearless free fall.

My own release a short time later relaxed me; all tension left my limbs. All of my grief and heartache and pain and anger and disappointment and sorrow and suffering, dammed up inside, poured out in a grateful torrent. I lay beside Françoise, exhausted and calm and contented.

Propped on one elbow, she turned toward me, and stroked my cheek again. "Feel better?" she said.

"Much, much better."

"*Voilà!* You really needed that. I could tell. *Bon! C'est bien fait! Bon travail!*"

Although I had studied French in college, my understanding wasn't very good, so I didn't even try to respond, even a little, in French. I read it better than I spoke it. Instead, I was thinking: Françoise is a giver. Her greatest pleasure is in giving.

I looked into her big blue eyes. "You know, I thought you had already moved to San Francisco."

"That is still my dream but so far no luck in finding work there. I'm afraid my competences, I mean my *skills*, are rather limited. An MA in English isn't worth very much these days; and it will mean next to nothing in France. So, as you Americans say, a bird in the hand is worth two in the bush, so I stay at Atlantic-Pacific Insurance. If I go back to school and get a Ph.D., I might do better. I thought of teaching, but I did some student teaching at UC Davis and didn't like it; so, that scares me. *Violà!* So there!"

While Françoise was taking a shower, I lay in bed with my eyes closed, thinking about my situation with Christy. What a mess!

I remembered coming home recently, after being away overnight at Folsom Lake, and finding a large pool of oil in our driveway. It wasn't there when I left.

I had taken the Subaru to work, parked it and taken the Bronco to

Folsom Lake. Christy's car was new and didn't leak oil. For a car to leak that much oil, it had to have been parked in our driveway overnight. Mario drove a late model Cadillac, so it was unlikely his. That left Clifford and his leaking car. Yeah, it had to be Cliff.

When I mentioned the oil to Christy, she simply ignored me and the silence continued.

Françoise came out of the bathroom drying herself said, "It's such a beautiful day! Let's go for a walk in the park."

It was a simple idea and it struck me as ideal. "I'd love to."

When I came out of the bathroom, Françoise was already dressed. I dressed and like two happy kids holding hands we trotted down the steps and rushed out to the street. The park was a short distance away.

"How is your writing coming along?" I asked as we entered the park.

"*Les choses pourraient être meilleures*. Things could be better! I'm learning a lot and I'm getting better. Yes, that is why I came to America and why I majored in English. I wanted to write like Flannery O'Connor, like Edith Wharton, like Kay Boyle."

"Like American writers?" I asked.

"I also love Virginia Woolf; I love her to pieces, as you Americans say."

"You love the English language?"

"Yes, because I can see it as a *construct*; because I wasn't born to it, I can *see* it better; *c'est devenu mon argile mouler*, it becomes my clay to mold or my slab of marble to chisel into what I want it to be. I grew up reading fiction written in English. These writers appealed to me so much more than did the French women: Duras, de Beauvoir, Colette, Yourcenar, Sarraute, and Weil."

"Oh?"

"*Le point que je fais*, I mean the point I'm making is the French women writers had such a heavy load of that postwar *vision tragique*, I mean tragic vision, or the disillusionment that came at the end of the nineteenth century, when the world to them seemed to be going absolutely mad as modernity set in with its machines and technology and war after war."

"And what was so appealing to you in the American women writers?"

"Their *humanity*, their hope, their *optimism*, their belief there were still possibilities for joy in life. I know O'Connor is thought to have had a *tragic Catholic vision*, but even in O'Connor, on some unspoken level, there is optimism."

"I think, when I was an undergraduate, I read one of her short stories for an English class, something about a killer and an old woman."

"'A Good Man Is Hard to Find'?" Françoise said.

"Yes! That was it!" We sat down on a park bench "You must have learned English early? How did you find American literature?"

"Papa was interested in Australian and British and American literatures. He read extensively, always looking for new ideas and plots for his films. *Papa a conserve une vaste bibliothèque.* I mean at home, I mean in our first home, Papa kept an extensive library. So, I was exposed early. I grew up bilingual."

"What an interesting family you have, Françoise."

"Yes, but it all seemed quite normal to me. *Maman*, her name, I think you remember, is Damela Beauchêne. She worked as a secretary at the American consulate in Rennes, a hundred kilometers away. She did a lot of commuting. She didn't have to work but she insisted on it because it made her feel better about life. She didn't want to be a stay-at-home wife or just a socialite living off Papa's money."

"You once told me she has a brother."

"*Had* a brother. He passed away two years ago from dysentery. We had to have his body shipped back to France. He had worked for years in Algeria, where he served in the French consulate. At the time that poor suffering country was undergoing another one of its many crises."

"I always thought Algeria would be an interesting place to visit."

"You would *not* want to go there. We went there several times to visit my uncle. I was a little girl at the time. The people seemed to me to be so sad, so unhappy. It wasn't a good experience."

A man walking a dog passed in front of us. The dog pulled at the leash as if he was trying to come over to us to be petted, but the owner, an elderly man, pulled him back, saying, "Come on, Tony, don't bother the nice people, come on, boy, behave yourself."

The man and the dog continued on.

I said, "How is the novel coming along?"

"Right now, it's really difficult. I'm writing it first in French, then I will translate it to English. That way I will have two versions. Beckett wrote first in French; then translated his things to English. I'm very hard on myself. It takes me a long time to perfect a story. *Je suis perfectionniste!*"

"Do you return home to France often?"

"No. I can't afford so much travelling; and I am no longer accepting money from Papa."

"How about your mother?"

"Maman recently retired and she's now happily canning apples and pears and tending to her garden."

"What is your father working on these days?"

"Papa is still dreaming up new stories for the cinema. He writes his own, and people also send him tons of scripts all the time to read."

I was enjoying this reunion with Françoise so much so that it suddenly occurred to me that I was a married man––a married man dreaming of a relationship with this remarkable woman. I said, "Are you involved with anybody right now?"

She said, "You mean a *copain*, a boyfriend?" She looked down at her hands. "Yes, I *was* involved. Two weeks ago, we had a big fight and now I think the affair is kaput!" She smiled. "I ended it. He wasn't ready to end it, but I was. Besides, all he cared about was going to the park and flying drones for sport." She looked into my eyes. "Are you interested in resuming our relationship?"

I thought we had just resumed it a little while ago in bed. Without hesitation, I said, "Yes."

Françoise said, "That's why I asked you to wait two weeks before coming here. I wanted to end my relationship with Gabriel first because, you see, I had a feeling you and I might get back together."

I decided to tell Françoise the whole rotten truth about my situation. "Look, Françoise, I made a foolish mistake. I got married this past October. It was the dumbest thing I've ever done. I married a girl I was involved with in high school. I let my romantic memory of our relationship blind me."

"What happened?"

"I caught her in bed with her art dealer; and I told her I am getting a divorce."

"I see."

"She's an artist, a painter, and quite good too. She's also very intelligent."

"Is she pretty?"

"Yes, she's pretty too."

"Has she agreed to the divorce?"

"Yes, she has."

"You know some women need to keep seducing men to prove to themselves they are attractive and desirable or worthwhile, that they have value. It stems from a deep insecurity. Society does that to many of us women. Exactly what did she *say?*"

"She said fine, 'You can have your divorce,' but when I asked her if she was going to move, she said no, she's staying in the house. The house is in my name and according to California law it belongs solely to me because I bought it *before* we were married."

"What else happened?'

"A lot of things. For example, I discovered she's on a porn website."

"*Pas bon.*"

"I know. There have been other signs she has been involved with other men, even with a friend of mine, Clifford."

"I remember your friend Clifford."

"I'm sure you do. Anyway, Cliff drives a car that leaks oil. A large puddle of oil was in the driveway when I came back from being out of town overnight. I asked her about it, and she didn't deny it."

"Wow, infidelity, so soon after marriage?"

"Yes."

"So, you came and had sex with me *se venger*, to get revenge?"

"I hope you don't seriously think that."

"No, I don't," she said, thoughtfully, "but on the surface, it looks that way."

"I care a lot about you, Françoise, and if you are willing, I would like to see if our relationship, this time, can deepen and last."

"I'm hopeful, too. I was just wondering if you were feeling that way. Mark, when we were making love, I felt closer to you than ever before. I also felt your sorrow. I think you have matured a lot since we were together two or three years ago."

I nodded but said nothing.

40

I seemed to be emerging from that fourth stage of grief, *depression*, over Mother's death, heading, I hoped, to the final stage, *acceptance*, but separating that depression from the one I felt over the demise of my relationship with Christy was hard.

I spent the following Saturday afternoon with Françoise. She knew I wasn't ready or able to move into her tiny apartment with her. I still had responsibilities to my job, my house, and even to my wife.

I said, "I'll see you Monday afternoon, after I'm finished with work. Maybe we will feel like seeing a movie or something?"

Françoise kissed me. "Yes! *Au revoir*, Mark! *Adieu!*"

When I got home, Christy was in the kitchen. She was wearing a pullover and jeans. Her long, beautiful auburn hair hung down her back. She was wearing no makeup and none of her usual jewelry. She was sitting at the kitchen table drinking a Diet Coke.

I said, "Hello."

She didn't respond but after a few seconds she said, "I'm leaving tomorrow to visit my parents."

"Are you coming back?"

She gave me an incredulous look. "You bet I'm coming back. This is my home as much as it's yours. Even if you don't live here you have to pay the mortgage."

"That's where you're wrong. I can default and let the house go. Then where would you be?"

She didn't respond.

Again, I said, "Where would you be?"

"You would cut off your nose to spite your own face?"

Instead of responding to the comment, I said, "Are you driving your car to the airport?"

"No, I'm taking a cab."

I was still legally married to this woman, a woman I had cared for, now a woman whose very presence turned my stomach and made me anxious. Even in my sleep I worried. If I wasn't careful, I might soon need hypertension pills.

Monday morning Christy was all packed and ready to go. When the taxi arrived, I helped her carry her two pieces of new luggage out to the curb. The driver put them in the trunk.

Christy looked at me as if she half expected me to kiss her goodbye. She was frowning and smiling at the same time. I stared at her, almost tempted to embrace her. Suddenly she lunged toward me and tried to kiss me on the lips, but I turned away, and the kiss landed on my right cheek.

"Have a good visit with your parents, Christy."

"I don't even get a proper goodbye kiss?"

I put my arms around her and hugged her, but I didn't kiss her. She gave me a quizzical look after a released her.

"How long will you be gone?"

"A week. I'll be back next Monday. I think the flight gets in something like eight o'clock at night."

Then she got into the car and I closed the door.

I saw no immediate way out of this emotional labyrinth. I went to work and did my job. I saw Françoise as often as I could. I took her to her first Kings game. I tried to fall into a regular pattern. I didn't want to feel like a lab animal running a maze.

Although I was sleeping most nights at Françoise's apartment, it was difficult because my things weren't there. I thought I was taking steps to extract myself from the domestic entanglement I was in, yet it felt like I was sinking deeper into a morass.

Sunday, the day before Christy was to return, it dawned on me she had been gone a week and hadn't called and I hadn't attempted to call her. I felt her absence but at the same time I was happy to have the house to myself. She had become a habit but, like smoking, a habit that had become dangerous, and habits are hard to break. I cared about her, though. I wished her no harm.

Monday evening, driving to work with the car radio tuned to NPR news, I heard the announcer say, "A United Airlines passenger plane has lost contact with Utah Air Traffic Control. Two hundred and thirty people are on board." The plane was headed for Sacramento.

There was no need to assume the worst. She might have changed her mind about her return flight. Christy's death wasn't the price I wanted to pay for freedom. That would've been wicked and cheap and mean and somehow too easy. My life wasn't a murder mystery wherein unwanted characters could be bumped off.

I wanted her to live as she pleased and me to be free to do the same-- as far away from her as possible. I wanted to forgive *myself* for poor judgment and move on. I couldn't even say my time with her was wasted time since I believed I was learning something valuable from the failed relationship. I consoled myself with such thoughts.

But when I pulled into the driveway and unlocked the front door, I saw the two pieces of luggage Christy had taken with her. I could hear water running in the shower. I was relieved. I believed I was finished with her, but was I? We shared the same house. I could have moved to a hotel or found an apartment, but I hadn't. Part of it was stubbornness. It was my house. Part of it was my inability to extract myself from my own suffering.

I was in no mood to make up to her, mainly because I didn't believe she could change, and I knew I couldn't tolerate her the way she was.

When she came out of the bathroom, wearing her robe, she said, "I *thought* I heard you come in."

"How was your trip?"

"It was good to see Mommy and Daddy."

"Glad it went well for you."

She gave me a quizzical look; then said, "How long are we going to keep this up?"

"Keep what up?"

"You know what I'm talking about."

"Christy, we've had this conversation before. You know where I stand, and I know where you stand."

"Where do *I* stand?"

"You insist on sleeping with other men while married to me. I find that unacceptable."

She blushed. "I don't insist on anything."

"Are you saying you've changed?"

"I'm not saying that. I don't know why you're always so bent out of shape about other men. I never thought you were the jealous type."

"Listen, Christy, I've nothing more to say to you about this subject."

"Are you in love with another woman?"

"By your actions you've already made that none of your business," I said and walked out.

After work the next day, I stopped at Françoise's place. I sat on the couch and she brought me a glass of white wine, then sat down beside me.

"Mark, I'm thinking about moving to England."

41

Françoise said, "Papa has made me an offer, *difficile a baisser*, that is hard to turn down. He says I can go to our villa in Italy to write my novel, but I don't like the villa. The rooms are too cold, or I can stay in the apartment in Paris, although it's occupied right now by one of my cousins. I can't write in Paris: too many distractions. I want to continue to speak English. He knows I've been trying now for several years to get my novel written. He says if I move to our cottage at Newquay, Cornwall, he'd support me until I finish my novel. I know I said I didn't want his money, but it's beginning to look like I'm not going to be able to finish this novel without his help."

"What about us?"

"That's just the point: I want you to come with me. Please say you will, please, please!"

I didn't respond.

"Newquay, do you know it?" she said.

"No."

"It's a coastal town in Cornwall; it's a *station balnéaire*, a seaside resort town, a fishing port on the North Atlantic, about thirty kilometers from Bodmin and about twenty kilometers from Truro. *Très belle!*"

"How do you propose I would make a living?"

"I'm sure, with your education and skills, you'd have no trouble finding engineering work somewhere in England and London is three or four hours away by car. It's not far at all."

"Four hours by car is a long way. That's two hundred miles."

"Maybe two hundred," said Françoise. "But sometimes it takes that long given traffic to get from one side of Sacramento to the other."

Françoise was in a class different than I was. I knew she didn't like to think in terms of class. In fact, she had once questioned my tendency to use the word "class."

I wasn't at liberty to uproot myself and go live in a seaside tourist town in the southwestern part of England. Doing it at her expense was out of the question. I needed to work for a living. I was of the professional working class. I had a career––a career with a promising future. I couldn't move to Cornwall and just trust in providence.

For one wild crazy moment, I considered the idea. I wondered: would it be totally idiotic, totally foolish, totally preposterous, totally harebrained-and-ill-conceived, for me to trot off with Françoise on a fluke and trust everything would somehow workout?

Had I been twenty-one I would have done it without a second thought.

It didn't take long for reality to sink in: it would be next to impossible for me to get a work permit in England; and even if by some weird luck I did get one, finding a job in my kind of engineering would be unlikely. I wasn't willing to take just any kind of job available. I had spent many years training to do what I was doing and for me to throw it all away would be absurd.

I had heard how hard it was for foreigners, even well-educated foreigners, to find work in England. According to the news lately the British resented foreigners, especially ones taking good jobs. Other factors were too obvious to belabor.

In England there was talk of withdrawing from the European Union. This "Brexit" signaled a dramatic shift in England to the right, which I interpreted as a turning inward.

No, my best bet was to stay in California. I had a good secure job and I had just gotten a raise from $90,000 to $100,000. In many ways, I was a dreamer, but not a fool; I was adventitious but not *that* adventitious. I was willing to take chances but only chances that held promise or gave advantage. I was not a big gambler.

I said, "When do you think you'll leave?"

"I must give notice at work. Probably in a week or two."

A week later, the first Monday in May, I was talking with Marie about trying to sell some of Mother's things to a used furniture store. She said, "I've already tried that. A couple of people came out and looked at the furniture. One was interested in the dining room set and the other was interested in the living room furniture. Neither one wanted to pay what they were worth. I don't know what to do."

I said, "Why don't you ask some of Mother's neighbors if they want Mother's furniture after Elsie leaves? Even if you aren't ready to sell the house, we could at least start thinking about how we're going to get rid of things after she leaves."

"Why don't *you* call them and ask them? You're way the hell out there in California! You expect me to do *everything?*"

"You're right. I will call them. Do you have phone numbers?"

"No, but you can look them up, I'm sure."

"Okay, okay."

She was right. I needed to help more.

I found most of the phone numbers in the online white pages. That night I called Miss Carla Ann Carter, and she was delighted to take the bed in Mother's bedroom. Mrs. Anna Belle Johnson would take the living room couch and matching chairs. She would donate her old set to charity. Mrs. Ruby Mae Williams agreed to take the bed in the guest room where Elsie slept.

They all agreed to wait until Elsie moved out before picking up these gifts. I had the notion Elsie might want many of the items in the house she had called home for so many years; but Marie didn't want me to talk with her about moving or about taking some of Mother's things. On that score Marie and I were deadlocked.

The next day I called Marie and said, "I think it's time to put the house on the market. It's been over a year since Mother passed."

"Well," she said, "Why don't *you* make the arrangements?"

Wow! This was a step forward. It was unanticipated. Marie could be unpredictable. There was a glimmer of hope. I was learning something new about my twin sister. In the past she had always said it was too soon because it would be unfair to Elsie. "I'll find an agent today," I said.

I got online and located about ten real estate agents on the North Side of Chicago; I wanted one on the North Side so Marie would have easy access to the agent.

In one hour, I narrowed the list down to one: Lucien March, at Thyrza & Baruch, on West Grand Avenue near Willow Street.

"I'll go out and take a look at the house," said Mr. March. "I'll then make a document listing the particulars of the house, and we will take it from there."

I gave him my and Marie's contact information. "Just so you know when you get there, there is still somebody living in the house. Her name is Elsie Jones. I'll let her know. She was my mother's caretaker."

With May it was beginning to feel more like spring. People were wearing fewer clothes. My allergies were beginning to kick in. The plants and trees around the house were beginning to bloom. Some days were balmy; others were breezy or hot and dry with clear or cloudy skies.

Christy and I ate at separate times and still didn't sleep together. She went her way and I went my way. One day I said, "I'm going to file for a divorce."

She said, "You're still talking about a divorce?"

"It's the logical thing to do. We don't have a healthy relationship. Why continue to live this way?"

Christy smirked.

I said, "I've reasons the court will accept. I don't need your consent. I've looked into it. If you agree, we can file a joint petition; if you don't agree, I will file a regular petition for a contested divorce."

"What would be your reason?"

"I think you already know. At the very least I can say we have differences that can't be bridged."

"Do you know what's involved in a divorce: alimony, property division, asset distribution? Are you ready for those things?" she said.

"I'm ready."

"Well, I just wanted to hear what you would say. I am not interested in filing for alimony or even temporary support. This house? You can have it. I'll give you your divorce, Mark. I don't need to hold onto a man who thinks I'm a slut. It's just that I'm never going to get pushed around again by a man; never going to let a man make me feel less than human; never going to let a man beat self-respect out of me. I'm an educated woman, a liberated woman, a feminist, a good artist, whose philosophy of life you can't accept. I don't believe sex has anything to do with love. I love you, or at least I used to love you. That love is now dying. You're killing it with your narrow thinking, with your puritan ideas. So, yes, we can file an *uncontested* divorce any time you're ready." Proudly she said, "If you can't love me, I want nothing from you."

That afternoon, I tried to make an appointment online at the Sacramento County's Superior Court of California on 9th Street, but I couldn't figure out how to do it. I was hoping I could take Christy at her word and wanted to move quickly before she changed her mind.

"Let's just go there and make the appointment," she said. "The sooner we do this the better. At least we can get the documents we need."

I couldn't help but wonder why her tune had suddenly changed;

but I didn't say anything. Had a happy little leprechaun whispered in her ear? Odd to say but I liked this new icy charm of hers.

At the courthouse, the clerk, a nervous little man in a white shirt with the sleeves rolled up, asked us what we wanted. I said, "We want to make an appointment for a divorce hearing."

"Will this be a contested or uncontested divorce?"

"Uncontested," said Christy.

Bravo! Christy was really coming through.

"Then you don't need a hearing," the clerk said. He handed us a sheaf of papers. "You fill out these forms and bring them with you at the appointed time. An officer of the court will meet with both of you in one of those rooms over there." He pointed to a sequence of doors.

Christy said, "We were married last October; and since we haven't been married very long, just seven months ago, we thought maybe all we needed was an annulment for irreconcilable differences?"

I didn't know we had thought that!

The man said, "To qualify for an annulment you must prove incest or bigamy or one of you was underage or one of you was of unsound mind at the time or one of you committed fraud or you were forced into marriage or one of you are incapacitated in some way."

"I see," said Christy. "Then we just want a *regular* divorce."

He said, "In a regular divorce you have to disclose assets and fill out a schedule of debts and a schedule of income and expenses. If you have property, such as a house or automobile, you might want to consider getting a lawyer. A regular divorce *is* a contested divorce."

Christy said, "We don't want a *contested* divorce. I'm not asking for anything from my husband, and he's not asking for anything from me."

"Then, as I said, you come here at the appointed time and talk with an officer of the court and sign the documents. In three months the divorce will come through, but a word of caution: if you turn down spousal support or alimony now you won't be able to come back to this court and request it at a later date. Keep that in mind."

"I understand," she said.

When we got home, we worked on the forms. I was glad we didn't have to disclose our assets. Christy was sitting pretty. She had more than nine hundred thousand dollars in the bank. I knew she had received money from Todd's life insurance, the sale of his dental practice, and other monies from the settlement of his estate. The profit from the sale of her Evanston house alone was substantial.

She also freely spent money. She paid cash for the Toyota Camry. Since arriving in California, she frequently ordered expensive shoes, clothes, and jewelry from online sites. She also shopped at Macy's and other Sacramento stores.

She was financially independent. Which wasn't to say she would not need to get a job again, probably in advertising as she had in Evanston.

I kept checking the Thyrza & Baruch website to see if Lucian March had posted Mother's house. In my second conversation with him, I suggested the house be listed for three hundred and fifty thousand dollars. He said it was too much for a "high crime" area.

It was a house, he said, worth four hundred thousand but only in a "safe" neighborhood. He wanted to list it at two hundred thousand. We settled for two hundred and fifty thousand.

Two days later the house was listed with pictures of the interior and exterior of the house and the front and back yards.

"We're getting a lot of interest already," Lucien said when I called him to compliment him on the pictures. "I think this one will go fast, but I'm pretty sure we will have to drop the price a bit."

"Okay," I said.

Through May, I continued to see Françoise. On days when I was home from work and we were sitting on her couch, I told her I was in the process of getting a divorce.

She said, "That's great news, Mark! You will be free to come to England with me?"

"Françoise, we've gone over the reasons why I can't up and leave without some reassurance that I can find my kind of work in England and it's unlikely given the political and social climate there right now. I see every day on the news people there and in European countries complaining about foreigners coming with no skills or coming and taking good jobs. The no-skills people they see as a burden and the skilled ones are unwanted competition. They resent it. It's hard to get a work visa there."

"That's true but you would be an exception."

"I don't see how I would be."

"Because *I* want you to be."

"Françoise, that makes no sense."

She laughed. "You're correct about that."

"I'm glad you understand."

"It's just that I would *love* having you there. *Je te veux avec moi.* I mean, I want you with me."

I said, "It breaks my heart we have to separate, but you must do what you must do, and this is a great opportunity for you to get your novel written. I encourage you to take it."

"I take time out from working on the novel to write an occasional story. I just finished one where I use the French actress Isabelle Huppert as my model for a character. I call her Stephanie."

I said, "Do you know Isabelle Huppert?"

"Not really. When I was a teenager Papa used to give a lot of parties in our Paris apartment. She was one of the guests. I was introduced to her but that was all."

"You must have met many famous people."

"Yes, back then many famous actors and writers came to Papa's parties: Le Clezio, Modiano, Depardieu, Thurman, and I can't remember them all, but my sense of Isabelle is mainly from her movies. *That* Isabelle is my motif."

I waited for her to tell me more.

"The actors and writers were adults, and I was a child. I didn't pay much attention to them."

"Where do you send stories written in French?"

"Just recently I sent one to *Lire*, three to *Le Litteraire*, one to *Muze*, and two to *Long Cours*. I can't wait to hear from them. These aren't stories I wrote for my thesis. I wrote those in English. I revised these, and they are much better. The stories were all rejected but sending stories out boosts my spirit; gives me more confidence I can become a *published* writer. Sometimes I get an encouraging note from an editor."

"You're so talented, Françoise."

She said, "My big dream is to sell a story to the *New Yorker*."

"Have you ever sent them anything?"

"*Oui! Des centaines de fois!* Hundreds of times! I always get printed rejection letters but once the fiction editor wrote in the corner of the letter, '*Thank you. You're a gifted writer.*' That was encouraging!"

"Yes! When are you leaving?"

"Wow! *C'était changement abrupt de sujet.* I mean that was an abrupt change of subject. Please excuse my lapse of thought, Mark. Sometimes I think first in French; but I'm working on it and trying to think more consistently in English."

"Oh, I understand! Sorry. It's just you've talked about moving to England for weeks and I've never had a clear sense of *when* you plan to do it."

"The cottage is being painted inside, and Papa wants to put in a writing *bureau*, I mean desk, for me. There was some repair work to be done. Papa is also buying a new bed, too, I mean, a new mattress. The cottage also needs Wi-Fi, which it didn't have. I think it was installed this week. When those things are done, *voilà*, I will be able to go there." She smiled her sad sweet incisive smile. It was a smile with a certain vibrancy and defensiveness about it. It endeared her to me.

On May 25, at ten, Christy and I walked into the Sacramento courthouse to complete our divorce. We were directed to small, dimly lit room and took seats at a wooden table facing a worn swivel chair.

About five minutes later a middle-aged man in a blue suit and power-red necktie entered. He looked like he hadn't had a good night's sleep in quite a while. There were bags under his eyes. His suit was shiny thin on the elbows and on the seat.

He flopped down in the chair and said, "My name is Basil Ludlow. I'll be walking you through this process. Any questions?" With a sarcastic expression he waited for a response.

"No," said Christy. "No questions."

"I see you won't have to have your name restored. I assume Werner is your original family name?"

"That's right."

"You aren't asking for spousal support. I hope you understand you won't be able to come back to this court and later ask for it?"

"I understand," said Christy. "We were told that the first time we were here."

"Very well. Let's get started then."

The rest of the meeting went smoothly and was over in less than thirty minutes. I was so happy that I wanted to do a Nijinsky dance on the tabletop, but I kept my joy concealed.

She and I drove home in silence. I felt like I'd been cured of a deadly disease and told it would never return. I was intoxicated with happiness. How often can one correct one's stupid mistakes so easily?

42

That night when I returned from Françoise's place, I asked Christy, "Why did you change your mind about divorce?"

"Because I *love* you, that's why. I don't want you to be my caged bird; and I know you're seeing someone else. You're free to do what you please. I don't approve, but it's none of my business. If sleeping with another woman is what you want, then..."

"That is not what you were saying a month ago."

"I didn't say anything a month ago." She turned her back to me, walked to the sink and filled a glass with tap water. She took a sip then said, "I'm moving next week."

"You're moving—moving *where?*"

"Isn't that what you want?"

"Sure," I said, "But not so long ago you said––"

"I *know* what I said."

"Are you going back to Evanston?"

"No, I'm moving to Davis."

"Davis? Why Davis?"

"I'm moving in with Cliff."

"Oh, I see." It all began to make sense. The red hair in the bed! The puddle of oil in the driveway! She had changed her mind about the divorce because she and Clifford had a plan: she would get her divorce and come to live with him. Well, that was just hunky-dory!

I felt good about her moving in with Clifford. Under my breath I sang praise to his hospitality!

I said, "What about your painting?"

"I haven't been able to do much painting lately. Things have been too unsettled around here for me to do any work."

"What about Mario?"

"Forget Mario. You're lucky he didn't file charges against you for the way you treated him."

"He got what he deserved."

"Let's not argue. It's pointless."

"Will you have a place to paint at Cliff's?"

"Yes. I'll have a studio. You've seen his house. It's big, plenty of room."

"Well, I'm happy for you and for Cliff, too."

"And I'm sure you're happy with your other life," she said.

"What do you mean?"

"Your life with whoever you're seeing."

I didn't respond. I felt she was fishing but I wasn't going to bite. I wanted our relationship to remain as congenial as possible. We were no longer entrenched in daily conjugal warfare. Were we now affirming each other's humanity or did this calm foreshadow bitterness worse than we'd so far known?

Christy had all of her things, her many clothes, shoes, purses, and some of the furniture we'd bought together, moved while I was at work. She took with her all of her paintings, her easel, her drawing table, stacks of drawing tablets, a supply of fresh canvases, supply cart, paints, and things I can't even remember. I never saw the truck. She took the bed she and Mario had made love in. Apparently, Cliff had room for it. I was glad to be rid of it.

When I got home that night the house seemed empty although it wasn't. Christy had left most of the living room furniture, the couch and chairs and lamps and end tables. The bed in the guestroom where I slept was still there.

The house also had about it a silence and stillness it hadn't held before Christy's departure. The quietness was both peaceful and alarming. It continued for days till I grew used to it, slowly relearning the value of tranquility. I spoke just to hear my own voice: "She's gone," I said out loud. Again, I said, "She's gone," just to hear the echo; and, in a muffled voice this time, I said it again: "She's gone."

Françoise was more than a source of comfort at this time; but I was learning no one could be your emotional mainstay. In the brief time you are alive, you must be your own all-purpose mainstay. I remembered Vladimir Nabokov's well-known words: "The cradle rocks above an abyss, and common sense tells us that our existence is but a brief crack of light between two eternities of darkness."

At the end of May, a week after Christy moved, Françoise called me at work: "The house is ready. Papa says I can go there now. Are you sure you won't come later? Maybe you will change your mind?"

After work, I stopped at her place. We went out for dinner at the Firehouse restaurant, on 2nd Street, and the conversation was a repeat of what we'd already said before. Françoise was sure I would find suitable work in England. I was equally sure I would not find work as an engineer in England. We were still deadlocked.

The issue of certain unspoken attitudes among some in England was never voiced, but I was aware of it, and I was sure Françoise was also aware of it and of its possible role in whether or not I might succeed in England in finding suitable work. It was the little monster in the room.

I spent the night with Françoise. After making love we held each other. This was unusual because Françoise wasn't the cuddling type. She was rather matter of fact and aggressive about lovemaking.

This night was different. She was going away. In my arms she cried a bit and Françoise wasn't the crying type. I wasn't sure why she was crying; and I was reluctant to ask, but I did anyway: "What's the matter?"

"*Je ne pourrais peut-être...* Sorry, I was about to say I may never see you again. That makes me sad."

"Oh, we'll see each other again. I'm sure."

"Then, you will come visit me in Newquay?"

"Yes, I will. Will *you* come back to visit me?"

"*Oui!* Yes, I will, I will. Actually, I plan to move back to the California at some point, perhaps after my novel is finished."

On the first Monday in June, I drove Françoise to Sacramento International Airport, and with a kiss we said goodbye just before she went through security. Once through security she turned and waved and with a teary smile threw me another kiss.

I was surprised that tears came to my eyes. Was I afraid I had lost her or was I regretting my unwillingness to muster enough courage to move to England?

I no longer seemed to have the kind of reckless courage that propelled me from Chicago to Berkeley so many years before. Losing courage and being too cautious were the hazards of growing older.

Wednesday, Marie and I got our first offer on Mother's house. I kept my fingers crossed. The prospective buyer had his "expert" inspect key elements of the house such as the roof and the hot water heater and the furnace. The expert said no, don't buy the house; so, the prospective buyer changed his mind. The expert said the house needed a new roof.

For the record, the roof was new, the furnace was in fine working condition and so was the hot water heater.

"Onward," I told our agent, Lucien March.

I started getting two or three texts daily from Françoise. The first one came while she was flying thirty-five thousand feet above the Atlantic:

"Mark, miss you already. Please come! Love, F."

Marie called, "Listen, we've another prospective buyer. His name is Luther Moses, a community organizer. He wants to help rid the South Side of gangs and street violence and he's interested in buying Mother's house."

"I'm listening."

"Our agent showed him the house yesterday. Elsie was there. I like it best when the agent can show the house while she's out, but she doesn't agree. She feels like she has to be there to protect Mother's things as if somebody's going to steal something. It's silly."

"She has to do what she has to do."

"Luther Moses is well known on the South Side. He's been working with gangs and young men fresh out of prison, those living in halfway houses as well as those out there in the streets getting into trouble. He's trying to show them they can become productive members of society."

"I'm glad he's doing it."

"Luther wants to show them how to overcome disadvantages and he has the financial support of the mayor and other people downtown."

"Sounds good."

"He's helping to stop very young boys from joining gangs."

"Well, if he buys Mother's house, he will plant himself right in the middle of the problem. I guess it's where he needs to be."

"Fingers crossed," said Marie.

"Yes, fingers crossed."

Three days later Marie called again. "I talked with our agent this morning. Moses's loan application has been approved. We're one step closer."

"Bravo!"

Sacramento was still blisteringly hot and it was only the middle of June. July and August promised to be broiling. Summers in Sacramento could be feverishly scorching. Many people headed for the hills.

At work we had good air conditioning, but by the time I drove home in the roasting heat of the late afternoon, the interior of the Subaru was over a hundred, so intensely hot I could barely stand it, and the air outside was sizzling. Once in the house I turned on the air conditioner and set it to seventy-five.

Françoise kept sending me text messages: "At least come over and see what you think. Can't you take at least a week off and come to see if you like it?"

I checked with Herb's secretary, Babette Dudley, and learned I had almost two months in back vacation time. "But," she said, "if you're planning to take off, best to check with Herb first." I did just that. He said he had no problem with me taking vacation time.

Hearing the good news, I booked off July third to thirty-first to go to England to visit Françoise. It would be a perfect time to get out of the fierce furnace of summer in Sacramento.

I sent Marie an email: "I'm taking about twenty-five days of my vacation time just to get away for a while. You can contact me by email or text. Love, M."

Françoise texted me and said, "Rather than you taking the commuter flight from Heathrow to Newquay, I'll come and pick you up. It's a four hour drive each way, but it will be fun."

43

I arrived at Heathrow late on the fourth, American Independence Day, and there was Françoise at the luggage claim, waiting for me. She was wearing a jersey and jeans and ballet shoes.

I was lucky to spot Françoise. Like many airports, Heathrow was a glittering affair, bright with glass and light and polished floors reflecting everything. I put down my carry-on just as she walked into my arms.

"*Bonjour*, Mark!"

"*Bonjour*, Françoise!"

We hugged and kissed. "Oh, it's so wonderful to see you, Mark! I'm *so* excited!" she said.

"So am I."

"Let's go!" she said, gently taking my hand.

After retrieving my luggage, we walked quickly to the parking lot. It was eight at night local time; I was still on California time and feeling jetlagged but going on nervous energy.

"Papa bought me this nice car. I feel so guilty accepting things like this from him. I should be able to take care of myself." Her smile was sad.

"It's a nice car," I said of her new silver mini-SUV Nissan Qashqai as we stored my luggage in the truck and got into

Françoise was a fast but expert driver. We hit the road south on the M3, and it was smooth sailing past the exits for the small towns and villages. Once we reached the Exeter area, Françoise said, "Not long now."

Before long we drove into Newquay and parked in front of the Germaine cottage. I checked the time. It was eleven-fifteen. We made good time from Heathrow.

The large stone cottage was set slightly below the road and was surrounded by an array of trees and shrubbery. A classic English cottage, probably built in the eighteenth century. it was well kept and sturdy, with a look of permanence. I couldn't help wondering how many generations had lived there and restored and updated its interior before Françoise's family bought it.

Once inside, Françoise said, "*Voilà!* You must be bushed. Do you want to turn in right away?"

"I'd like to shower first."

When I came out of the shower, Françoise said, "How about a nice cup of tea before we go to bed?"

"That would be delightful."

"*Bien!*"

Most of Wednesday morning I slept a long time before waking. When I did return to consciousness, Françoise came into the bedroom and said, "*Salut*, Mark!"

"Good morning, Françoise."

I sat up in bed and stretched, surprised I was actually in England. I felt slightly ruffled from jetlag and still sleepy, with vague memories of swimming through miles and miles of dreams, not all of them bad.

"It's past noon," she said. "I've made some lunch for us. It's all set up in the garden. When you're ready come on out."

"Okay," I said, wearily climbing out of bed.

"Also, you should know, a local woman, Nellie, comes once a week, on a Wednesday, to clean and mop, dust and polish. She's from Dublin. So, if she arrives and I'm not here you'll know who she is. She's been with my family for many years. Even when there is no one living here she comes to clean."

"Got it!"

Another shower felt wonderful, almost ritualistic, but I was still groggy from the flight and the time change.

I felt I could lower my sails here, now that I was far from the Elk Grove emotional battlefield exchanging verbal artillery fire with Christy or living in dead silence. Here, I could surrender to comfort and casual generosity.

I dressed in a cool white cotton shirt and soft brown slacks and white tennis shoes and stepped outside into a sunny English day. I felt refreshed and invigorated.

"Beautiful flower garden!"

"Thank you. Nigel does a good job of tending to it."

"Nigel?"

"Yes, my family's gardener."

The garden was surrounded by an ancient stonewall. An old walnut tree stood by the wall.

Françoise said, "There is an underground spring running under the garden. All of the stone pottery and figurines you see there, have been here since the house was built."

The garden consisted of a small lawn and stone patio surrounded by an amazing profusion of blooming plants at their peak: Queen Anne's lace, penny royal, yellow cowslips, purple foxgloves, summer snowflakes, purple pasques and cuckoos; and there were blue spring gentians, dog roses and red poppies, primroses, and a thicket of thriving bilberries.

Françoise walked to the bilberries and touched one branch. "This garden is my favorite place. Sometimes I sit out here and try to write but all I end up doing is daydreaming. It's *too* beautiful." With both hands Françoise gestured toward the flowers, their fiercely appealing colors erupting all around us.

With a laugh, I said, "You need a dungeon in which there are no distractions."

"*Voila!* Exactly!" She smiled approval. "Feel free to look around. Lunch can wait a few minutes."

Bees were buzzing about, one hummingbird danced in the air, moving from flower to flower. Three or four butterflies floated by.

I walked around the cottage, Françoise following me as though seeing her family's cottage afresh through my eyes. On one side were dogwood in bloom and hedge yews, oxeye daises and cranesbill geraniums.

"You must love it here?"

"I'm beginning to appreciate it more."

We carried on into the front yard, through flowerbeds of oriental poppies, sweet rockets, foxglove and lady's mantle and pink roses climbing the side.

I looked more closely at the house, which was as enchanting as the garden: it was a traditional Cornish cottage made of stones fitted unevenly together, which gave it part of its charm. The tile roof was a layer of sloping umbrella shapes.

We returned to the garden. The patio was in the center. On it was a glass-topped table surrounded by four white metal chairs with colorful cushions. Off to the side were three armchairs and a wooden bench, all with cushions. On one armchair were various magazines and paperback novels.

"I had this food delivered by the local *épicerie fine*––delicatessen I guess they say here, just some local *charcuterie*."

"It looks delicious."

We sat across from each other. There were slices of roast lamb, pâté, sausage, salami, cheese, green beans, and rolls in a basket and a pitcher of punch. With the back of her hand, Françoise fanned a fly away.

"What a feast!" I said, conscious for the first time in many hours that I was hungry.

"I'm so happy you came, Mark. We're going to have such a delightful time. There is so much I want to say. I don't know where to begin."

"Like what?"

"Well, I'm thinking of things we can do while you're here."

"Like what?"

"We could take the Nissan and go to France and drive down to the south. We can share the driving. It's very beautiful. Did you go there when you came over with your mother?"

"No, we didn't go south; besides, I was too young to appreciate the experience."

"Well, we can do that now if you like, or we can do something else. What would you like to do?"

"I'd love to go to the south of France with you."

"*Voilà! D'accord!* We'll take the Eurotunnel; it's faster than the ferry."

"It will be an adventure," I said, really warming to the idea.

"Papa and Maman are staying at the farmhouse in Bordeaux. We can stop for one night there and say hello. *Non?*"

"Yes!"

That afternoon and the next morning, Françoise and I made passionate love. It was good to hold her in my arms again, to feel her heart beating against mine. We were beyond conventional gestures of affection, feeling a joyous harmony. I was feeling much better. I appreciated and enjoyed her kindness.

I gazed at Françoise. I knew how moody and introspective she was. She required a lot of alone time. I would have no trouble keeping myself occupied in one way or another. The house was full of interesting books and paintings and figurines. I looked forward to sitting in the garden reading while Françoise worked on her novel.

Saturday morning, Françoise and I were on our way. Once we crossed into France, we stuck to the autoroutes, carefully following our marked map. We made the journey, not the destination, the *object*, and enjoyed every precious minute together. Blissful nights in clean motel beds on crisp white sheets were just as much fun as joyfully freewheeling along the bright autoroutes. We savored each stop as if it were our ultimate destination. Driving through the plush green countryside was delightful. I liked seeing the clusters of old white stucco farmhouses with orange roofs, the rivers reflecting the blue sky, and catching a glimpse of a castle high on a hillside.

Monday morning, I did most of the driving. The traffic on the AB37 through Saintes was light. We stopped to see the Sainte-Marie Abbey and the old Roman Arch of Germanicus; we drove by the Saintes Cathedral, then crossed the Charente River. As we approached Bordeaux, Françoise said, "Both my parents speak English very well, although understandably they prefer to speak French."

I nodded.

"Papa and Maman bought this farm a few years ago. It has a small vineyard, but it doesn't produce much wine. I think right now there are only two or three farmhands working the vineyard. Papa has his own label, but it's just for private use. He uses an image of Monet's water lilies on the label."

At the entrance to their property a sign said: CHÂTEAU GERMAINE PROPRIÉTÉ PRIVÉE. We drove on the private road and I saw a great stretch of farmland with hundreds of rows of grapevines propped up with stakes and, in the distance, the steeple of a provincial church. As we pulled up in front of Château Germaine a friendly looking Airedale came running from the side of the house. Françoise said, "That's Xavier!" The dog danced happily, barking as we stepped out of the car. A red tractor sat at the edge of the vineyard.

An elderly man wearing a large straw hat and a blue smock was clipping hedges alongside the house. A woman wearing a large white apron and a big smile opened the front door and crossed the yard to the car, her arms raised, ready to hug Françoise.

She and Françoise spoke quickly in French, then Françoise introduced me in English: "Mark, this is Madam Venda Durand. She's my family's housekeeper."

"*Bonjour, madam,*" I said and reached for her hand. She seemed surprised at a handshake. Obviously, this wasn't the usual protocol.

"*Bonjour,* Monsieur Smith," Madam Durand said, her accent heavy, "From America, welcome to France."

"*Je vous remercie,*" I said, trying not to screw up my college-learned French.

Françoise called over the man clipping hedges. She spoke to him in French. As he smiled, I could see that his skin was badly weatherworn. She introduced us. "Mark, Monsieur René Aylwin."

Monsieur Aylwin, too, seemed surprised I had reached for his hand to shake. His smile was rather sad.

Madam Durand led us inside the foyer, down the hallway and into the living room announcing us in French to Monsieur Germaine.

My first view of the great man: he rose from an armchair by the unlit fireplace, put down a book he was reading, and approached me with a smile. I felt quickly at ease.

He was tall and slender with a long handsome face and thinning hair. He was wearing slacks and a purple pullover.

"*Bonjour,* Monsieur Germaine," I said as Madam Durand left the room.

"Hello, Mr. Smith. Françoise has told us all about you. It's good to meet you." He reached for my hand and we shook. "Won't you have a seat?"

"Thank you," I said taking a chair opposite to the one he'd just vacated. "It's a pleasure to meet you, Monsieur Germaine. I'm a great admirer of your films."

I regretted my tone. I sounded too worshipful, like a star-struck kid meeting his favorite superstar, though it was an awesome experience meeting someone of his standing. I *was* star-struck.

Françoise and her father kissed each other on both cheeks. He spoke to her rapidly in French, which I couldn't follow entirely, though I understood he was asking her about our drive from Newquay, then about her novel-in-progress.

"*C'était un bon depart*," she said, sitting on the Catania sofa, crossing her legs, leaning forward elbows on knees, looking at her father who returned to his chair.

"My apology, Mark," Monsieur Germaine said. "Do you speak French?"

"*Un petit peu*. In college I had French, but I read it better than I speak it."

Monsieur laughed politely. "Ah, college French!"

Françoise said, "Papa, we're just staying till tomorrow morning. We're going on from here to the Côte d'Azur."

"You kids will have fun there. Been there before, Mark?"

"No, sir."

"Oh, you don't need to 'sir' me, Mark. Just call me Maurice, if you don't mind."

I nodded. I didn't think I could call him Maurice, not this soon. This put me in a bind. I would not be able to address him at all.

A woman I assumed was Françoise's mother, Damela Beauchêne-Germaine, entered the room. She was a bit shorter than Françoise and a bit heavier, and despite her slightly stooped shoulders she was strikingly beautiful. She was wearing a white sweater and a gray skirt. Her smile was bright and energetic.

She said to me, "*Bonjour!*"

"*Bonjour*, madam!"

Françoise got up and rushed to her mother and they kissed each other's cheeks as they hugged.

Madame Beauchêne-Germaine turned to me and said, "*Tu dois être* Mark?" Her eyes were friendly, and she had a beautiful feminine face.

"Yes, I am, and you must be Françoise's mother?"

"*Oui!* Yes, I am."

We shook hands.

"Well, it's a great pleasure to meet you, Mark, and welcome to Bordeaux. Françoise has talked so much about you..."

That night the four of us went for dinner at an elegant little seafood restaurant on Rue Courbin. Monsieur Germaine requested the "English" menu. Françoise ordered some type of goby fish. Her father ordered red mullet and so did her mother. I ordered a type of mackerel native to the Mediterranean. The food was delicious and we had a splendid evening. Monsieur Germaine did most of the talking. The economies of Europe––France and England in particular––were on his mind. He was worried about England. To him it looked like England was moving toward extreme nationalism, which wasn't good for England, Europe, or the world.

"*Et peut-être aussi la France*," he said. Then in English he said, "Extreme nationalism, it's no good. *Les gens apprendront-ils jamais?*"

I didn't say anything in response, but I was thinking about the prospect of someone like me finding a job as an engineer in the political and social atmosphere he was describing. Françoise saw this too but didn't want to acknowledge it.

Later, Monsieur Germaine talked about the goings-on on the set of his film in progress. "This is my first film that also tries to grapple with the, the...divisions *culturelles et raciales*... cultural and racial divisions. I set it in Paris as a kind of microcosm of the world's situation."

"Interesting," I said.

"Also, I want to show how when a nation gives in to fear it becomes easily seduced by extreme nationalism, otherwise known as fascism; and there is always a corrupt bully waiting to be the leader."

Françoise said, "This is new territory for you, Papa."

"Yes, it is, but I want it to be a farce, a comedy."

"And Paris is the perfect setting," said Françoise.

"You see, I want to treat the subject humorously."

I said, "I'm looking forward to seeing it."

"Thank you, Mark," said Monsieur Germaine.

Françoise said, "Papa, I'm happy you're making such a film."

Madame Germaine said, "He's been very, very busy. We're just taking a little break right now."

Monsieur Germaine said the film would also be a cross between a romantic comedy and a thriller. He said, "*Ce sera mon meilleur film!*"

And we all said bravo and wished him luck.

Tuesday morning, Françoise's parents saw us off and wished us well on our drive to Nice. At the last minute, her father said to me, "Be careful in Nice, Mark, some of those anti-Arab locals might take you for an Arab. They've been known to shoot them off those little motorbikes right on the boulevard in Nice."

Françoise said, "Ah, Papa, don't say things like that." She frowned at him.

Although Monsieur Germaine was smiling when he spoke those words, they left in my chest a tight feeling. I took the warning to heart.

He said, "Just be cautious."

We took our time. We were in no hurry. We stopped after three hours of driving and checked into a motel at Montpellier. We got a good night's sleep.

Wednesday morning, we again headed for Nice driving by the turn-off for Arles– Aix-en-Provence regions then on into Nice. It took about seven hours, with only three stops.

It was early evening when we checked into the Hotel Cote d'Azur, a four-star hotel on the Promenade des Anglais. We had a little balcony with a couple of chairs and a table; our room looked out onto the Mediterranean Sea. In the distance, we could see early evening sailboats moving along in the breeze; below us, across the street, young couples, children, and elderly people strolled along the promenade.

By the time we were settled in the room it was seven. We unpacked a few things and decided to go down for dinner and then take a walk along the sea. We were in the hotel restaurant, menus in hand, but before we could make selections, we heard a massive explosion outside. The room shook.

44

I felt dizzy. I could see the water in the pitcher shake as everything on the tabletop danced around. The lights flickered. I felt the pressure in my head and my heart beating faster. There was screaming and shouting. The restaurant turned into bedlam as people scrambled under tables. We had no idea what was happening.

I grabbed Françoise's hand and we dropped to the floor and ducked under our table. Was it an earthquake? Were bombs dropping from the sky? The beginning of World War Three?

When the room stopped shaking, we gingerly came out from under the table to a chorus of shouting. "They're saying a car exploded just outside," said Françoise.

We headed for the lobby. Then we saw it: The entire front entryway of the hotel was blown away. Smoke and dust and toxic fumes floated on the air, entering the posh hotel lobby. The sound of approaching sirens grew louder. In French the concierge said, "A bomb went off in a car parked in front of the hotel."

Through the rubble, we could see the twisted metal of the automobile and flames dancing high. The smell was horrible, unbearable. When the toxic smoke cleared a bit along the ground, I saw bodies.

How many? At that moment, I couldn't say. Later, it was reported five people were killed instantly. At least thirty were injured, ten, seriously. Three of the ten later died; the other seven were maimed for life.

People stood stunned and speechless in shock, some leaning against walls. When the emergency vehicles arrived, a scramble began as workers collected bodies and tended to the wounded. Those who could walk were taken by the arm and led to the ambulances; those lying on the ground outside were moved onto stretchers. Fire fighters struggled to douse the car fire, which burned with a horrific toxic smell.

Because of the rubble and the pandemonium at the entryway, there seemed no way to get safely out of the building. In no mood to go upstairs to our room, Françoise and I retreated to the back of the lobby where some sat in stunned silence and others quietly wept. We remained there for hours, commiserating with the other hotel guests. Françoise placed her head on my shoulder and cried. Her whole body shook, and I tried to comfort her as best I could. Later, still in shock, we went back to our room, but went to bed without undressing, fearing we might have to suddenly flee the hotel. We slept fitfully until daylight lined the edges of the heavy dark curtains.

I lay motionless for a moment, not remembering where I was or what had happened. I did not trust the daylight. I knew the world had changed. It seemed cursed and broken and hopeless. I felt some muddled upheaval had happened.

Then memory returned: the horrible reality of last night flashed back. I groaned, remembering the explosion and the bedlam. Some of the fumes had seeped into our room.

While Françoise remained fast asleep, I stumbled to the bathroom and showered. When I came out, she was sitting in the armchair by the window. She had opened the curtains, letting in the bright morning sunlight. She looked destitute and stricken with sadness.

"*Bonjour,*" she said.

"*Bonjour*, my dear," I said.

I leaned down and kissed her on the mouth. She had tears in her eyes, and they were running down her cheeks. I tasted the salt of her tears. She reached up and hugged me.

I went to the window looked out at the sea. It was as calm and as blue as the sky. People were strolling along the promenade. On the avenue, cars and trucks were shooting by in a normal way.

Françoise said, "*Cela semble irréel.* It all seems so *unreal,* yet I don't think I will ever feel fully secure again."

"Yes you will, sweetheart."

"I didn't sleep well. How about you?"

I said, "No, I didn't sleep well either. I had bad dreams."

"*Je ne me souviens pas de mes rêves.* I don't remember my dreams. It's just as well. They're probably awful."

I said nothing. I was watching a little woman walking a little dog along the promenade. They seemed so normal. That puzzled me. Was she unaware of what happened?

Everything before the explosion seemed unconnected to the present moment. Now we seemed to be in a different era, the la-di-da world gone. I was a child at the time of 9/11, but I remembered we felt the la-di-da world suddenly disappeared--*zap!*-- unlikely to ever return.

"I'm going to take a shower," Françoise said, putting her cup down on the table beside the chair, standing and slowly stretching her arms above her head.

She went in the bathroom and closed the door. I could hear the water pounding in the tub. I was concerned but she was going to be okay. I, too, was going to be okay. But my emotions were scattered like debris on a battlefield. I tried to collect them and restore harmony. I didn't succeed, not then.

On my phone I checked my email. Among the spam, there was this: "Mark, where are you? I stopped by the house twice! Are you okay? I'm worried about you! I hope you are well. Remember, I care about you. You haven't seen the last of me. Love, Christy."

I groaned and shut off my phone.

Then I turned on the TV. News reporters were talking about the explosion at Hotel Cote d'Azur. I found an English-language channel based in Monte Carlo where the reporter described in detail what had happened. But, he said, "We've no word yet on who is responsible for this horrific act or why they did it."

A little later, in the elevator, one of the other occupants said to us, "*A quoi appartient le monde?*"

We all nodded agreement, as though the question was a pronouncement. What is the world coming to?

On the way to breakfast, Françoise and I passed through the lobby and noticed the rubble was still in place. A woman with purple hair holding a Yorkie terrier was asking at the front desk why the debris hadn't been removed.

The clerk said, "*Madam, c'est une scene de crime*" and pointed to the side door. "*Utilise la porte laterale.*"

Bodies had been removed but the sidewalk and the driveway along the front entrance were stained with blackening pools of human blood. The toxic smell of gasoline, gunpowder and oil, plastic and synthetic still lingered heavily on the air.

After breakfast we had the car brought up from the underground parking lot to the side doorway.

"*Je vous remercie,*" I said to the driver as he handed me the key to Françoise's car obviously assuming I would be the one driving. I tipped him well.

"Do you want to drive?" I said to Françoise.

"No, you drive. I still feel a bit shaken."

We pulled into traffic along the Avenue des Anglais, heading in the direction of Villefranche-sur-Mer and Beaulieu-sur-Mer. I turned on the radio. They were talking about the bombing, but there was still no word on who was responsible.

I kept driving, somewhat aimlessly. We weren't really back to normal. We hadn't discussed where we were going. I was sure we were both still in shock, trying now to simply recover some sense of normalcy.

I said, "Where should we go?"

"Just go," she said. Then she thought for a minute and said, "If you turn around and go back in the other direction, we can drive up to Saint Paul de Vence. I went there with my family years ago. It's a *charmant* village. It sits high on a hillside and on a day like today the sunlight there is likely to be lovely on the whitewashed walls and the red rooftops. There is a museum and a chapel there."

I turned around into the marina's parking lot and headed in the other direction.

"I suppose after last night you're feeling even more hesitant about moving to Europe?" said Françoise.

"Oh, no. The thing that happened last night can happen any place. You know it happens in America, too."

She said, "And Paris and London and Madrid and Amsterdam."

"This is the world some historians predicted years ago."

"So, what do you think? Do you want to try to be together in Newquay?"

"Do you *own* the cottage in Newquay?"

"No, my parents own it."

"Well, Françoise, we would not be able to *live* there. We would have to have our *own* place, and I don't know where that would be. The problem remains: where would I work?"

The traffic on the avenue was slight.

"We could live in London or Paris?" She said it as a question.

"Yes, but it takes lots of money to live in London or Paris." I paused. "And I don't have lots of money."

She was silent for a while.

"Besides, you're supposed to be writing your novel."

"I *am* writing my novel."

"I just can't see any way for us to *live* in Newquay or London or Paris."

"You paint a very grim picture. Mark, I think I'm in love with you. Doesn't that count for something?"

"Yes, of course."

"Do you love me?"

"Yes, I love you, Françoise," I said, but I wasn't really sure of it. I *wanted* to believe I loved her. So, I said it again with more conviction: "*Of course* I love you!"

"Let's not talk about it anymore today," she said grimly.

"Okay."

"Did you want to inquire around in England to see if you might find work?"

"I thought we weren't going to talk about it anymore today."

"It was just a thought." Her smile was sad.

"You know as well as I, such a move for me as a foreigner would be extremely complicated. I would need to apply for residency."

"Yes, but having a job offer makes it a lot easier."

"That may be true but getting the offer is what is so unlikely. But I'm willing to try."

"You are? Terrific! It wouldn't have to be on this particular trip. We both could do some research online and in newspapers and see what is available," said Françoise. "When we find some possibilities, we can arrange for interviews, and you can come back for the interviews."

"You make it sound so easy."

"You're back to that old argument, huh?"

"Sorry. Reality is reality."

We drove on for a while without talking.

When we reached the mouth of the road up to Saint Paul de Vence, I reached over and took her hand, pulled it up to my mouth and kissed it. "I *love* you," I said, and I believed it this time.

We had started the climb up into Saint Paul de Vence when Françoise said, "Mark, if you tried, I think you would be hired right away. You have highly desirable skills."

"I thought we weren't going to talk about that subject any more right now?"

"Okay! My lips are sealed," she said.

After parking the car, we walked the short distance to the center of the village of stone buildings and countless fountains. Holding hands we strolled past art gallery after art gallery, and restaurant after restaurant, and gift shop after gift shop. Here and there tourists were milling about taking pictures.

We stopped at a fountain. My shoelace had come undone. I sat down on the ledge of the fountain and retied it while Françoise took my picture.

We found Fondation Maeght, a museum of modern art, and toured the galleries and the grounds. As we wandered around, I thought of Christy and her love of art. This place she would have loved.

Back to the village center, tourists were everywhere we turned, in the narrow passageways and in doorways taking pictures. I checked the time. It was five minutes to three; we would have a late lunch; so, we started stopping at the little restaurants to check the menus posted outside or in windows. Most of the restaurants had outside tables dressed in white tablecloths and set with cloth napkins and good silverware.

We chose Restaurant de Chagall, with tables under a great old tree. A young man in a white waiter's jacket and with very dignified posture led us to a table at the edge, always better than in the middle, and pulled the chair out for Françoise, then for me. We thanked him.

Lunch! We ate the same thing. Our entrée was mixed salad and cold soup with a bit of paté; *le plat principal* was white fish, rice, and mixed vegetables, followed by a plate of various cheeses. For dessert we shared an ice cream cake roll.

As we were finishing, my phone chimed. I said, "It's my sister."

"You should answer it," said Françoise.

"Mark! Guess what?" said Marie.

"What?"

"We sold Mother's house!"

"Bravo!"

"Luther Moses is a happy man; but we still have to finalize things before everything is set. I think I told you the bank approved his loan, and I've faxed the proposal to Attorney Berg. You need to sign some papers. Once everybody has signed, we will get something they call an Acceptance of Transfer of Beneficial Interest and Ratification of Trust Agreement. When are you coming home? I need your help!"

"I'm coming home on the twenty-fifth. How about Elsie?"

"Elsie is moving back to Atlanta to live with relatives. She's been very understanding about the house. Can you stop in Chicago?"

"No, I can't stop. I'm glad Elsie has a place to go."

"And she has her social security," Marie said. "How come you can't stop in Chicago?"

"I've got to get back to work on the thirty-first. Any papers I have to sign can be signed online or by fax, and I can do those things from home."

"Okay, okay, don't get huffy."

"I'm not getting huffy I'm just telling you what I have to do."

"Aren't you happy we sold the house?"

"I'm ecstatic! How much did it sell for?"

"We had to come down on the price a bit. Still, we got a lot for it. It's a great house. It just happens to be in a neighborhood recently turned bad."

"Yes."

She continued: "Moses accepted the counteroffer. It's a bargain for him. Who gets three bedrooms and a big kitchen with two big walk-in closets for two hundred thousand dollars?"

"I'll send Lucien an email and let him know when I'm coming home. Thanks, Marie."

"Okay! Talk with you soon!"

She hung up.

I looked at Françoise and said, "We sold my mother's house."

"*Toutes nos felicitations!* Congratulations!"

We spent two more days in and around Nice. We drove up the Old

Roman Road, bumping on its cobblestones. At a little theater company, we saw an opera, *Four Saints in Three Acts*, by Gertrude Stein. We danced in a nightclub. We went to the Musée Matisse and the Muséum d'Histoire Naturelle, to Terra Amata, and to the Musée National du Sport.

At one point Françoise and I were sitting at a sidewalk café talking and drinking coffee when a car slowed down and a young Frenchman leaned out the window and shouted in French some obscenity or racial slur I didn't understand.

Françoise and I looked at each other. She said, "It's everywhere! Yes, even in my beloved France! *Hatred* is everywhere."

What the young man did, made me feel sad—sad for the world we lived in. His vulgar, insulting words weren't the problem: his *need* to fling them was. It was depressing.

We weren't in a hurry when we left Nice and headed up, so we made the return trip as much of an adventure as the trip down. We stopped a few times to sample local wines and food and to see in passing a few sites we'd missed, such as Roman ruins and chateaus and castles. En route, Françoise got a call from her mother. Her father was busy in the streets of Paris directing his new film.

At Le Havre we crossed the English Channel on a ferry and landed at Southampton. In Portsmouth we spent the night; the next day we continued to Newquay.

We were no longer talking about the chance that I might move to Newquay. That conversation was on a backburner.

45

Françoise said, "I think we should do something; but I don't want to go any place where there are crowds. I'm afraid of bombings. Too many horrible things are happening."

"I understand."

"I was thinking..."

"Yes?"

"I was thinking maybe we should drive to Sussex?"

"What's there?"

"Virginia Woolf's house. You know her books?"

"No."

"You should read her books, especially *To the Lighthouse*. We can spend the night in a bed-and-breakfast there and come back the next day. *Bien?*"

"Sure." Why not? I thought.

It was good seeing Françoise happy again. Sussex wasn't a destination I would have chosen, but because she wanted it, I had no objection.

Françoise telephoned and reserved a room in a garden studio holiday cottage. "I'm so excited! I've never been there, and I've always wanted to go," she said.

Early Friday morning we hit the road. When we arrived in East Sussex after a four-and-a-half hour drive, we parked the car, Françoise used the outdoor restroom, and then we walked across the grounds to Monk's House, Virginia and Leonard's Woolf's summer retreat.

We reached the cobbled path to the entryway, walking past the greenhouse attached to the cottage. 'Isn't it lovely?" said Françoise.

"Yes."

Inside, the attendant greeted us. The ceiling was low, and the interior was quaint with rustic furniture, sturdy wooden tables and wooden armchairs and wooden rocking chairs with well-worn cushions on the seats.

The walls were washed green and the windows were small. Two large mahogany wooden beams from floor to ceiling stood in each room. A bowl of flowers from the garden sat on the table beside various copies of Virginia's novels.

Françoise whispered to me, "I can just *imagine* Virginia and her sister Vanessa, Leonard, Roger Fry and Duncan Grant, in this cozy little cottage." She held tightly to my shirtsleeve. Imploringly, she said, "Can't you just sense the amazing artistic and intellectual life that took place under this roof?"

I nodded, trying to imagine it.

She whispered again: "I've read all of her books. Virginia went *deep* into herself. I think of what Kafka said. One has to go deep into the 'cold abyss' of self in order to find the best." Françoise looked into my eyes. She said, "That's what I'm trying to do with *my* novel."

A few other visitors were milling about in the cottage and on the grounds. One elderly man with white hair smiled at us and said, "Did you folks hear about the bombing?"

I said, "*What* bombing?"

"About two hours ago in London twenty people died in a bomb explosion. They are saying it was a suicide bomber. About fifty people were wounded."

"Oh, my God," said Françoise, holding her face with both hands. "Is the world going crazy?"

"Where did it happen?"

"I think it was at some kind of concert," he said. "And earlier this morning there was also a radio report of an incident in Barcelona. I didn't catch the details."

Françoise and I were still in shock from the car explosion in Nice; now here was news of more bombings.

The terrorists wanted you to give up normal life and live with fear. We were not going to give in to fear. We took a look at Charleston, Vanessa Bell's country home in East Essex, overgrown with wallflowers. This quiet countryside area felt safe––safe from danger.

Vanessa's studio was there. We went inside the great old house and looked around at the crowded rooms. I felt like I was invading somebody's private space. The rooms gave me the feeling the people who lived there had just stepped out for a walk and would return shortly.

We walked in the plush garden Vanessa created, admiring the profusion of zinnias and tulips, sweet peas and sunflowers, hollyhocks and dahlias, globe artichokes and red-hot pokers and other colorful plants and shrubbery. I hadn't been excited about coming here, but now I was glad we had.

In West Sussex, we walked around the nineteenth-century Nymans gardens at Staplefield Lane in Handcross. We sat on a bench by the wall of the great stone castle, looking out at the grounds. After the bad news about London and Barcelona, sitting there was a calming moment.

Françoise said, "*Je pourrais m'asseoir ici pour toujours*—I could sit here forever, forever and ever, and daydream."

I took her hand and held it.

Later, we ate dinner in a local restaurant.

Our small attic room for the night in Virginia's garden cottage, with its low-pitched ceiling, was quaint and perfect; so was the little bed with its crisp white sheets and fluffy pillows in white pillowcases.

Saturday, we drove back to Newquay.

Sunday, after breakfast, instead of working on her novel, Françoise wanted to walk. As we went along, Françoise explained things. "I love walking these paths when I am *triste ou déprimé*; you know, sad or depressed, when I want to quiet my mind and my emotions. Walking here, I find it very soothing."

We followed footpaths through the village and along the coast that Françoise knew well. They were profuse with wildflowers high on cliffs above the Georgian sea. We walked for a long while on golden sand along the sea, past folding rock strata, continuing on winding footpaths up and down and along the sea then up and down again.

Walking for the sake of walking was new to me. I never did it in Chicago and I never did it in California. Along the way, Françoise and I greeted birdwatchers with cameras. We walked along the Watergate Bay. We passed the Whipsiderry sea caves.

I was surprised I was enjoying walking in a natural environment. It was a strange new experience. In the distance I saw a coastal medieval church and a castle and quaint fishermen's cottages strung along the way.

At Lusty Glaze beach and the Iron Age hillfort on Trevelgue we stopped to rest for about five minutes then continued on.

On this last day together, holding hands and walking, we enjoyed simply being together. If it wasn't love it felt like it.

46

On Tuesday, I flew back to California. At airport security, I was searched thoroughly, and so was my carry-on. They had to be careful of people entering the country, even American citizens. I sailed through with a smile.

It took me a full day of sleep to recover from jetlag. I called Françoise right away and, despite the eight-hour time difference, we talked for an hour.

She said, "*Tu me manques*, Mark." She missed me.

I said, "*Tu me manques aussi*, Françoise!" I missed her too. I imagined she got lonely there.

I went back to work. I'd adjusted culturally to being in England and France when I was with Françoise; now, at home, I needed to readjust. Though everything was unchanged, I was seeing it––and myself––with fresh eyes. The language and the customs were still mine, but it felt strangely ironic having to adjust to something so familiar and comforting.

To finalize the sale of Mother's house, estate and trust business had to be settled. Lucien March sent documents by email for me to sign electronically as did Attorney Berg. Luther Moses's lawyer also sent us documents to sign. Apparently, some minor work was needed on the back stairway and he insisted Marie and I pay for it. We agreed and the work was done.

Some final documents I needed to sign before a notary public, which I took to my bank. I even signed documents to allow Marie to have full access to the money in Mother's two bank accounts, to investments, and to the benefits from Mother's life insurance policy. She already had access, but this made it official.

Marie had to oversee the dispersal of Mother's belongings; she had to gingerly handle Elsie's departure from the house. She had to deal with the real estate agents, both Luther Moses's and ours, and she had to also deal with Attorney Berg. If there was anything left over after expenses, Marie deserved it.

I had in mind I would now live a monastic life––at least till I saw Françoise again. In my crazy fantasy life, she would come back to California, or somehow I would return to her somewhere in Europe. It was all nonsense. In reality I suspected we were finished with each other but basking in the memory of my time with her I hoped with all my heart I was wrong.

The first weekend back from England, I had in mind catching the River Cats baseball team playing another minor league team from Las Vegas. I bought my ticket online.

Wednesday afternoon, as I was leaving the house, car keys in hand, Christy pulled into my driveway and parked her Toyota Camry behind my Subaru, making it impossible for me to back my car out.

"So, you're alive. Where were you? I've been trying to contact you!" she said angrily as she stepped from her car.

She was wearing a gray windbreaker and a green skirt and sandals.

"Hello, Christy. What do you want?"

"Is that any way to greet your *wife*?"

"We're divorced."

"It's not final yet, so I'm still your wife." She stepped closer.

"I've got to go. Your car is blocking my––"

She grabbed me by the crotch. "Where were you? Are you giving *this* to somebody else?"

I knocked her hand away.

"What difference does it make to you? You're living with Cliff. Isn't he giving you enough of what you need?"

"Never mind Cliff." She looked around. "Let's go inside. You wouldn't want your neighbors to see us fighting our here, would you?"

"Move your car, Christy."

"No, I'm not moving the car until we go inside."

"For what? We've nothing to say to each other."

"I'm not going to let you treat me this way, Mark. Let's go inside. You know I still have a key to the house."

"I'll have the lock changed."

She laughed. "You want nothing to do with me?"

I didn't respond.

"You used to love me. What happened?"

"You know what happened."

"You're like a scratched record repeating the same old thing all the time."

"Maybe you're right but I know what I feel."

"I gave you a divorce, Mark, *because* I love you. It was what you wanted. *I* didn't want a divorce. I wanted to stay married to you."

"Stay married to me and go to bed with other men."

"So what?" She paused. "We've had this discussion many times before. Let's go inside and talk. You owe me that much. I gave you your divorce, so you would be happy. I never thought the divorce meant we would no longer be friends."

"You want to be my friend?"

"I thought we were friends. Remember the agreement we made when we were kids? We agreed to *always* be friends."

"You have Cliff now for a friend. Go talk with Cliff."

"That was a cruel thing to say."

"I'm asking you for the last time: move your car."

"And again, I'm saying no." She grabbed my hand and started pulling me toward the walkway to the front door.

I resisted. "I've a ticket to——"

"*Screw* your ticket," she said angrily. "Come on inside."

I noticed a man across the street walking his dog; he stopped to watch us. Rather than continuing the verbal warfare, I gave in. I didn't want neighbors witnessing this. "Okay, we'll go inside and talk for only a few minutes. Okay?"

"Okay," she said. "A few minutes."

Christy sat on the couch in the living room. I remained standing.

"Sit down," she said.

"No, I'd rather stand."

"You're afraid to sit beside me? How did I become so poisonous to you? You used to *adore* me?"

I didn't respond. She was right. I did adore her, but I became disillusioned. I was bitterly disappointed in myself for all of those years of perceiving her to be someone other than the person she was. I wasn't angry at, or disappointed in, her, just *myself*. Obviously, my perception was faulty.

"Mark, please sit beside me."

"Why?"

"Because my minutes are ticking away."

That did it. I sat down at the other end of the couch. The minute I did Christy slid over again touched my crotch.

"I'm not doing anything with you, Christy."

"Then can I have at least a kiss for old time's sake?" She moved closer, trying to kiss my lips. I turned my head away.

She backed away. "You're in love with someone else, aren't you?"

I didn't respond.

"Is she pretty? Who is she?"

"Does Cliff know you're here?"

"Cliff is sweet, but this is not about Cliff. This is about *us*. I still have feelings for you, Mark. I can't believe you've turned off your desire for me so quickly. I just can't believe that."

"Why don't you and Cliff get married?"

"I'm not *ever* marrying again," Christy said. "I'm getting a job at an ad agency in Sacramento. Mr. Freedenberg wrote me a nice letter of recommendation. I did good work there."

"Well, congratulations. I'm happy for you."

"No, you aren't," she said sarcastically. "I can tell by your tone."

"My tone? There wasn't anything wrong with my tone."

Christy stood up and sat on my lap facing me.

"Get up, Christy!"

"No!"

"Yes!" I gently pushed at her.

She tried to kiss me again, but I turned my head and her kiss landed on my neck. She bit my neck then sucked the bite.

Christy straddled me. She sucked my earlobe. I felt the hot rush of blood building in lust and anger. Using both hands, she gripped my face and forced a hard kiss on my lips. Her tongue plied my teeth apart and shot into my mouth, seeking my tongue.

If I pushed her off, she'd land on the floor. I didn't want to hurt her. I felt myself giving in to lust. She kept up the pressure, moving her bottom around rhythmically on my lap––an uninvited lap-dance. Against my will, Mister You-Know-Who was responding enthusiastically. I was at the bridgehead about to fall over into the lake.

Christy was unzipping and pulling at my clothes. I resigned myself to it and closed my eyes. Then I felt wet warm pleasure fill my senses.

When we finished, she said, "My love belongs to you, Mark, but you do *not* own my body. You never did. *I* own my body. No man owns my body; and no man ever will. I do with it whatever I please."

Needless to say, I missed seeing the River Cats play baseball. I felt guilty when I thought of Françoise.

The next day I had the locks changed.

47

August that year was very hot. I worked steadily. I made frequent trips to the Klinkhoff Dam. Water storage always needed attention. I also did work at the Jansen power plant, checking the pumping capacity and flow. We were working on rebooting. Repair work was still being done on the spillway.

Runoff into the Orlena River was something we always monitored. This time I was there to check the pump-storage capacity and the hydro-electric pumping mechanism. As state employed engineers, we were also entrusted to protect fish and wildlife water sources. That was one of my own top priorities.

I was one of the engineers assigned to also keep a close eye on Lake Kasper, north of Clear Lake, because Kasper was known to have a severe blue-green algae problem. The cyanobacteria that gathered largely around the edges of Kasper smelled awful. People complained about the odor. We used a herbicide but like all herbicides it carried a danger of toxins. The battle was endless.

I also drove up to Tahoe to test the lake. On the way, I sometimes stopped in Truckee for lunch or gas or both. It was a good little rustic town. Often motorcycle groups stopped there too. Most were friendly.

Once a group of bikers, with shaved heads and Nazi tattoos along their bare arms, rode into town. One had a Nazi tattoo on his forehead. I got back into the Bronco and drove farther up the road to have lunch at a diner just off the highway.

But Truckee was a town in which you saw many young men in cowboy hats and cowboy boots and guys wearing leather jackets with Harley-Davidson on the back. Most of these guys were not looking for trouble.

Because of my type of work, I wore jeans or khakis and denim jackets. I imagined I fit right in in Truckee, but sometimes my imagination played tricks on me. Once a guy said to me, "Where is your Harley?" I smiled and said, "It's in my stable with my horse." He laughed.

One Saturday morning I was up on the ladder changing a burned-out light bulb on the side of the house by the driveway when Christy drove up and parked in the driveway. She was dressed like she'd just come from the health spa.

She got out and came over as I was climbing down.

"Guess what?" she said.

"What?"

"Cliff and his friend Robert and I had a threesome."

I sighed. "So, you had your threesome. Why tell me?"

"Why not?"

"I don't need to know about it."

I walked away and climbed the steps and entered the house. She followed me into the kitchen where I had a pot of coffee on the electric heater.

"May I have a cup of coffee?"

"Sure," I said and poured us each a cup.

"The threesome happened two days ago but I really came here to tell you about the dream I had last night. I want your opinion about what it means."

"Okay."

I sat down at the kitchen table across from each other.

"You were in my dream." She took a sip of coffee, burned her tongue, then put the cup down. "I was still married to you and we were a happy couple. We were living in some place like New York in an apartment. I got pregnant, but you said the baby couldn't be yours. I knew it was and I insisted that it was. You said no, it's Cliff's baby. Then I said it couldn't be Cliff's baby because you are my husband."

"You don't have to be a husband to make a baby."

"That's true. Anyway, I had the baby, and it grew up overnight. He was a handsome young man. At this point you seem to have left me and I was living with another man--not Cliff, not Todd. He adopted my son; then my son went off to college. He finished college got married and had a son; then they wanted to move in with me. Then a doctor told me I needed a knee replacement. I said but I'm too young for a knee replacement."

I said, "How odd. A knee replacement?"

"Yes. I *know* it's odd but maybe not. Mommy thinks she might have to have one. I am afraid for her. Could that be it? I had the knee replacement. When I looked in the mirror, I was an old woman with gray hair. I *looked* like mommy. The dream was so vivid, so real. What do you make of it?"

"You want a child, and you fear loneliness and old age."

"Is that all?"

"Sure. That's it."

"I don't think so."

"Then what do you think it means?"

"I don't know. Maybe I need to get back to painting. I don't have bad dreams when I'm painting."

I didn't say anything in response. We sat there and finished drinking the coffee; then I stood up and took the cups to the kitchen sink. I turned to her and said, "I've got things to do, Christy."

She got up and came over to me and aggressively stuck a finger inside my shirt and flipped it; then she said, "All work and no play makes Marksie a dull boy."

Then she turned and walked out. I heard the door slam behind her.

Françoise and I hadn't made any promises to each other about any kind of relationship, about loyalty or otherwise. We did say we would stay in touch. I said I would make an effort to find my kind of employment in England or France. She said she would do the same on my behalf. But nothing so far had turned up.

She and I kept in contact by email and texting and once or twice a week by telephone. The weekend following my departure, she had flown to Paris to spend a couple of days with her parents. Then it was back to Newquay where she resumed working on the novel. "I'm making great progress," she said.

She was writing her novel on her computer and worried a lot about losing material, so she was backing up about every twenty or thirty pages. "Very wise," I said. Françoise was also counting the words as she wrote. She wanted a novel of about eighty thousand words––not too short, not too long.

She said it was autobiographical. I never talked with her about the subject of her novel, although once in an email she hinted it was about a French girl at the Sorbonne who goes as an exchange student to a school in California she was calling Paxton University. The rest of it was predictable.

On my days off, I routinely jumped in the Subaru and drove out of the city. Getting out was good for me. It cleared my head, and it gave me a chance to breathe fresher air, the kind of air I'd inhaled in the countryside of England.

I drove sixty miles to Nevada City once and ate lunch in a little diner on Commercial Street. It felt good being in a small town again. I walked around a bit then drove back home.

I realized I was fighting loneliness; I was fighting a kind of heartache; I was fighting desolation. I needed broken parts of me to mend. I was looking back at my mistakes and trying not to; I feared the future but held stoically to hope.

Once with colleagues from work, I went whitewater rafting at South Fork on the American River. On hot days, I swam there, but because many people had drowned, I always wore my big red Superlite life vest.

Another time I drove up to Lake Shasta, stayed overnight in a motel and drove back home. I did some hiking in Yosemite Park.

On weekends, to fight the emptiness, I felt I had to keep active. I walked under the great redwoods, breathing in their delectable aroma. I drove Highway 1 down the coast, sometimes stopping at Half Moon Bay and Santa Cruz Beach and Monterey and Carmel and Big Sur and Cambria.

I enjoyed the drive on a clear day with the sky cloudless and blue-green and the Pacific Ocean a slightly darker blue-green and calm and stretching all the way out to where it seemed to meet the sky.

There were also days filled with toxic smoke from fires in the hills or remote areas blowing into the Valley. On those days, if I could, I stayed home.

48

At the beginning of September, I woke at three in the morning realizing I needed to go to my mother's and my father's graves. It was an urgent and powerful feeling and I had a hard time getting back to sleep. When I did fall asleep again, I dreamt I was there, kneeling down at their graveside.

In a few days the dream turned into reality. Without telling Marie I was coming, I flew to O'Hare, rented a car, and drove to Manifest. I stopped at Lemuel & Kester Flowers and bought two large bouquets of white carnations and returned to the car.

Memorial Gardens Cemetery was just as I remembered it. It was a lovely place with a pond in the center and a profusion of tall mature trees that lent a cool and comforting feeling. The dark red stone of many of the headstones contrasted beautifully with the green grass and the trees. I parked alongside the cemetery road and walked over to the two graves near the front fence.

I felt this pilgrimage was my way to settle a grievance and gain closure, I wanted to forgive my parents but mainly I wanted to forgive myself. Yes, to gain *closure* so I could move on with my life, whatever that might entail.

Marie or someone had recently placed a bouquet of fresh roses on each of my parent's graves. A gentle breeze was blowing through the tall oak and through the weeping beech and the sycamores and cedars; and I could hear the nearby traffic on Ridge Road, reminding me the world was still going about its business as it passed this burial site in this sleepy town.

I placed one bouquet of the white carnations on Dad's grave, the other on Mother's grave. I remembered Dad saying: "We're all just trying to survive: the lizard on the rock, the bird in the tree, the guy on the bus with his lunch bucket going to work."

I thought of Viktor. Why did I think of him at *this* moment: sky and earth, life and death, his theories of math and match?

Although the ground was slightly wet from the groundskeeper's watering, I knelt down before the two graves and I stayed there for a while. I looked over at the pond and saw the glint of light on the surface reflecting the trees in a shimmering, dancing pattern. I now *accepted* Mother's death, as I had, somehow, when I was younger, learned to accept Dad's, too.

It was a profound moment. The aroma of new-mown grass and wet earth and the balmy scent of the trees and the perfume of the roses and carnations were sweet to my senses. For the first time in a long while, I felt contentment.

I got back in the car and drove away.

—

Photo: Neil Michel

Among CLARENCE MAJOR'S previous novels are *Dirty Bird Blues* (a Penguin Classic), *Such Was the Season*, a Literary Guild selection; *My Amputations*, winner of the Western States Book Award; *Painted Turtle: Woman with Guitar, a New York Times Book Review* Notable Book of the Year; and *One Flesh*. He has contributed to *The New Yorker, The New York Times, The Harvard Review*, and dozens of other periodicals. He is the author of sixteen collections of poetry. A Fulbright scholar, Major won a National Book Award Bronze Medal, the Western States Book Award for fiction, a National Council on The Arts Award; in 2015 he won a "Lifetime Achievement Award for Excellence in the Fine Arts" from the Congressional Black Caucus Foundation, and in 2016 a PEN Oakland/ Reginald Lockett "Lifetime Achievement Award for Excellence in Literature." He was elected to The Georgia State Writers Fall of Fame in 2021. Major is a distinguished professor emeritus of twentieth century American literature at the University of California at Davis.

Thanks for purchasing this book and for supporting authors and artists. As a token of gratitude, please scan the QR code for exclusive content from this title.

A Note on the typopgraphy

Garamond is a family of many serif typefaces, created by and named for sixteenth-century Parisian type designer Claude Garamond. Garamond typefaces are often used for book printing and body text because of the lasting elegance and legibility of the design. Fine tuning of the typeface has led to the creation of digital fonts within the family to satisfy the changing landscape of publishing.